"MEETING YOU MADE ME QUESTION EVERYTHING."

Ben's eyes held hers as he poured the wine. "Until we met, I thought I liked being a bachelor again."

"I think I understand what you mean," Sara said quietly. "I've had my own adjusting to do. You're quite different from the type of man I thought I'd fall in love with. Then again, in some ways, you're really not."

"What were you looking for?"

"I wanted someone who'd accept me precisely as I was, who would adapt to me."

Ben nodded. "I wanted the same thing. I wanted a woman who'd accept me completely, and someone who'd depend on me for everything. Only... somehow, I've ended up depending on you, too."

Sara smiled and touched his arm. "That's what people in love do for one another."

Ben raised his wineglass in a toast. "You know something? I think you're right. We two make just the right combination. Sara, now and always, let's drink to us."

ABOUT THE AUTHOR

The author of sixteen romance novels,
Aimee Thurlo has written under the pseudonyms
Aimee Martel and Aimee Duvall, as well as her
own name. When she isn't at the word processor,
Aimee can usually be found riding one of her two
horses or practicing her skills as a marksman. A
native of Cuba, Aimee has spent most of her life
in the United States. She now lives in New Mexico
with her husband, a teacher, and their five dogs.
For inspiration, Aimee finds staring at an entire
wall of Timothy Dalton photographs and posters
enhances her creativity. *The Right Combination*,
her first Superromance, is dedicated to the
handsome British actor.

Aimee Thurlo

THE RIGHT COMBINATION

Harlequin Books

TORONTO • NEW YORK • LONDON
AMSTERDAM • PARIS • SYDNEY • HAMBURG
STOCKHOLM • ATHENS • TOKYO • MILAN

Published June 1988

First printing April 1988

ISBN 0-373-70312-0

To Timothy Dalton,
because it was your photograph
that triggered my imagination.

CHAPTER ONE

BEN LOWELL LEANED BACK in his chair and glared at the two men who were standing on the other side of his desk. "You're my top executives. Are you trying to tell me that one woman operating a business out of two tiny basement offices has *both* of you stumped?"

"We've tried everything, boss, really." Marc Winger leaned forward and rested his hands on the conference table. His gray hair looked almost white in the diffused fluorescent light. "First of all, it's been impossible so far to find her. We're not even sure what she looks like. No one working for us has any recollection of ever having seen her. Sara Cahill has an answering machine, not a secretary, so we're stuck leaving messages that have never been returned. I've tried to go talk to her in person several times, but I've never once found her in her office." He rubbed his face pensively. "I think she was inside there somewhere, but no one would answer my knock, and the door was latched. One time I waited there until after nine in the evening, but not a soul came out."

Joe McCallister loosened the jacket that hid most of his ample girth. "Ben, I've been a businessman for fifteen years, and I've worked for you for the last five. You know that I don't admit defeat easily, but in this case we have no choice. The woman has an ironclad lease that she signed with the former owner. Before this downtown section of Albuquerque became fashionable and the city started turning old buildings into fancy offices, it was almost impossible to get anyone to rent space here. She moved in two years prior to the downtown renovation project and practically dictated her own terms."

Joe stood up and walked to the window, facing a panorama of the Sandia Mountains. Although the foothills were twenty minutes away, the evergreen-capped peaks rising from the desert floor seemed much closer in the clear air of the mile-high city. "You bought this building because Classic Parts Incorporated needed the extra room, and because it was a great buy. However, we all knew about our downstairs tenant beforehand. The former owner told you she'd never move out, and we agreed to let her stay unless she violated the agreement. She likes it down there, obviously, and has been ducking our calls. I guess we were wrong in assuming that we'd be able to make her an offer and get her to leave."

The man behind the desk nodded. "I was prepared..." Ben Lowell paused, then corrected himself. "I *am* prepared to cover all the moving fees, plus pay the first month's rent on her new offices. That's more than reasonable. Our business dealings are proprietary and I don't want strangers looking over our shoulders. I intend us to have this building to ourselves. Just what kind of operation does she run down there, anyway?"

Joe shrugged. "I'm not really sure. All we know is that her company is listed as Mousetrap Incorporated."

"What the hell does that mean? Is she an exterminator?" Ben Lowell squared his powerful shoulders, then stood. For several seconds he said nothing, his blue eyes taking in the men before him. "You two are going to have to find a way to cut a deal with this woman downstairs. Is she doing so well financially that she's indifferent to a sound business proposition? Offer to find, or help her find, even better offices. We'll make up the difference between what she'd be paying here and what her new rent would be for one year. That should convince her. If not, then I want you to dig up every shred of information you can about her. Maybe there's something she wants or needs for her business that we can provide. There's got to be some ethical way of persuading her to move out.'' Ben's eyes grew hooded, and his expression changed from impatient to stoic.

To the other men in the room, his body language was a definite signal that the meeting was over. Joe stood. ''I'll have something concrete for you in a few hours. You're right about this, Ben. It's absolutely ridiculous to allow this woman to run rings around us.''

Marc shot his colleague a cynical look. As they strode to the door, he added in a harsh whisper, ''Great words, Joe. I hope they taste just as good when you have to eat them.''

Alone in his office, Ben Lowell smiled, then began to laugh softly. His two top men, stymied by this woman. A lady exterminator? Well, if worst came to worst, maybe he could hire her to keep the building free of vermin. He didn't want anyone in his building who wasn't working for him. His competition was full of cutthroat people, and he didn't want any outsiders hanging around when they were discussing business.

As he recalled the look on Marc's face he began to laugh again. Joe had told him earlier that Marc had even tried having one of the company attorneys write the woman a letter. He'd received a response from a prominent attorney in town explaining that Sara Cahill, his client, was entirely within her rights as a tenant to stay in the building. Once again the elusive Ms Cahill had won the battle.

A buzzer sounded from the telephone beside him. "Yes?"

"Mr. Lowell, your son is here."

"Send him in."

Ben Lowell's face lit up as the round-faced, bright-eyed eleven-year-old boy bounded into the room. As usual, Jimmy was wearing one of his favorite sweatshirts. This one was white with a robot frog printed on the front. His worn blue cap with the NASA logo and a red backpack completed the image. "Yo, Dad! I hate to bother you, but I'm working on this really neat project for science class and I'd like to use your computer. Yours runs twice as fast as the one at home. I like the one you bought for me, you know that, but it doesn't quite have the math capability I need for this."

Ben smiled, his expression softening. Rosemary had died two years ago, and if it hadn't been for Jimmy, he doubted he could have survived the loss. Like himself, his wife hadn't been perfect, but she'd understood him. Her tendency to be disorganized had blended well with his predilection for taking charge. They'd complemented each other well, and despite their occasional differences, he'd loved her deeply.

"Okay, you can use the terminal here in my office, but stay out of everyone's way. Remember, we have a business to run here, too." He walked to a desk off in the far corner, switched on the computer, and gestured for his son to join him. "Sit, and for Pete's sake, try not to blow it up." He gave his son a wary look. "You're not going to do anything strange to it, are you? Like maybe try out one of your inventions, or maybe some super-duper electric gizmo that's going to short-circuit the entire building?"

Jimmy pushed his eyeglasses farther back on his nose with a fingertip, and adjusted the creased bill of his cap.

"Jeez, Dad! Give me a break. All I need is to use your big number cruncher to test my data. If I can figure out how much pressure the spring needs so it can catapult a pencil from a wristband right into my palm, then I'll be all set."

"Okay." Ben sighed, then returned to his desk. Jimmy was his only child, and as far as kids went, he was the best. Last year, his teachers had asked that Ben give serious consideration to sending him to a special school for gifted children.

That, however, would have required sending Jimmy out of state to a boarding school. Neither he nor Jimmy had been too enthusiastic about that prospect. Fortunately, the school district had what they called a "magnet school" that anyone in the district who qualified could attend instead of a neighborhood school. The teachers hadn't seemed too hopeful about Jimmy's chances of enrollment, for Dewey Middle School had quite a long waiting list. But Ben had taken Jimmy in for special testing in advanced math and sciences and within a month, they'd received notification that Jimmy would be accepted.

Ben watched his son program the computer, proud of the fact that they were so close. He liked keeping track of everything in Jimmy's life. No surprises there. He knew what to expect from Jimmy, and Jimmy from him. Ben found the thought comforting.

Ben opened a thick file crammed with papers, then began to study each in turn. Though aware in a pleasant sort of way that his son was working across the room, Ben mentally shut out all the office noises coming from outside his door, and began to review the projected sales quotas for the month.

The next hour slipped by quickly. By the time he heard a soft knock at his door, he was almost finished with the report. "Come in."

Joe McCallister walked into the office. Hearing a noise to his left, he turned his head and smiled, recognizing Jimmy. "How's it going, Jim?"

"Just fine, thanks." Jimmy glanced at his dad. "Do you want me to shut down the computer and take off now, Dad? I can save my data on a floppy disk and come back later."

Ben shook his head. "No, just go on with what you were doing. That is, if our talking won't bother you."

"Heck, no! All I need is another fifteen minutes and I'll be out of your way. Just forget I'm here."

Ben watched his son for a minute. Sometimes he wasn't sure if Jimmy was more adult than kid, or vice versa. He didn't act up like other boys his age, and he seemed so mature—most of the time.

Ben waited for Joe to sit down, then focused his attention on him. "What's up?"

"I've been doing some checking on available office space, comparable to what our tenant has downstairs. I think I've found a place that would be perfect for her—if I can get her to talk to me. It's in the Riegger complex down the street. The basement layout is almost identical to what she has here, except they modernized the entire building and it's got brand-new carpeting and office furniture. The rent's slightly more, but if you're willing to compensate for that, I think we might be able to sell her on the idea. Of course, this is providing we can find her and make our pitch."

"Have you learned anything about her business yet?"

Joe shook his head. "When I mention her company name, Mousetrap Incorporated, all I draw is a blank.

None of the businesses around here has ever used her services, whatever they are. Our out of town contacts haven't reported back yet, but I bet you're right. She's an exterminator, or some kind of environmental health consultant. I wonder if she's got one of those crazy vans with a plastic bug on the top parked somewhere around here?"

Ben walked to the window and looked outside for a few minutes. "Well, at least it isn't in our parking lot." He turned around, and shoved his hands into his pants pockets, pushing his suit jacket out of the way. His men weren't getting anywhere with Sara Cahill. The time had come for him to take over. "Neither of you has had a heck of a lot of success dealing with Ms Cahill. I'm going to handle this from now on."

"Whatever you say." Joe stood up and grinned. "Actually, I think this is an excellent idea, boss. It'll be a humbling experience for you. Then all of us guys can get together for a drink after work and commiserate."

"Fat chance, buddy," Ben teased back. "I don't intend to lose."

Joe laughed. "I love your optimism, boss."

As soon as he left the office, Jimmy turned around in his chair. "What a neat name for a company! Mousetrap Incorporated," he repeated thoughtfully. "Dad, I just bet she's an inventor. Like me!"

Ben cringed. He'd seen some of the results of Jimmy's experiments. If his son was right, the lady could be concocting almost anything in the basement! The thought of having his mail forwarded to kingdom come didn't exactly thrill him. "What makes you think she's not an exterminator?"

Jimmy shrugged. "She could be, I suppose, but she sure sounds like an inventor to me. Haven't you ever heard the saying 'Build a better mousetrap and the world will beat a path to your door"? That's the slogan for our spring science fair at Dewey."

Ben brooded over the possibility. Inventors... Besides his own son, whose creations usually spelled disaster, he'd never met one. What kind of woman was Sara Cahill? Unusual, stubborn and obviously intelligent, if she'd managed to counter the wiles of his most experienced executives. Exterminator or inventor, he was going to find out more about her.

SARA CAHILL REFASTENED her auburn hair into a knot atop her head, then covered her shoulder-length locks with a baseball cap. She was glad she worked alone. Wearing loose jeans and a sweatshirt might not do much to flatter her five-foot-six model-trim proportions, but the outfit sure made her feel a lot more comfortable. She put her safety goggles on, protecting her emerald-green eyes, and loosened the rubber strap so that they didn't press too tightly against her nose.

Tonight she was going to test her new invention for durability, and that required special precautions. A leading cookware manufacturer had offered her a contract to create an improved handle for their pots and pans. Her expertise with ceramics and epoxy materials had made her the best candidate for the job.

The handles, made of the ceramic-epoxy blend she'd formulated, were light, sturdy and so heat-resistant that one could actually remove a pan from a hot oven by the handle without risking a burn. The patented process she'd developed produced a material similar to the heat-proof tiles on the space shuttle, but stronger and less expensive to manufacture.

Placing one of her prototype saucepan handles in a special vise, she stepped behind a Plexiglas shield and activated a switch that raised the pressure to two thousand pounds per square inch. Sara increased the force, squeezing the ends of the handle in the metal jaws. Suddenly the handle snapped with a tremendous crunch, sending fragments flying around the room. She ducked instinctively as a large chunk ricocheted off the protective barrier. Exhaling softly, she pushed her safety glasses onto her forehead.

Now for a more down-to-earth test, Sara thought. Consumers might not relate to scientific tests like the one she'd just conducted, but they couldn't argue with what she was going to do next. Gathering up a double boiler and frying pan equipped with her special handles, Sara stepped into the long hallway.

The basement floor was tiled over concrete, creating a surface harder than most kitchen floors. Bringing her arm back like a major league pitcher, she threw the frying pan down the hall as hard as she could. With a mighty clatter, the pan bounced and tumbled along the floor, coming to rest just beyond the foot of the stairs.

From where she was standing, the handle appeared to be undamaged. Now for the double boiler. Twirling the large pan like a massive Frisbee, Sara sent the cookware rattling along the tiles. Just as the container tumbled past the stairs, someone's head appeared from around the corner.

"What the hell?" A man stepped into the hallway and glanced warily from one side to the other. "Lady, what's going on? I was upstairs on the way to my office when I heard this deafening crack, and then a lot of clattering racket. I run down here and find pots and pans bouncing along the floor. Did your stove explode or something?"

Sara stopped to appraise the stranger. He was handsome, dressed in the traditional three-piece suit. He looked like a bank president or company executive. "You were lucky not to get hit by my frying pan."

He stood without moving for a few moments, watching the young woman wearing a pair of goggles on her forehead gather up a pot and frying pan from the floor. If this was Sara Cahill, she was a strikingly beautiful woman. Her features were delicately proportioned, like those of a porcelain figurine. Yet there was an earthy quality about her that was accentuated by the baseball cap she wore and the faded jeans and sweatshirt.

She was preoccupied, inspecting the pans carefully for damage as she walked, so Ben said nothing as he went toward her. He hadn't the foggiest idea why she would have thrown the cookware down the hall. Maybe she had a violent temper. She entered an office and he followed. After placing the pot and pan on a desktop, she turned and smiled at him hesitantly.

Sara tossed the baseball cap that had kept her hair in place onto one of the chairs, along with her safety goggles, then finger-combed her hair, allowing it to drape over her shoulders. "Well, that's it for me for today." She pulled her sweatshirt over her head, revealing a long-sleeved oxford shirt with a delicate floral pattern that exactly matched the color of her jeans.

The result was startling. A few seconds ago, she'd looked almost tomboyish, but now he was face-to-face with a most appealing woman. He cleared his throat. "I'm Ben Lowell."

"Hello, Ben Lowell." She extended her hands. "What brings you here to Mousetrap Incorporated? I'm Sara Cahill, owner, manager and staff."

"I work upstairs. I came to find out who you were and what you did down here. After hearing that commotion and seeing the frying pans, I'm more curious than ever.

Do you restrict your attacks to vacant hallways, or are the other occupants of the building in danger of being beaned by a pot?''

Sara laughed. "Hardly. I'm an inventor, and I was testing the strength of the handles, that's all. Nothing to worry about. I hardly ever throw objects down the hall.''

"I'm sure your husband's grateful for that," he answered.

She smiled. "I'm not married.''

"That's good to know." So Jimmy had been right about her profession. She seemed friendly enough, but she *had* stymied his best, hard-boiled executives.

"Are you here only to satisfy your curiosity about me, Mr. Lowell?'' She locked the door to her lab, then placed a few files in the safe. "Or are you one of the storm troopers that are trying to run me out?''

"At the moment, I'm just wondering how safe it is to have you in the building.'' He grinned slowly. That was the truth, in more ways than one.

She laughed, a hearty laugh that was fresh and uninhibited. "I never conduct any major experiments in my design shop, Mr. Lowell. I use National Laboratories for that. I just try my ideas out here on a very small scale.''

He felt himself waffling. Yes, he had come down here to persuade her to leave, only now he wasn't in such a rush to help her vacate her basement offices. Sara Cahill was a very unusual lady, and she intrigued him. It had been a long time since he'd met a woman he'd honestly found this interesting, as well as appealing. "Why don't you let me buy you a drink? We can get to know each other. Now that you're sharing the building with Classic Parts Incorporated, it's the neighborly thing to do.''

Sara met his eyes. She'd never seen eyes that particular color, a unique mixture of turquoise and blue. His gaze was direct. Sara playfully challenged him by holding it for a moment or two longer than custom dictated. Realizing that he wasn't going to look away, and that at best the little game was at a stalemate, she turned around and reached for her purse. "I appreciate the offer, but I'm going home. I have to plan the final heat tests for my new formula."

"Okay, but let's talk on the way to your car," he suggested without any hesitation. "If you won't have a drink with me tonight, maybe we can have lunch tomorrow. Or if not, dinner. If we both try, I'm sure we can come up with a time that's mutually agreeable." He wasn't letting her off the hook that easily. He never distrusted his instincts, and right now they told him Sara would be worth the trouble of getting to know her.

She almost laughed. She liked aggressive men, and something told her that Mr. Ben Lowell was a prime example of one. She had a feeling that it would take a major miracle to get him to take no for an answer. "We have nothing to talk about," she persisted good-naturedly, matching his stubbornness. "But let me save you some time. If you're another one who's going to ask me to move out, the answer is still no."

She walked into the hall, then waited for him to join her. As she bent down to lock the door, she stole a sidelong glance. Ben Lowell was impeccably dressed. His suit and maroon silk tie were both tasteful and expensive. Only in his mid-thirties, he had about him the undefinable look of authority and assurance that usually came from power, money or both. He was also extremely handsome, though not in a conventional way. His features were too chiseled to be perfect, but they conveyed a certain strength that she found appealing.

"If you don't feel like having a drink with me this evening, how about a late snack? I know a great little spot not too far from here," he offered, watching her place the key in the lock. A figure like hers begged for tighter jeans than the ones she was wearing. And what he saw as she stooped verified that conclusion. He took a deep breath.

She straightened and turned around. Instinct told her what portion of her anatomy had captured his attention moments before. She smiled. It made her feel good to know that even though she was wearing an old pair of jeans, a man this attractive still thought she merited closer inspection. "Are you always this persistent?"

"I try." He laughed. "Does that mean you'll accept my invitation and share a late snack with me?"

"It's not late," she retorted. "It's only eight-thirty. Besides, you don't seem to understand. I'm through at the office, but I intend to keep working once I get home. I'm usually in my laboratory until two in the morning. The only reason I'm leaving early tonight is because I'm not ready to go on with the next phase of my work. The drive home will help me unwind, and I need a break. Sometimes it's best to stop after a successful test and think about something else for a while."

"Exactly my point," he argued. "And as luck would have it, here I am, at your disposal." He smiled, eyes twinkling with devilish merriment.

Sara studied him. He was very determined in a cool and well-mannered way. And he did have the most devastating smile.

"Why are you being so adamant?" she asked, avoiding any suggestion of pretense. Maybe she'd get a straight answer if she managed to shock him by being direct. "What is it that you want from me? So far all I know about you is your name, that you work in the building, and that you're curious about my work."

"All true." He grinned. "However, I have to admit you've taken me completely by surprise. I expected the head of Mousetrap Incorporated to be quite different."

"How so?" Sara led the way up the basement stairs, keeping her pace brisk. There was a blend of pushiness and pure virility about him that made her uneasy. If she kept moving with a spring in her step, she'd be able to disguise the effect his presence was having on her.

To her surprise, it took him several moments to answer her. He didn't seem like the type to hesitate. She stopped at the first-floor landing and gave him a quizzical look. "What did you expect?" she repeated.

"I thought you were an exterminator." He shrugged. "That's not an occupation a man associates with gorgeous women."

She laughed easily, flattered and amused at the same time. "An exterminator?" She caught her breath, then added, "But if you thought that, why did you come downstairs? Did you want to see if I was some kind of gnarled old crone who cackled every time she zapped a cockroach?"

"Well, actually, it was my son who suggested we were all wrong and that you might be an inventor. He's quite gifted in science and he's always inventing something or other. He was thrilled at the possibility that there might be an inventor right here. In his eyes that would mean there was someone *really* important in his dad's new building."

Disappointment washed over her. So he was married. Well, that took care of romantic fantasies. It took another second for the rest of the information to hit home. Ben Lowell wasn't just an employee! He was the owner of the building, the man behind the troops who'd been trying to get her to leave her own comfortable offices! "Now I get it! You didn't come down out of curiosity. As I suspected, you really came to talk me into leaving." She pursed her lips and tried to control her temper. Once it got to a certain level, she'd explode like Vesuvius. "Well, Mr. Lowell, I'm comfortable right where I am. I happen to like the rent I pay, and most important of all, my lease stipulates that no matter what the new owners decide to do to the rent, my lease agreement holds for two more years. I wrote those terms myself, and I'm not giving you an inch." She squared her shoulders, then faced him. "Now, if you'll step aside, I'm leaving."

"Wait a minute. I admit, I did want you out, but I was willing to discuss the matter," he protested, blocking her way.

"There's nothing to discuss. I'm going home. You can go to... wherever you were planning to go tonight."

"Are you afraid I'll change your mind? Is that why you refuse to even talk to me about this?" he challenged.

His statement took her completely by surprise. Her mouth dropped open slightly. "I'm not afraid of anyone, Mr. Lowell. Least of all you." Her tone was belligerent, more out of habit than any real sense of outrage. She'd always had to fight the tendency to be too nice to people. It was natural for her to accommodate others. The problem was that giving in meant that someone else would do the taking. Sara had seen what had happened to her mother, the perfect example of a good-natured person. Her dad had simply taken over, and her mother had lived her entire life in the childlike state of adapting to someone else's rules. Sara was determined never to let her own good nature lead her down the same path.

"Great. Since you don't find me intimidating, then there's no reason we can't get together, talk and get to know one another." This woman certainly had a lot of fire in her. The fact that she was being so difficult only strengthened Ben's resolve. He'd always believed that nothing easy was worth going after.

"We've talked," she said with finality. "Go home to your wife and family. As you said, it's late."

He stopped suddenly, a wave of darkness passing over his eyes. "I don't have a wife now. She died. And my son is with the housekeeper, probably doing his homework."

Sara's mouth fell open with embarrassment, but she quickly recovered. "Sorry. Your private life is none of my business," she muttered, turning away quickly. Keys in hand, she headed for the revolving doors.

"Give me your keys," he offered, catching up to her again, "and I'll unfasten the lock at the bottom of the doors. It's after hours, so they're shut tight."

"I know that. I always leave after everyone else does," she replied tersely. "I can get it."

"I know you can," he insisted, "but I feel better when I act like a gentleman."

Sara smiled, though she really hadn't meant to. Playfully turning his words around she added, "Does that also mean that even though you feel rotten about it, there are times when you aren't a gentleman?"

"Most definitely," he retorted with a roguish grin as she handed over the key ring.

He wasn't to be trusted. Not one little bit. After all, he did want her out of his building. Yet it was hard not to be affected by him. He seemed so sure of himself and so undaunted by her efforts to brush him off. Men had been known to find her intimidating, but this man's will matched her own.

She waited for him to unlock the doors. A second later they stood face-to-face. A glittering intensity sparkled in his eyes as he held her gaze. For a split second, Sara was afraid that he was about to kiss her.

Without hesitation, she entered the segmented interior of the revolving doors. It was time to get away from this man.

She pushed the doors forward, anticipating a speedy exit. The door moved half an inch, then stopped abruptly. She started to push again, when she heard someone directly behind her clearing his throat. Startled, she jumped and turned around quickly.

"You're supposed to take the next compartment," she said, her throat constricting. "That's the way revolving doors work."

Ben smiled as he continued to lean against the back of the compartment, holding it securely in place. "I wanted to talk to you."

"Don't you ever give up?" she asked, aghast. In the cramped enclosure his presence was overwhelmingly seductive. Only the soft glow of the street lamp illuminated the area outside. Her heart raced and her skin tingled with anticipation.

He watched her in silence for a moment. There was a flush in her cheeks that suggested that she found him as big a temptation as he found her. "If you'll give me a chance, I think we can work something out that will benefit both of us."

"Hardly," Sara retorted, trying to sound cool. She wondered about lips like his that smiled with tenderness, yet hinted at an iron will.

"I admit my first inclination was to try and persuade you to move out of the building. However, even if I could do that, I'm not so sure I'd attempt it anymore." His voice was low, heady and intoxicatingly seductive.

Her mouth went dry. How long had it been since she'd had a relationship with a man? A year? More? Maybe that was it. It was like sampling a teaspoon of rich chocolate ice cream after months on a diet. You'd forced yourself not to think about it, but once you got the taste on the tip of your tongue, you'd remember all that you'd been missing. "Look, we can't stay in here. Be reasonable."

"Have dinner with me," he replied.

"And what if I say no? What would you do then?" she countered. Sara should have hated it, but the more he stood up to her the more attracted to him she became.

His smile was sensual. "I always do whatever needs to be done," he said suggestively.

For a minute she thought her knees were going to buckle. Had the situation been reversed, she might have said the same thing. Yet there was something else happening, something she couldn't quite pinpoint. The attraction between them was mutual, she realized with sudden clarity. And it was growing more potent by the second. "Fine. Dinner," she blurted.

He stepped away from the back of the compartment.

Sara turned around and quickly pushed the doors forward. Air. She needed air. The colder the better. Scarcely aware of how fast she'd moved, she gasped when she heard a thump and Ben careered forward, pinning her to the front of the compartment.

She was aware of everything, though her thoughts were jumbled and coming too quickly for her to focus. Sara felt the tautness of his body pressing intimately against her, and caught the masculine scent of his cologne. The heat of his breath seared her neck. She fought the irresistible urge to turn around, welcome his embrace, and see what it would be like in his arms.

It took a second for him to recapture his balance, but in that brief time he felt his body respond to the yielding softness of hers. Sara's hair brushed his face, the scent of it like apple blossoms. He took a deep breath and reluctantly moved away. "Sorry about that. You pushed the door forward so fast, you didn't give me a chance to get out of the way. Are you all right?"

He'd stepped back, but not far enough. Her body throbbed. "I'm fine."

"What is that perfume you're wearing?" he asked, his voice a lazy drawl. "It suits you."

"Eau de laboratory," she retorted quickly, trying to lighten the mood.

"I knew I recognized the scent," he responded and they both laughed.

A moment later they emerged. Sara felt her heart drumming with excitement.

"Where shall we go for dinner?" he asked, trying not to think sexual thoughts.

"I have no intention of going out to dinner with you, Mr. Lowell." She wouldn't take any more chances. The feelings he'd awakened in her were too disturbing to ignore. "I agreed only so I could get out of those revolving doors. Like you, I also do whatever has to be done. I would have promised to make love to you in a vat of pickle relish if that was what it took. But now that we're outside, forget it, buster."

"Really?" he replied. A smile played over his lips, tugging at the corners of his mouth. With deliberation he held up her keys. "How do you intend to drive home?"

CHAPTER TWO

ONE DAY HAD PASSED since Sara had found herself tricked
into having dinner with a man every instinct warned her
to avoid. Ben Lowell was successful, aggressive, likable,
extremely appealing—and a cartload of trouble. Ben's
mind was always at work, never missing a nuance or an
angle to get whatever he wanted. The dirty trick he'd
pulled with the keys was a prime example of that. Yet,
instead of rejecting the man outright, she found herself
liking the challenge of trying to stay one step ahead of
him.

She walked across the office and picked up the handle
of a Dutch oven, slightly discolored, but undamaged from
exposure to a six-hundred-degree furnace temperature.

Worst of all, she was having trouble concentrating on
work. Her thoughts invariably drifted back to him. With
a sigh, she plopped into the nearest chair, and set the
handle on her desk. Her reaction to him left her baffled.
She was becoming a stranger to herself.

Until a few days ago, she'd been happy, though most
people considered her life-style unusual. Being different
from others had never bothered her. For instance, she'd
learned early in life that she was a late-night person, so
she'd always be at her peak of efficiency when the rest of
the world was asleep. Also, unlike most of the women
she'd met, Sara enjoyed living alone and depending on no
one but herself. Eventually, she expected that she'd fall in

love and get married, but it had always seemed something that belonged to the distant future. It was an event to look forward to, but she definitely wasn't in any rush. There was plenty of time. At twenty-eight, the world was ahead of her, and the possibilities were infinite.

In her fantasies Sara envisioned finding a man who, like herself, was a night owl. They'd have a bunch of night owl children, and give them the type of home life she'd dreamed about, where they'd all be very close—not just people who lived under the same roof. She'd become the old-fashioned "heart of the family" to her brood, and enjoy the sense of belonging that came from being needed, and being part of a circle of love.

Her scenario wasn't terribly realistic, but inventors weren't known for dreaming up the usual or the mundane. Her fantasy was simply her idea of perfection.

The empty spot within that had gnawed at her since childhood, the core that longed to be filled with love would remain in a state of quiet expectation, knowing that inevitably the time would come for satisfaction.

So why had meeting Ben Lowell made her feel so restless? Why was she questioning her decision not to rush into relationships? Why had that empty spot started to ache with such acute longing?

She pursed her lips and furrowed her eyebrows. She'd been inhaling too many epoxy fumes, that was why.

"Hi!" a small voice greeted from the front door of her office.

Sara glanced up. A thin boy about four foot six with thick, circular glasses and a blue NASA cap looked at her with the same intensity and eager curiosity a boy his age might reserve for a national sports hero. "Hello, yourself! Did you take the wrong turn at the elevator?"

"Oh, no! I *tried* to find you!" He stopped, glanced at his sneakers, then cleared his throat, nervously shifting his red backpack over one shoulder. "Dad said . . . I mean, I found out that . . ." His face turned a deep crimson. "You're an inventor!" he managed to say at last, as if the statement explained everything.

Sara blinked, then laughed. "Wait. Let me guess. You're Ben Lowell's son, right?"

He nodded. "Yes, ma'am, I'm Jimmy. Wow, this is so neat!" He walked farther into her office, then peered into the small lab in the next room. "This is exactly the way I want my office to look someday. Laboratory stuff in one room, lots of papers scattered everywhere, and a big desk and swivel chair just to make it more business-y."

Sara gaped at him incredulously. "Wait a second. I'm not sure I should be flattered with that description. Papers *scattered* everywhere?" she repeated, feigning outrage.

"Oh, bug dung," he muttered. "I didn't mean to insult you or anything," he blurted out.

Sara laughed loudly. Ben's kid was quite a character. She found herself really liking the boy. "You didn't. It's okay. You want me to give you a tour?"

"Yea, that would be great!" His eyes lit up as he followed her through the office.

She was okay, Jimmy concluded. At least she wasn't telling him to get out, or waiting impatiently for him to finally get bored and leave. Some of his dad's girlfriends acted that way. Then again, she wasn't his dad's girlfriend—yet. Most women his dad met usually applied for the job sooner or later.

"This is my lab," Sara explained, showing him the length of a long table filled with Bunsen burners, beakers and flasks. A large metal cabinet spotted with safety labels contained many of the chemicals she used for her work. "I don't do any elaborate experiments here, but this is usually where it all begins."

"Is that a centrifuge?" Jimmy asked, pointing to a piece of equipment across the room.

She was surprised that Jimmy was so well-informed. "Yes, it is, as a matter of fact. I use it sometimes to separate materials of different density, like solids from liquids. You must have seen one before."

"Sure did," he replied with a smile. "My Integrated Studies class visited the university's Biology Department on a field trip, and we got to see one being used to separate plant pigments." Jimmy kept his eyes on her face. She was beautiful. Maybe that's why Dad had acted so strangely when he'd asked him if he'd managed to talk her into leaving the building. Dad had probably taken one look at her and changed his mind. Jimmy smiled.

"What's that grin all about?" Sara asked. "I hope you don't think I'm some kind of crazy scientist. Your dad was afraid I'd blow up the building or something."

Jimmy laughed. Dad could be such a fuzz-brain sometimes. "Naw, I don't think you're crazy or going to blow up the building. Dad'll realize it too, after a while. You just have to be patient with him. He's a great guy, but he just hates it when things don't go exactly the way he plans. He's not big on surprises of any kind."

Sara was about to reply when she heard footsteps down the hall.

Jimmy turned quickly and peered outside. "Hi, Dad!"

"Jimmy, I've been looking all over the place for you. I thought you were going to join me in the lunchroom. School's been out for an hour already. I believe you mentioned something about dying of starvation."

"Aw, you knew I'd come down to the basement," the boy replied with a grin. "That's why you looked here."

Sara laughed. Jimmy was outrageous. In fact, between his candor and his interest in science, he was precisely the type of kid she would have wanted.

"Hello, Ben." She watched him lounge in the doorway, his eyes fixed on her. As his gaze dropped, taking in the rest of her appreciatively, she suddenly became self-conscious. "Come in. Would you like a soft drink? I keep a few colas in my lab refrigerator."

"Next to what green and growing things, I wonder?" he teased.

"Hey, I'm just an inventor. This isn't Frankenstein's laboratory, you know," she returned good-naturedly.

Jimmy was at her computer stand, looking at the software she'd arranged in plastic flip files. "Dad, this place is just like the one I'll have someday. It's perfect!"

"I hope you realize that he sees you as a kindred spirit," Ben told her, giving his son a wink. "Why don't you come upstairs with us and share an afternoon snack? That is, unless Jimmy's driven you crazy with questions, and you'd rather we both disappeared."

"I'm due for a break, but I'll have to make it a short one." Sparks flew between them as she met his steady gaze. His eyes weren't turquoise blue at all. They were greenish blue. Like the color of the ocean on a clear day, the soft hue shimmered, fluctuating with the currents of his thoughts. Sara felt the magnetic pull of his presence, and for a moment or two she could barely breathe. "I'm having a problem with my current project," she explained. "It isn't exactly progressing at the rate I'd hoped."

"Did the pan handles break after all?" he asked.

She laughed, remembering the volley she'd fired down the hall. "No, but they're not holding their color tint. They're turning from black to brown when I expose them to six-hundred-degree temperatures. That just won't do."

He glanced around quickly. "You're not heating any skillets in a furnace around here, are you?" he asked, a bit too fast to sound casual.

"No. You don't have to worry about your building going up in smoke."

"Good." He grasped his son by the shoulder. "Son, let's leave while the going's good."

"What's all this stuff about pots and pans?" Jimmy asked.

TWENTY MINUTES LATER they were sitting around an empty table in the newly installed lunchroom on the top floor.

Ben and Jimmy finished their candy bars while Sara ate a cupcake. She studied the vast array of vending machines and all the treats they contained. She could get an entire dinner up here. "Would you mind if I used these machines from time to time? Before you moved in, I'd either have to bring my own stuff or go to the deli down the street."

"Use them as often as you like," Ben answered.

"Does that mean she's staying?" Jimmy asked his father, cutting through the unspoken references.

"What can I tell you, son?" he asked and shrugged helplessly. "She won't go." Ben suspected she wasn't the least bit interested in his business dealings. As a tenant, she was probably a good risk.

Sara smiled. "If I recall correctly, you bought me a very nice dinner last night, but you never did ask me to move out."

Jimmy beamed them both a bright, hopeful smile. "Dad, I'm going home now. I have to get some homework done before supper. I'll see you later." He gave his father a thumbs-up gesture.

Before Sara or Ben could say another word, he was on his feet, walking to the door. "See ya!"

Sara blinked. "Did I miss something here? What was that all about?"

"My son, the matchmaker. Subtle, isn't he?"

The huskiness of his voice settled on her like a gentle caress. Her heart quickened. "He wants you to remarry?"

"Actually, I think what he really wants is to be the one who selects my bride. Once he decides he's got a potentially qualified candidate, he does all he can to make it happen. In all fairness, though, he's very selective. You're only the second one in the past twelve months."

"I'm flattered." She paused. "I think."

"By the way, I'm glad we're alone in here now. I want to make you a proposition."

For one wild moment Sara thought he was about to ask her on a very intimate date. Would she be able to bring out the gentle side of him, that tenderness she'd glimpsed in him when he was around Jimmy? Realizing that his eyes were focused intently on hers, and afraid that he might have read her thoughts, she glanced at her lap and pretended to brush away nonexistent cupcake crumbs. "I'm listening," she managed to say.

"My company, Classic Parts Incorporated, is a mail-order business. It's our job to find rare, out of production car parts for dealers and private collectors. Noticing some of the materials you work with gave me an idea, but I really need someone like you to help me develop it." He recognized the stirrings of desire within himself and acknowledged them with reluctance. This woman distracted him too much. He couldn't think clearly around her. Last night he'd meant to persuade her to move out of the building. Instead, he'd found himself persuading her to have dinner with him. Now, when he was supposed to be asking her to work for him, he found himself wondering what it would take to get past that reserve she'd erected to keep him at bay.

"What is it that you need?" she offered, noting his silence. "I'll be glad to help if I can." He looked as if he was fighting some inner battle. Didn't he want to ask her for help, or was it something more? A thought formed slowly in her mind. Was it possible that he found the attraction between them as disconcerting as she did?

"As an inventor, you're in an ideal position to help my company. You see, there are times when a client asks me to locate an automotive part that is no longer available. I do my best, but if I can't track one down, that means we all lose. I've missed the business, and the client has to do without, or I lose him to a competitor. The cost of individually casting and machining metal parts for a car is unbelievably high. Most of the time it just isn't worth it to the client." He leaned forward, his face taut with concentration. "However, if I could employ some new molding or a casting method that's affordable, and get my clients the parts they need this way, I'd be offering an exclusive, more comprehensive service. Classic Parts could double or triple its business. That material you created for those handles might be adaptable to our needs, but if not, maybe you could come up with something specifically suited for us."

"And you want to hire me to find this alternate material and casting method, right?"

"Yes, if you think the idea is feasible and not just a pipe dream."

"Oh, it's possible, all right." Sara mulled the idea over in her mind. "The key lies in finding the right chemical substance to mold into the desired product; something as strong and heat tolerant as metal, but cheaper and easier to work with. The material I used for the handles doesn't have all the properties you'd need for automobile parts, but that doesn't mean I couldn't come up with something else that would work." She felt more at ease concentrating on business matters around this man. At least on this ground, there were no emotional intangibles and no uncertainty.

"Will you take the job then? If you agree, then I'm sure we can work out financial arrangements."

"I'll accept—providing we can negotiate a mutually acceptable contract." Sara paused. "Write me a specific proposal explaining what you want, and I'll tell you if it's practicable and what it'll cost. After that, we can settle on terms."

"That's great. By the way, you said that National Laboratories provides you with facilities for your major tests. I suppose they are trustworthy."

"Certainly. Their owner and I have been friends for some time now. Why do you ask?"

"I'm just being cautious, that's all. Some of my competitors are very ruthless businessmen. They'd love to know as much as they could about my plans, so they could try to undermine me."

"Well, you don't have to worry about Mike and National Laboratories. I trust him implicitly, and you will too, I'm sure. Is there anything else?"

"There is one more thing. I would like you to keep me informed of your progress. Although in essence you're an independent contractor, the fact that you share the same building with us should make it easier for us to stay in touch. I've worked very hard to make Classic Parts the company it is today, and I like to keep tabs on everything. That way, there are no surprises."

Sara remembered Jimmy saying that Ben hated surprises. Of course, anyone would hate bad news, but too much sameness could lead to a horribly predictable life. In or out of business, such dull consistency couldn't be a good thing. She started to ask him about it, when she saw him glance at his watch.

"I have a meeting with the Customer Order Department manager in a few minutes. However, I want to talk to you later and work out some details. Is that all right with you?"

"Sure. My time's flexible. Just let me know when." A curious sensation of heaviness washed over her. To her own surprise, Sara realized it was disappointment. She didn't want their meeting to end. Annoyed with herself, she stood and gave him a level look. "I'll be in my lab. Give me a call when you're ready to discuss this project at length."

Ben watched her walk out of the lunchroom. Her change of attitude had taken him by surprise. One second she'd been relaxed and friendly, then all of a sudden he'd been face-to-face with a cool businesswoman looking for the bottom line. Had he said something to upset her? He clenched his jaw. The real question, of course, was why her mood change had bothered him at all. He'd never been overly sensitive. Besides, she was still too much of an unknown quantity for him to let the attraction between them blossom into anything more serious.

He remembered Rosemary. Their ten-year marriage had been a happy one. Rosemary had understood his need to take charge and make the decisions. She'd known instinctively that it was his way of keeping their family safe. Yet, as it had so many times throughout his youth, the unexpected had shattered his world. Rosemary's death of a heart attack at the age of thirty-two had devastated him. A youthful bout with rheumatic fever had left her heart in a weakened condition and she'd pushed herself beyond her physical limits. The hardest thing to face now was the knowledge that he'd been partially to blame. If only he'd been more alert and had watched over her better, she might still be alive. He tossed the empty can of soda into the trash can with a vengeance, then strode down the hall.

He'd learned his lesson well. Control and alertness were the keys. You couldn't take precautions against what you couldn't foresee, but you could minimize the risk by always being prepared and well-informed. The more information you had, the more control you could exert over events, and in that way lessen the chance of the unexpected turning your life upside down.

By the time Ben reached his office several men were waiting, and he banished all thoughts of the past from his mind. "Hello, gentlemen," he said briskly and continued to his desk, showing no sign of the torment he'd known only moments before. "Let's begin."

SARA SAT IN HER OFFICE and reviewed the notes on her last experiment. Her mind, usually so disciplined, continued to play hooky. She felt a constant, straining alertness that invariably pulled her thoughts back to Ben. She was bewildered.

Sara had always prided herself on being logical, not at all the sort of woman who'd be swayed by an infatuation. There had been men in her life before, and she'd liked some more than others, but had never felt this inexplicable surge of conflicting emotions. She wanted to know more about Ben, yet to know more might deepen an involvement she wasn't at all sure was wise.

Any woman who'd let a man like Ben into her heart was asking for trouble. He was a strong man, determined to have his way. He'd compel her to surrender all of her heart, yet would be very hesitant to respond with the same totality. He liked being the one in charge. The only problem was, so did she.

The telephone's ringing brought her out of her musings. "This is Sara Cahill."

"Hello, Sara Cahill," Ben's familiar voice drawled over the wires. "I'm going to be tied up for the rest of the afternoon, but I can have that formal proposal brought to your office in another hour or so for you to look over. I know you work late, and although I seldom stay after hours, tonight's going to be an exception. Jimmy's off at a friend's house. How about meeting me for a working dinner, say at about seven? We can go over the details of our business deal then. I'll pick someplace quiet where we can talk without interruptions."

"That sounds fine." Sara placed the receiver back in its cradle.

The proposal was indeed delivered—thirty minutes later. With renewed determination, Sara began her experiments. She had several samples of handle material she was going to heat test in the flame of a blowtorch.

Hours later, grasping the final test sample with metal tongs and wearing a protective glove, Sara held it in the blue cone of flame until it began to glow. A few seconds after she removed it from the flame, it was cool to the touch, yet retained its color.

"Yes!" Sara yelled triumphantly, shutting off the torch and setting it down to cool.

"Hello!"

Startled, Sara jumped and whirled around. "Ben! What are you doing here?" She pulled up one edge of her glove and glanced at her watch. Good grief! At first she hadn't been able to get to work without thinking of him. Then she'd forced herself to concentrate, and had lost track of time completely.

"That's a new style of mitt!" He ran a finger upward from her palm, tracing the length of the asbestos glove on her left hand. "Are you starting to play catch with your frying pans now?"

Her skin prickled beneath his feather-light touch as he continued his caress up her arm. The heat from his fingertips seemed to penetrate the light material of her shirt. "Don't tease," she ventured, thinking that the word was appropriate in more ways than one. "I am making progress. I've finally found the ideal formulation for a non-heat-absorbing handle material. This probably has hundreds of other applications beyond the cookware industry."

He stood before her, admiration shining in his eyes. "That's terrific. It must be wonderful to know you can create things that will make other people's lives better. It's quite a special talent."

Sara felt her face begin to redden. "Quit, you're embarrassing me. Let me go to the rest room to wash up. I'll be right back."

She practically ran out of the office, purse in hand. Safely behind closed doors, Sara exhaled softly, waiting for the beet-red color to fade from her cheeks. Praise was something she'd never known how to accept gracefully.

By the time she returned to her office a few minutes later she felt more relaxed. "Did you want to go out for a sandwich?"

"Actually, I had a sandwich for lunch. If you don't mind, I'd rather have a more substantial meal right now. I'm hungry. I thought we could have dinner at Maria's. It's convenient because it's close by. It's also my favorite place. You always get more than enough to eat."

Her eyes widened slightly. Maria's was one of the best restaurants in town. "Fine." Her body tingled with excitement and apprehension. Being with Ben seemed to add a dash of adventure to everything.

"By the way, how come you didn't answer your phone? When you didn't show up at my office, I tried calling you several times, but all I could get was your machine." Ben studied Sara's face as he spoke. He liked the way she wore her makeup. She applied only enough to enhance her features. A bit of color to the cheeks and peach-colored lipstick blended in well with her light coloring. It gave her a wholesome, healthy look. He smiled, thinking of how she'd blushed when he'd complimented her. He'd meant what he'd said, but perhaps it was best not to apologize for embarrassing her. It might only result in making her feel awkward all over again.

"I'm sorry. I didn't hear the telephone when you called. I turn down the ringer when I'm running experiments. That way, unless I'm really listening, the sound won't interrupt my work." She led the way out of the office.

They walked down the hall together, and took the elevator to the ground floor.

Ben shifted uncomfortably as they stood quietly side by side. There was a subtle sexiness about Sara that made him feel uneasy. His body reacted to her on a purely physical level that he was unaccustomed to experiencing.

He'd dated his share of women, but he'd never felt the pull, the need that Sara evoked. If this was chemistry, he needed it like a hole in the head.

"As far as I'm concerned, Sara," he said, back to business, "the fact that you'll be doing work for Classic Parts makes it important that you know a bit about us. I'd like to give you a feel for what it is that we do. You'll be able to understand our procedures and our goals if you can see Classic Parts through my eyes."

She wanted to do just that, but not for the reasons he'd cited. A compelling sense of curiosity drove her to learn as much as she could about him.

As he walked her to his car, Ben continued. "When I bought this company, it was in a financial mess. That was eleven years ago. Today, Classic Parts is respected, and we have a steady profit margin. This company is very important to me. It's come a long way, but I've still got lots of plans. This past year we started getting so much business that it became very difficult for us to handle the load. I knew we had to expand or start losing to our competitors. If we couldn't keep up, we'd risk being squeezed out of the market in the long run. So we decided to take the chance and expand. I have a great deal of faith in Classic Parts. By the time I retire, I believe my son's financial future will be more than just secure. He'll be able to do or be whatever he chooses."

So it was more than money. Jimmy was Ben's primary motivation for constantly striving to make his company better. She wondered about his relationship with his son. It was obvious he loved Jimmy a great deal. For an instant she found herself wishing her own family had felt that way about her. She shook her head as if to rid herself of the unwelcome thought, and focused on what he was saying.

Ben held his car door open for her, then walked around and slipped behind the wheel. "Actually, I have a confession to make," he said, as he turned the ignition switch. "This afternoon I checked you out with some of the major companies I know, to see what results you usually get for your clients. I expected that in your line of work it would be fifty-fifty at best. I was really surprised to find out that you always deliver," he added with genuine admiration, as he eased into the street, merging with the downtown traffic.

Sara studied the way his hands gripped the wheel. His hands looked strong, yet they also possessed grace and sensitivity in their touch. "The problem is, the results don't always meet the client's expectations," she replied with characteristic candor. "I'll give you an example. I was hired at one time by a housing contractor. He wanted me to see if I could come up with a paint that had reflective qualities. He wanted this paint to bounce back room heat and act as an energy-saving device. All I could promise him was that I'd try for three months, and see what kind of progress I could make. Well, I found the right chemical balance, only when I added it to paint, it would turn the color metallic silver. There wasn't much of a market for glossy silver interior paint, so he wasn't satisfied with the results." She paused. "However, he did get what he asked for."

Ben pulled into the parking lot the restaurant shared with the museum next door, and started to search for a parking space. "You're trying to warn me, aren't you?"

"Yes, I am," she answered.

He drove up and down the rows of parked cars, but every spot seemed to be filled. "This place is never that crowded on weeknights," he commented, perplexed.

"I think the museum has a special function going on tonight," Sara said, directing his attention to one side. "See?" She gestured toward a large group of people gathered around the museum's front entrance.

He hoped that all those people wouldn't decide to drop by the restaurant for drinks or dessert later. He'd wanted this to be a quiet dinner, one that would help put her in a relaxed frame of mind so that they could negotiate the details of their contract.

"I'm afraid we're going to have to do a bit of walking. I can't find a parking space near the door," he said apologetically.

"It's okay. It's a beautiful, clear evening." The faded orange lights of the street lamps combined with the brilliance of the full moon, adding touches of color and life to the gray of the night. The pavement beneath her feet, like the canopy of stars above, glistened with flecks of silver that eluded her as they walked.

Their stroll was pleasant, but the gathering at the museum still irked him. He'd wanted everything to flow smoothly this evening. Discovering annoying last-minute surprises was not a good sign. Well, at least she didn't seem to mind. "You're being an awfully good sport about this. I'm sure you didn't expect a forced march before dinner," he joked.

"It's not that far. I can almost see the restaurant outlined on the horizon," she quipped, pretending to strain her eyes ahead in hopes of getting a clearer glimpse.

"I was expecting you to sympathize with me, and offer a few words of comfort," he countered with a grin.

"Let that be a lesson to you." She could feel the warmth of his body beside hers, and was acutely aware of her attraction to him. "You have to be careful with expectations. Unless you build in a margin for play, you often end up disappointed." She grew serious. "That's basically what I was trying to tell you before about the type of work I do."

"Don't worry. I always try to include play in my expectations," he drawled, giving her a wink.

She chuckled softly. "I really mean it."

"So do I," he said, baiting her again.

CHAPTER THREE

WHEN THEY ENTERED Maria's, Ben and Sara were seated almost immediately, despite the gathering crowd. As they followed the hostess, she noted the old style Spanish decor, from the viga beams that framed the ceilings to the adobe walls decorated with folk art. They were seated at the most secluded table in the room. Outside their window, a water fountain tinted with blue and lavender lights cascaded and gurgled in a steady rhythmic pattern.

The muted glow from the single candle at the center of the table sent speckles of dancing light across the tablecloth, bathing it with touches of golden warmth.

The maître d' seemed eager to please Ben, making sure he was satisfied with their location. "The table is perfect, John, thanks," Ben replied.

"I've paid special attention to details, Mr. Lowell. I trust you'll have a memorable evening."

When he moved away, Sara gave Ben a puzzled look. "Memorable? That's an odd choice of words, don't you think?"

"Yes, it is," he conceded. "I can't imagine what he meant. All I said to him was to make sure we had a nice table. I'm a regular customer, though, and I bring a lot of clients here for lunch. That's probably the reason he's always especially attentive. John is the type who likes anticipating your needs before you voice them. I remember one time when I mentioned that one of the dishes had been overseasoned. John not only replaced my lunch, but those of my guests who'd ordered the same thing."

Ben dismissed the matter with a casual wave of the hand. "Now, as far as the warning you were trying to give me about my expectations, I don't want you to worry about that." He lowered his voice slightly and continued, weaving added meaning into his words. "I'm aware that there are risks involved," Ben drawled as his eyes strayed over her intimately, "but I believe the stakes are high enough to warrant them."

The unspoken awareness between them pulsated and shimmered with a life of its own. Sara sat very still, afraid she might inadvertently let Ben know just how thoroughly he affected her. Her gaze drifted across the room in an effort to divert her thoughts. Couples, young and old, holding hands or gazing into each others' eyes, seemed to fill the dining area that surrounded them.

The waiter came to take their cocktail orders. "What would you like?" Ben asked her, his mind filled with renegade thoughts as his eyes settled on her lips.

"A glass of red wine, please."

"Scotch for me," he added, his gaze never leaving her.

She liked the way he made her feel, wonderfully feminine and almost alluring. Forcing herself to remember that they were there to discuss business, she schooled her thoughts. "I believe I have a very good grasp of what it is you want me to create for your company, Ben. What I'd like to do is work on your project for one month. That'll be a trial period. Then at the end of that time we can sit down and review the progress I've made."

Ben wished he could pull her out of the chair and kiss her. He really hadn't thought of anything else for the last fifteen minutes. He wanted to crush her against him and feel her respond when he caressed her. He took a deep breath. "That sounds fine...."

He was about to say more when a guitarist came by their table and began to serenade them with Spanish love ballads. Ben sat back and listened, glad of a chance to watch Sara without seeming obvious. She appeared to be enjoying the music. He wanted her to have a good time and to relax. Every once in a while he'd notice small signs that she was starting to feel comfortable around him. Then, without warning, she'd suddenly retreat behind talk of her work. Her efforts to remain emotionally distant made him even more determined to get past the barriers she'd erected. He wanted very much to get to know her.

As the guitarist moved away, Ben smiled. "How's your wine?"

"Wonderful," she answered politely. She didn't know much about wine, and for all she cared it could have been red sludge left from a chemical spill. She couldn't taste a thing. Her heart was hammering.

When their dinners were brought to them, Sara stared at her food, wondering how she'd ever eat all of it. She could barely swallow. Still, she made a good show of eating her filet mignon.

Ben held the bread basket out to her, and watched her take one of the dinner rolls. Her hand trembled slightly. "Sara..."

The musician came by their table again, interrupting him. Ben watched him in puzzled silence. He'd been at this restaurant many times, but he'd never seen a guitarist before. He glanced around the room and noticed for the first time that instead of the usual lunch crowd of businessmen, the room was filled with couples having dinner. As the singer strolled away once more, Ben rubbed his chin, still perplexed.

"What's wrong?" she asked.

"You know, I come here at least two or three times a week, but I never knew how different the atmosphere is in the evening."

"I remember reading an article in the Trends section of the newspaper a few weeks ago about this particular restaurant. The reporter touted it as one of the most romantic dinner spots in town."

"Maybe fate's decided to step in on our behalf tonight." His gaze was intense and penetrating.

With a great deal of effort, she tore her eyes away. "You're certainly treated like a VIP here," she ventured, subtly changing the subject.

"Too much so," he observed. "There's something odd going on here tonight. I can't quite pinpoint it though."

"What do you mean?"

"Our table's practically off by itself. Yet the guitarist seems to come by quite often. I've also noticed the maître d' looking at us strangely, and then smiling. I wonder what it's all about?"

The waiter approached them. "If you want to celebrate after your dinner, we offer an excellent list of champagnes, both domestic and imported," he said, as he took away their empty plates.

The guitarist returned a moment later. Ben glanced at Sara, then back at the musician. The man sang a haunting and romantic love ballad, then with a nod moved on to another table. "They must think we're in love," Ben concluded after a moment's pause.

"If that's all it is, what exactly do they figure we'll be celebrating after our dinner?"

He laughed. "You're right. That doesn't sound quite right, either." He rolled his eyes. "Oh, good grief, I think the music is headed this way again!"

"What on earth did you say to these people when you made your reservations?" Sara asked, sharing his laughter. "Did you try to wangle a secluded table by telling them that you were going to propose to me tonight?"

The waiter came to their table and presented a wine list. "I thought you might like to see our champagne selections."

Ben and Sara exchanged glances. "For our celebration?" she asked.

The waiter smiled happily at them, then nodded and went away.

"Quick, before we get serenaded again," she insisted. "What did you tell them?"

He narrowed his eyes in a pensive gesture. "When I spoke to John, I asked him to find a secluded table for us. I explained that I had some very important matters to discuss with you." He shook his head. "No, wait a minute. That's not quite right." He paused. "I remember what I said now. I told him that I was bringing a special lady tonight. I commented that if everything worked out, you'd be playing an important role in my future. I was speaking in terms of business, though. I guess I must have spoken too vaguely. John obviously got the wrong idea."

She smiled broadly. "That explains it. They wanted to please you, but they misunderstood. They thought you meant I was special to you in a personal way."

"You are that too, you know." Ben sat back in his chair and studied her. "I'm just not sure to what extent yet."

"Be careful. Curiosity didn't do much for the proverbial cat."

He raised his eyebrows. "Are you telling me to proceed at my own risk? Or are you trying to warn me off?"

Her pulse was beating double time. "You figure it out," she replied recklessly.

"I already have," he acknowledged, looking mischievous.

His voice, deeply resonant, made her body tingle with a primitive awareness of him. Before she could recover, he switched the topic of conversation.

"John went to a lot of trouble tonight. I almost hate to clear up his misconception. I think he'd be so embarrassed if I told him this was a business meeting that he'd probably want to let us have dinner on the house." Ben's voice was nothing more than a low whisper that heightened the sense of intimacy that was growing between them.

"So don't say anything," she replied, forcing her tone to remain casual. She found it oddly disconcerting to know that those around them had been thinking of them as a couple. It wasn't an unpleasant fantasy, she realized, and was bothered even more by the thought.

"Let's play along," he suggested, then added, "unless you find that too difficult." He reached for her hand across the table and covered it with his own.

Tension coiled in her, making her body throb with a pleasant, undulating warmth. "No, don't be concerned about me. I see nothing to worry about," she said, aiming the tiny barb directly at him.

When the waiter approached again, Ben ordered the champagne.

"Are congratulations in order for this celebration?" the waiter asked politely.

"Only in terms of progress," Ben replied enigmatically.

Sara would have laughed, but the swirling sensations left by the way his thumb caressed the back of her hand were too distracting.

She tried to take back her hand, but he tightened his hold. "Don't tell me you're changing your mind," he teased her.

This was turning into a contest of wills, and the competitive spirit in her refused to yield. "Not at all." She'd meant her answer to come out sounding smooth, but her voice cracked.

He gave her an infuriating grin, and entwined his fingers between hers.

The chill in her stare only made his grin broader. "You're supposed to make it look as if you like me," he chided, "not as if you're about to commit murder."

She chuckled softly. "Forgive me. I never realized that acting was so difficult."

He laughed, completely enchanted by her. "You're always ready to meet any challenge, aren't you!" he observed.

The crazy kaleidoscope of emotions that she felt as his hand shifted and entangled once again with hers made a shiver run up her spine. "I think that it's all very well not to hurt the maître d's feelings, but we're missing the point of this meeting."

Ben drained his champagne glass and refilled hers. "We can talk about business, if it'll set your mind at ease." He liked holding her hand, and knew that the physical contact was working the same magic on her. "To be honest, I'm very glad you're interested in working on this project for Classic Parts. As I see it, there's only one problem. You asked for a trial period of one month."

His fingers curled and uncurled around hers, trailing a gentle caress over her skin. She struggled to concentrate on his words. "I need that time to get a project off the ground, Ben. It's not an unreasonable request."

"I wasn't faulting you," he said. "It's just that I don't want to wait an entire month to find out how you're doing with it. All my department heads make out weekly progress reports. Yours wouldn't have to be anything lengthy, just enough to let me know how it's going."

There was something so enticingly masculine and compelling about him that Sara almost agreed. But then, forcing herself to remain rational, she shook her head. Weekly progress reports? She grimaced. Half of the time she got so wrapped up in her work, she didn't even know what day of the week it was! "I'm not much for that type of red tape, Ben...."

He interrupted her. "That's okay. I'll go to your office and find out myself."

Great. Now he'd be making periodic checks on her. The thought made her cringe. Gently she took back her hand and pretended to fold the napkin with meticulous precision. She hated the paperwork mentality. Creativity needed a certain amount of freedom in order to flow smoothly. "I'd love to work on this project for you," she replied, matching his stubbornness, "but I work my own way. If you try to tamper with my M.O., then you'll only end up making me less efficient. Besides, the basement isn't exactly on your way in or out of the building, and if I'm caught up in a project, I won't even answer the door."

"Speaking of your basement offices," he began again as he settled the bill. "I had an idea about that. After seeing where you work, I'm surprised you don't die of claustrophobia. Good grief, you don't even have windows down there! I've been meaning to have the boiler and the pipes checked, but to be honest, I've been so busy it just slipped my mind. Until that's taken care of, I'm not at all sure it's safe for you down there. I've cleared away two suites on my floor. It'll be about double the size of what you're renting downstairs, and you'll even have a view. I'll have my people help you move your stuff up there just as soon as you're ready." As they stepped outside in the cool of the evening, he fell into step beside Sara.

Progress reports, moving her office...everything seemed to be getting out of hand. "Whoa! You're hiring me as an inventor, not as your humble servant. My office stays right where it is, and I do the work my own way, thank you." Dealing with Ben was like trying to stop a tidal wave. Did he always move into people's lives with the subtlety of a hurricane? "I realize that we both like to do things our own way. That's been rather apparent, but you're going to have to do some adapting. One of the reasons I like operating my own business is because I hate having other people telling me what to do."

"I thought you'd be happy. You'd be getting much better offices for the same rent you're paying now. What's wrong with my offer?"

"It wasn't an offer. You took it for granted I'd agree to everything you said." Sara gazed at him levelly. "If you want an inventor, someone to develop a new product, then you've hired the best. But if what you want is someone who'll take your orders, and abide by all your rules, buy yourself a cocker spaniel. All the charm in the world isn't going to get me to change the way I work, not to mention where I work."

He reached for her arm as she strode ahead of him, heading for his car. "Wait. I didn't mean to make you angry. First of all, I really don't think those pipes down in the basement are in good condition. And in my opinion, offering you the chance to move up to the top floor was like giving you a promotion. I'm sorry if you didn't take it that way."

Ben placed both his hands on her shoulders, turning her around to face him. "Accept my apology?"

Suddenly, Sara's world narrowed to the space Ben occupied. He was so close. She felt disarmed, as vulnerable as a young girl on her first date. She wondered what it would feel like to lace her fingers behind his neck and pull his mouth to hers. Her lips parted slightly, instinctively.

Ben gazed down at her. She looked so soft, so inviting. His hands trailed down her back, his gentle touch turning into an embrace. He brought her to him, and slowly lowered his head, taking her mouth with his own. Ben half expected her to push him away or maybe even sock him in the nose.

At first Sara couldn't even think. His lips coaxed and teased, and slowly his kiss deepened. Her heart pounded. Using all her willpower, she moved out of his arms. "Do you always apologize like this?" she managed to ask.

"No, but I could take up a new habit," he said, grinning at her.

"Then I'd better take up self-defense," she replied, trying to even the ragged sound of her breathing.

"You didn't struggle," he pointed out.

"True," she admitted and laughed. "Okay. We'll consider this a no win round, but just in case you're wondering, this is not going to happen again. I don't get involved with my clients."

"And if I fire you?" He stopped at the rear of his sedan and leaned against it. He watched her, a ghost of a smile on his face.

"I especially don't get involved with people who fire me," Sara said, trying to keep from smiling but not succeeding.

"Will you at least consider moving your office to the top floor where mine is? It really is much nicer."

"I'll stay where I am, thank you," she said curtly.

He exhaled softly. "Are you angry?" He pushed away from the car and began to move toward her. "If you are, I could apologize again."

This man was a walking danger zone. Even as she took a step back, Sara felt herself being pulled toward him. "Now see here. We can't keep doing this sort of thing. You're just asking for trouble."

"Really? Do you consider yourself trouble?"

"I wasn't talking about myself," she said, surprised.

"Then you don't have to worry. I'm no trouble at all." As Ben slowly approached her, she moved to one side of the car, keeping it between them.

So, there were times when she would back down rather than confront a challenge, Ben observed.

"Behave, will you? What would your son think if he could see you now? We're in a parking lot, for Pete's sake! It's practically immoral."

"Oh, now, if that's the sort of thing you have in mind," he teased.

"Of course not!" She closed her eyes and shook her head. "You're taking me back to my office right now. Things are less confusing in my laboratory." Not giving him a chance to react, she opened the car door and slipped into the passenger seat.

SARA SAT AT HER DESK, staring first at the contract she'd signed with Ben, then at the pot handles. If she could alter the formula slightly, she was certain she'd end up with something that would suit his needs. Of course, it was a rather large "if."

For now, she'd really be happy if she could just concentrate. Meeting Ben and facing the feeling he'd awakened in her had left her bewildered. She'd always considered herself self-possessed, the type of person who could be completely happy alone. Now she'd started thinking more about the things that were absent from her life. She was acutely aware of a need to share, to be wanted and loved.

The telephone rang but instead of picking it up, Sara stared at it, allowing the machine to answer.

"Hi, it's me." She heard Ben's now familiar voice. "If you don't start answering my calls, I'm going to phone the police and declare you missing."

At the sound of the dial tone, she smiled slowly. It might be fun to see if he would.

The telephone rang again. Sara remained at her desk as she listened for her machine.

"And by the way," Ben's voice said, "don't even think of calling my bluff. I'll have the entire SWAT team down there if you force me. I'll just tell them that I think you're experimenting with illegal substances."

Sara picked up the telephone quickly. "You wouldn't dare."

He laughed. "Thought that would jolt you."

"If you're calling to find out if I've made any progress since yesterday afternoon when you came down here, the answer is no. And I probably won't be, if you insist on checking up on me so often."

"Stop being so defensive. I was only going to ask you out for dinner."

"I can't. I just signed a contract with this lunatic businessman who expects me to deliver miracles in my spare time between his phone calls and visits."

"You're angry with me, aren't you?" he asked in a flat tone.

"I'm not going out with you, Ben. I'm just not ready to let anyone distract me from my work." Of course, it was already too late for that. He already had. Since he'd ventured into her life, he'd raised questions that were too disturbing to be brushed aside. Still, there was no sense in admitting it to him.

"Am I a distraction?" he guessed with uncanny accuracy.

"And a headache."

"'And?'" he mimicked. "I guess I'm making progress. At least you're thinking about me."

"You just don't understand. Your working hours are different from mine. You get up at six and get to work by eight. At six in the morning, I can't even walk without tripping over myself."

"Okay. My ego is ruined. You've rejected me three times in a row."

"You'll thank me when I can finally show you the results of my work here at the lab."

"Speaking of that…" He paused. "Sara, I'd really like to have some idea of your progress. It wouldn't have to be an elaborate report. A phone call and a few words would do. Or you could drop by my office and visit."

"I'll keep it in mind. Now I have to get back to work. I'll speak to you soon."

She replaced the receiver in its cradle and leaned back in her chair. The strength of her attraction to Ben scared her. She didn't want to feel vulnerable, yet that was exactly the sensation she was experiencing. He wasn't the type of man a woman like her could lower her guard around for even a moment. His predilection for being in control would mean he'd take any opportunity to make matters run in a way that best suited him. He'd certainly made enough demands already, despite her opposition.

Perhaps, Sara mused, she'd been out of the mainstream of life for too long. In a way, her work had insulated her from relationships. Dates usually happened at night, and that was when she was hard at work. Her mornings were usually free, but most people worked then. That left weekends, but being self-employed meant she normally worked then, too.

Sara walked to her lab and began to go over her notes. The formulation she'd worked on for Classic Parts showed promise. Of course, at this point she had little to go on except a few basic experiments and her gut instinct.

Hours passed slowly. Repeatedly she altered the formula she'd used on the handles, then experimented with each sample to see if she was getting the desired results. She'd succeeded in making the material even more heat-resistant, but when she tested it for strength, the mixture shattered after only a few hundred pounds of pressure. It had become as brittle as china. If only she could find a way to make it more durable.

She returned to her desk, papers in hand, and began altering the equations before her. Concentrating, she soon scarcely noticed the passage of time.

CHAPTER FOUR

A LOUD KNOCK AT THE DOOR made Sara jump. "Who is it?" she asked, feeling alarmed, then annoyed.

"Ben."

She pursed her lips. She should have known that he wouldn't stay away for long. He wasn't the type to passively follow guidelines he hadn't set up himself.

She stood and opened the door. "Come in, but I warn you I'm in a rotten mood. I've been trying to modify the formula I used on the handles so it can fit your requirements. However, I haven't even been able to get it to a workable starting point."

"Not the progress report I'd hoped for, but at least it is one," he teased good-naturedly.

She glanced at her wristwatch and sighed. "It's almost nine o'clock. What are you doing here so late?"

"Jimmy's science teacher took the kids out to dinner and a movie tonight. It's their reward for a project they've been working on as a team at his school, a competition of sorts between their classes."

"And you hate going home when he's not there?"

He smiled sheepishly. "Something like that. The house just seems so empty without him around."

"Jimmy's a great kid," she said, offering him a chair. "I really like him."

"He's special, all right." He glanced at the papers strewn over her desk. "Are all these part of the project you're working on for Classic Parts?"

"Yes, but you might as well not even try to read my writing." She took the notes gently from his hands and replaced them on her desk. "They're mostly a compilation of my thoughts."

He picked them up again. "Wait a minute. Don't be so hasty. Maybe I can help. Tell me something about the problems you're encountering."

"The biggest one is the client," she replied tersely.

"Come on, " he coaxed. "Hey, I thought you said that the formula you were using for the pot handles didn't have the strength needed for automobile parts."

"It doesn't. That's why I'm altering it, or trying to anyway."

Ignoring her wishes, Ben picked up another page of notes and a tug-of-war ensued.

"Look, you don't understand what's involved, and it would take me too long to try to explain it to you. Just trust me. If it can be done, I'll figure out a way."

He shook his head. "Wait a second. It says here that when you mix up a test batch of handle material and dry it in the oven rather than letting it air dry, you can run tests on it a lot sooner. Why not dry all the samples at an even higher temperature in the oven, and you'll cut your waiting period even more? Think of the time you'd save. You could test one batch right after another."

"I tried that once," she said wearily. "You see the star next to the comments in my notes? If you check at the end of the report, it says that the fumes created by oven drying are so strong I couldn't even stay in the same room." She took the sheets from his hand and placed them firmly on top of her desk.

"Come on, don't be so proud. I bet if you'd just let me read this over, I could help you."

"I've had a really hard day, Ben. What I need is to relax for a few minutes. I'm frustrated enough with the way the experiments are going. Don't add to it by trying to make suggestions about a process you don't understand. Let me do this my own way." Sara ran a hand through her hair. "There is nothing more annoying than having someone looking over your shoulder continually, and that's precisely what you've been doing to me all week."

"Oh come on. How do you know I can't help, unless you give me a chance?" he argued.

"I can't work your way," she answered, struggling to keep her temper. "If you're the type who can't let other people do the job you've delegated to them, we're not going to be able to get anything accomplished. You can either trust me to get the work done, or forget about the whole deal."

"Be reasonable," he insisted, undaunted. "I'm naturally curious about what's going on. You won't tell me how you're coming along, so what else can I do except check up on it myself?"

"That's it," she replied flatly, the last of her patience vanishing. She had no intention of bowing to unreasonable demands, no matter how well intentioned they might be. "I told you I wouldn't work under those conditions. As far as I'm concerned you've invalidated our agreement. You can tear up our contract. I quit!"

She strode to the door and held it open. "Now will you please leave my office? I have other projects that can use my time."

"You're just angry because you've had a bad day," he said calmly. "Let's talk. I'm not going to let you quit."

There were very few things in life more annoying than people who didn't react to anger. She felt her temper reach the boiling point. "You come in here, make me crazy, then act as if you can't figure out why I'm so mad. Will you please leave?"

Sara had quite a hot temper, Ben observed, and the fact that he remained calm upset her even more. What did she expect? Anger never helped matters. The only way to control a situation was to remain cool and collected. "Sit down and talk to me. We can work out whatever's bothering you."

"Fine. You don't want to leave?" Sara shouted, totally exasperated. She grabbed her purse from her desk drawer. "Then I will. Lock up when you're through playing inventor."

"Will you wait a second?" Ben dashed after her, but then turned back to lock her open door. It took only a second or two, but she'd disappeared around the corner by the time he glanced up. He muttered an oath under his breath. "Slow down!" he yelled, running after her.

She refused to answer him. With her eyes glued directly ahead, Sara jogged up the stairs and out the revolving doors. She had almost reached her car when he caught up to her.

"You sure make it difficult for a guy," he told her, almost out of breath. He paused, then added, meeting her eyes, "To be honest, I didn't mean to interfere with your work. All I really wanted was a chance to spend some time with you."

The admission took her by surprise. "You mean to check up on my progress," she said defensively.

"No." Bracing his palms against her car, arms outstretched on both sides of her, he held her trapped. "I wanted to spend time with you. I asked you out to dinner at least five times...."

"Three," she interrupted, then smiled sheepishly. "But who's counting?"

He gave her a roguish half smile. "So you see, you really didn't give me any other choice. Work was the only excuse left."

Her heart was pounding wildly. She was acutely aware of everything about him, from the fire-hot warmth of his body to the way his forearms were brushing against her hair. "You could have given up."

He chuckled softly. "No way. Everything about you is special and different, from your job to the way you live your life."

"And what would you know about that?" she countered, her voice a little unsteady. She placed one hand on his chest and gently started to push him away.

"Very little, and that's precisely it. I want to know more, I want us to be friends." He stepped away from her, but only slightly.

"And that's all?" she retorted, gathering up her courage. Did he have to stand so close? It was hard to concentrate, hard to breathe, and hard to talk through the obstacle her heart posed as it lodged in her throat.

"Let's say that'll be a good start." This woman had a gift for making him want to make her respond to him. It made him feel powerfully male to see the flush on her face and the expectant tremor in her lips, and to know he'd put them there.

She moved around him, managing to open up the gap that separated them. Taking a deep breath, she tried to settle her nerves. "You want me to give you an opening, a way into my life...." She stopped speaking, seeing his expression change.

"Opening..." He clenched his jaw. "Good grief! I left the building open!"

"Anyone can walk in...." she added, then almost in unison, they both started to run.

"Why did you park so far from the entrance?"

"All the good spots are taken by the time I get here in the morning," she answered, gulping lungfuls of air.

They were back in less than a minute. They dashed through the revolving doors, then slowed and finally stopped inside the lobby. Out of energy, Sara leaned against the wall and tried to catch her breath. "You're a bad influence on me, Ben," she said, her breath ragged. "You take me away from my work. You make me lose my temper, then you make me end up feeling guilty." She smiled, taking the sting out of her words. "What am I going to do with you?"

"You want to talk about bad influences?" He leaned over, hands on his knees and took several deep breaths. "I was so worried about catching up with you, I left my own building wide open. Every one of my employees was reminded again today to be extra careful. My top competitor has been trying to cut into my business lately, hoping to keep me from expanding and taking a larger share of the market. That means there are lots of people who'd love the chance to walk right in and read all my papers. I can imagine what the security guard who patrols the building at night would have said if he'd come in to make his rounds and found the front doors wide open."

"Did you think of closing the door to my lab?" Sara asked quickly. "If you didn't, I'd better get down there. I have a lot of research that pertains to your company."

"*That* I closed." He laughed.

Relieved, she gave him a long thoughtful look. Very few men ever matched her persistence and will, yet Ben seemed to do both effortlessly. As much as she hated to admit it, she was as curious about him as he about her.

"Let's close the doors, and go to the coffee shop a few blocks down. They're open all night. It'll give us a chance to talk," he suggested.

"Okay," she conceded, "but I'll have to keep the break short. Honestly, I won't get anywhere with my work unless I keep at it until I can find some answers."

Ben exhaled loudly. "You know what the real problem between us is?" He didn't wait for an answer. "We're both stubborn and like to get our own way." He walked outside with her to his car.

"So much for peaceful coexistence."

Ten minutes later, they arrived at the coffee shop and were seated. Nibbling on a piece of cheesecake, she lapsed into a thoughtful silence.

"Penny for your thoughts."

"You've already paid me more than that for them." She laughed. "I was thinking about your project. I'm sorry I was in such a rotten mood earlier. I really did have a miserable day. My work is interesting, but there are times when it can also be extremely frustrating. I should have listened to my dad when he told me to stick to a profession in which I could make a living without working round the clock."

"What did he have in mind? I have trouble picturing you doing anything less demanding." Maybe that was what appealed most to him about her. She was bright, and indefatigable when it came to her job. He'd always admired dedication. It was a quality he understood. Without it, he'd never have been able to turn Classic Parts into the company it was today.

"I'll tell you one thing. Even if I had chosen a different profession, I'd have still worked just as hard to be the best. I'm not much for half efforts." She finished her cheesecake in several quick bites. "I think that's why I've succeeded in a business as risky as mine. It takes a lot out of me, but I'm willing to pay the price it extracts because I love doing it."

"I get the feeling that the reason you like your work so much is because it's such a challenge. Am I right?"

She nodded. "I'd die of boredom in a job where each day was exactly like the previous one. I like variety and I love matching my intelligence against what seems to be an unsolvable problem. That's really what being an inventor is all about. When things go right, particularly if I've really had to work at it, there's a tremendous feeling of accomplishment." She paused and added, "Ask your son. I think he'd tell you the same thing."

"Jimmy loves to solve puzzles," Ben said. "He's quite bright, so he usually ends up succeeding. The problem is, his failures are often quite spectacular. Two months ago he was working on an automatic toothpaste squeezer. We had toothpaste on the ceiling, on the windows, and on the walls of the bathroom by the time he turned it off."

She laughed. "You're still lucky to have him." It was strange. Up to now she would have never described her life as a lonely one. Yet around Ben that was exactly the way it seemed. The richness of the life he shared with his son served to point out what was missing in hers.

"Jimmy can be a lot of trouble, but all in all I couldn't have asked for a better son," he said, a trace of pride in his voice. "He's the center of my life. He's always there in the back of my mind, no matter what I'm doing. But what about you? Would you like to have kids someday?" He sipped his coffee slowly.

"Sure, but to me that's all off in the future. There's a lot to be said for being single." She asked the waitress for a coffee to go. "It's nice to have the freedom to keep my own hours. I come and go as I like and I don't have to worry about anyone else." The words had a hollow ring even to her own ears. "I really should be getting back now."

They returned to his car. Ben watched her in pensive silence as she pried the plastic lid off her Styrofoam cup and sipped her take-out coffee slowly. "Tell me something. Is there anything about me you like?" he asked.

The question took her completely by surprise. She choked. "What?"

"I asked you if there was anything about me you really liked," he repeated.

"That's an odd question," she hedged. "What makes you ask that?"

"I'm trying to figure out why you refuse to go out with me. We get along well—" he grinned sheepishly "—when we're not arguing."

She laughed. "What more could two people possibly ask for!"

"My point exactly."

Sara was quiet as they traveled the silent streets. Moonlight gleamed over the skies, illuminating the darkened areas around them in soft hues of gray. She really didn't know how to honestly answer Ben's question without telling him too much. He was still a stranger to her, after all. "Why would you want to bother with me?" she said finally. "You have your son and he has you. You don't need anyone else. Your life is full." The words slipped out before she could stop them.

"I have a good life, but there are empty spots in it."

Remembering that he was a man who'd lost his wife, Sara bit the side of her lip. "I'm sorry. I seem to have a knack for saying the wrong thing."

"I don't understand why you'd ask me what you did. Is it that you don't want to get involved with a man who already has a family?"

She shook her head. "Not at all. Jimmy's a terrific kid. To be honest, I've never met anyone quite like him. If I ever did have a son, I would hope he'd turn out to be just like yours."

"Then why do you refuse to go out with me?" He pulled into the parking area beside their offices and met her eyes. "I hope you're not going to tell me that you're not attracted to me. I know differently. I've felt it."

"Up to a few weeks ago, I had my life organized exactly the way I wanted it," she said, measuring her words carefully. "I knew what my goals were, both long- and short-term. Lately I'm not sure what's come over me. I'm a stranger to myself. The only place I feel secure is at my lab. Until I work through the rest, I think I should stick to old, familiar ground."

They walked into the building together. "Maybe what you need is a friend. I've been told I'm a great listener."

She smiled. "You really are persistent."

"So, give in already," he countered.

She laughed. Well, why not? She had a really strong feeling that the adage Out of Sight, Out of Mind would never apply to Ben.

"I'm waiting," he said, following her into her office. "Of course, I could continue to visit you."

She groaned with frustration. "It looks like the only way I'm ever going to get any work done is to agree."

He grinned, but said nothing.

"All right," she said with a resigned sigh. "I give up."

He bent over slightly, then gave her a light kiss on the cheek. "Just to show you I'm keeping my end of the bargain, I'll leave right now and let you get back to work."

Sara stared at the closed door for several seconds after he walked out. Did he always get what he wanted? He'd come downstairs intending to get her to agree to date him, and had achieved precisely that by the time he'd left. Would trying to hold her own around him be as futile as sending a marshmallow to put out a bonfire?

Instinct told her that she was about to take the biggest gamble of her life. Ben was the first man she'd met whose strength and determination were more than a match for her own.

SARA STOOD IN the enclosed courtyard surrounding National Laboratories. It was well into spring. Maybe that was the reason for the peculiar restlessness she'd been experiencing. She felt a cool breeze playing over her hair and smiled. It was too bad she had to work today.

She stared aimlessly at the line of blue-green junipers that formed a border and screened out most of what lay beyond the wall. She had always felt secure in enclosures. Large, open spaces seemed to cry out with an emptiness that ached to be filled. She'd grown up in a large house, filled with expansive rooms. Yet the sparsely decorated interiors that emphasized works of art collected over the years had exuded an air of sterility. Tasteful furnishings had done little to hide the emotional void that had existed within those walls. Life at her parents' house had left a permanent chill in her heart. It made her long for fires in the fireplace and cluttered rooms symbolic of a life so full it brimmed over.

These needs had always been there in the back of her mind, but lately they'd been at the forefront. She stood and walked around. In front of the evergreens, a carpet of multicolored flowers looked dazzling in the bright sunlight. The stone walkway glistened with specks of silver as the sunbeams played upon its surface.

"You look as if you're in a trance," she heard a masculine voice behind her say.

"Hello, Mike," Sara said as she turned around. "I haven't seen you all morning. Where have you been keeping yourself?"

He sat down on the stone bench and invited her to join him. "Meetings. It's one of those days. Everyone has a problem they want solved."

"That's what happens when you're the boss. People are always coming to you for answers." She studied her friend thoughtfully. His brown eyes sparkled with intelligence. Mike would make someone a wonderful husband someday. He was caring, gentle and dependable. So why hadn't she reacted to him as she had to Ben?

Unlike Mike, Ben challenged her at almost every level. It was exciting just to be around him. He was constantly on the move, persuading or coaxing her into what he wanted. She had to stay mentally alert just to hold her ground.

There was also a vibrancy about Ben—a certain cockiness. Ben, simply put, was a man who knew how to get what he wanted. His attitude enhanced his maleness, and the combination was irresistible.

"You're a million miles away," Mike said at last. "I bet you haven't heard a word I've said."

Sara gasped. "Mike, I'm sorry! You're right. I'm off in outer space today."

He frowned. "This isn't like you. What's going on?"

"I've met a man who drives me crazy, is horrendous to work for and, irrational as it sounds, I think I like him too much for my own good."

Mike laughed loudly. "About time!"

"That's a terrible thing to say," she shot back with a scowl.

He shook his head. "Sara, my beautiful friend, I've been watching you for the past year. You never have time for anyone or anything except your work. You date, but in the end everyone seems to bore you. Remember Merv, the engineer I introduced you to? He was even willing to adapt to your crazy schedule without a word of complaint, but you only went out with him three times before dumping him."

"Dumping?" Her voice rose. "I've never done that to anyone in my life!"

"What would you call it? He kept trying to take you out, and you kept coming up with excuses until he finally quit."

"They weren't excuses. I was busy with a project," she replied slowly.

Mike gave her a long, skeptical look.

"Okay, okay. So I really didn't want to go out with him. But I did it in a nice way."

"Fine," he conceded. "You dumped him gently."

She exhaled softly. "He was a nice man, but Mike, just between you and me, he *was* extremely boring."

"So tell me about this Mr. Wrong you've just met," Mike teased. "He must have some good qualities if he's got you daydreaming about him."

"I wasn't daydreaming about him," she countered. "I was wondering about myself. I've been changing lately, and I can't figure out what in the heck's happening to me!" She stood and began to pace. "You used to tell me that I spent too much time working, and that unless I got out more I'd end up as loony as they come. Maybe you were right, and that's exactly what's happening to me now."

"Sara, darling, I hate to tell you this, but you're not making a whole lot of sense."

She sat down beside him unceremoniously. "I've been really proud of the fact that I'm independent and able to create my own happiness. I didn't need anyone else. Lately, though, I feel as if there's something missing." She paused, formulating her thoughts carefully. "It's as if I've got *too* much freedom." Her shoulders slumped. "You're right, I'm not making any sense."

Mike smiled slowly. "We've been friends for a long time, Sara. Maybe that's why I understand what you're going through so well. There's nothing wrong with you, sweetheart. What you're feeling is nature's way of telling you it's time to settle down."

"Oh, I don't know. Maybe I should go out and buy myself a hamster or something that would need me and want me around, if only to feed it."

He shook his head. "I think you're having these thoughts because you're falling in love."

She gave him an incredulous look. "And I think you've been out in the sun too long."

Mike was about to answer when his pager came alive. He reached for the switch almost absentmindedly, and turned off the beeper. "That's it for my break. I'd better go back to my office and see what the emergency is now. What a morning!"

Sara watched him leave, then stood reluctantly. She made her way past the security checkpoints strategically placed around the main section of the building, and returned to the lab she'd been using all morning. Mike was wrong, of course. She wasn't falling in love. Yet her heart ached with a most peculiar longing whenever she thought of Ben and Jimmy.

CHAPTER FIVE

BY THE TIME SHE LEFT National Laboratories, Sara felt she'd made some solid progress on the formula she needed for Ben's project. The heady sense of exhilaration she usually had after a productive day's work washed over her as she drove back to her office.

This afternoon she'd concentrate on the paperwork and detailed sketches that comprised a large part of Ben's project. It felt good to be on the right track.

Sara parked her car and strolled to her office. As she turned the corner, she saw a huddled figure wearing a familiar blue cap sitting by her door.

"Jimmy!" She smiled broadly, genuinely glad to see him. "What brings you down here?"

He scrambled to his feet. "Hi! I was hoping you'd come back soon." The boy stared at the floor, then shrugged. "It's not that I minded waiting. It would have been okay if you hadn't—" he added quickly "—come back, I mean. But I'm glad you're here." He knew he sounded stupid but he couldn't help himself. She was so-o-o perfect. If Dad would only open his eyes he'd see that she'd be great as part of their family.

Sara laughed softly. "What's all that?" she asked, pointing to his overstuffed backpack and a large cardboard box that lay at his feet.

"That's why I'm here. I want your opinion. This is my science fair project." Jimmy unzipped his pack and pulled out a worn sketchbook and three-ring notebook. "I'm working on a voice-activated robot that can sit on my desk and hold my book. When I tell it to turn the page, by giving it the command 'Turn,' it'll turn the page for me. If I can get it all to work the way I hope, it's going to be the neatest. I'm sure I'll win." He turned to a page in the sketchbook, and showed her a neatly penciled diagram.

"Well, bring your sketches to my office," she said, opening the door. "We'll go over it together."

"I've also collected the parts I think I'll need. I have them in the box. If you're busy, though, I could come back," he said slowly. "Dad would have a bird if he thought I was bothering you."

"You're no bother, Jimmy. Besides, think of it as a professional courtesy, one inventor to another."

Jimmy's eyes lit up so brightly, Sara had to struggle not to smile.

"That's great," he said as he set his things on her worktable. "I'm glad you're not like other grown-ups who think they have to talk down to kids. I hate that." He opened his sketch pad again, then unfolded the flaps on the cardboard box. "Here, let me show you what I had in mind. I raided stuff from garage sales and the junk that Dad had ready to be thrown out from his office."

As he began to lay out the endless row of parts, some of which were totally unrecognizable, Sara tried to study his sketch. "Jimmy, my man, you're going to have to explain some of this to me. Each inventor has his own way of doing things, and your method is different from mine. How about it?" She held out the sketch pad.

"I'm going to use the shell of an old car radio—you know, the part inside the dashboard that looks like a metal box—as the body. Then," he said, pointing to the bottom part of the drawing, "I'll glue it to a piece of wood to keep it from tipping over. I'll use a windshield wiper as the arm and build it to move just like it does in a car. Then I'll attach something sticky to the blades. That way it can sort of glom on to the page and turn it. I haven't figured out what to use for that yet. Maybe tape, or some sort of glue.''

''Let's start at the beginning. First, let me take a look at the construction materials you've gathered here.''

Jimmy pulled out a monstrous-looking plaster head. Seeing her expression, he laughed. ''I know, as a sculptor I'm a waste. We were supposed to make something out of papier-mâché in art class. This was supposed to be a bust, but it didn't turn out right so I made it an elephant's head instead. Only the trunk fell off. It's just perfect though. I can put it on top of the radio casing and make it my robot's head.'' He reached down inside the box and pulled out a metal tube with a handle. ''This is some sort of car part Dad had in a box of stuff he was throwing out. I figure it'll double as a trunk, and if I can get it to hang down just right it can stabilize the book my page turner robot will be holding.''

''Wait a second. You're going off in all directions at once. Let's work on one thing at a time.''

The next half hour passed quickly as Sara tried to help Jimmy while he drew his blueprints in detail. ''This step will save you time later on, and you'll be able to work out any mistakes before you actually start construction of your robot,'' she explained.

She was so neat, probably even better than his science teacher, Mr. McConnell. Jimmy erased a section of his drawings and started over again. She wouldn't do the work for him, knowing that it was supposed to be his project, yet she let him stay in her lab and ask her questions as he went along. It was almost like being partners with her. "Would you come to my school on career day and give a talk on what it's like to be an inventor?" he blurted out.

"Sure," she replied, not taking her eyes off her own work. "I'd like that."

"Maybe the kids at school will take me more seriously when they see you really can grow up and become an inventor."

Sara put her pencil down. "Do they give you a hard time?"

Jimmy stared at the box containing all the parts. "Sometimes, but it used to be a lot worse before Dad sent me to this special school. At my old school I was just the geek, a kid who always got straight A's, but wasn't much good on the baseball team."

Jimmy felt miserably embarrassed, but he'd never been much good at lying. "It was just that I liked doing things they didn't and they couldn't understand that. I have fun going to the library. I love the way it's always quiet in there, and it's never too hot or too cold. I like sitting there and reading, knowing that you can never run out of stuff to read, and that it's free. There's a whole world inside each book, and all you have to do is turn the pages. If you like it, then you can spend time in that place, if not then you just pick out another one."

"I used to feel the same way," she admitted. "In fact, I still do."

He watched her solemnly. He had to talk Dad into taking her out—often. She was an awesome scientist and a great person to talk to. Dad just had to see it! "I don't think Dad understands what it's like to want to go to the library rather than play football, but he doesn't say anything," Jimmy admitted slowly. "But he's a pretty neat guy all around. You'd like him, if you gave him a chance. I think he already likes you."

She chuckled softly. "Jimmy, are you trying to fix us up?"

"Maybe." He grinned. "I could do more if you wanted me to."

"No, don't," she answered quickly, not quite sure what he meant by "more." "Love isn't as simple as math and science are to you and me. It doesn't balance out like an equation. People aren't predictable, so what should happen doesn't always. Do you understand?"

"I think you're saying that I can't force it. Dad's told me the same thing." He was silent for a moment. "But then I see him at home alone sometimes. He just wanders around like he's restless and waiting for something, although he hasn't got anything planned. I don't want him to feel alone like that. He needs a friend, someone to share things with."

"I don't think he has any problems getting friends," Sara assured him. "Your father is one of the most personable people I know."

"Does that mean you like him?"

She was about to answer when a masculine voice interrupted her.

"Has he been driving you crazy?" Ben asked, and sauntered into the office. "You're not trying to play Cupid again, are you, son?"

"Aw, Dad, we were just talking."

Ben straddled a chair opposite Jimmy's and looked his son squarely in the eye. "The strangest thing just happened to me. I noticed that there are some things missing from my office. The oddest items, too, I might add. Everything that has glue on it, like Scotch tape, masking tape, even the peel and press labels have mysteriously disappeared. Also the throttle lever that was in the box of parts next to the file cabinet has vanished. It took me three months to get that for a client, you know."

"Oops." Jimmy smiled hesitantly. "I guess I borrowed the wrong things, huh?"

"Jimmy, what on earth are you up to now?" Ben smiled at his son, his expression becoming gentle. "I can tell you're on the trail of another one of your inventions. Son, you will be careful, won't you?"

"Dad!" Jimmy rolled his eyes. It was awfully embarrassing to have his own dad say something like that, particularly in front of a real live inventor. How was she ever going to take him seriously if he couldn't get his dad to? "So I've had a few problems with my inventions. I'm sure if you ask *any* inventor, she'd tell you it happens to all of us."

Sara noted his use of the feminine pronoun and had to bite her lip to keep from laughing.

"Besides, you know what?" Jimmy added, "I think you two should get together. If Ms Cahill could tell you what it's like to be an inventor, maybe you'd be able to understand what I'm trying to do a little bit better." He leaned over and whispered quickly. "Take her someplace dark and romantic, Dad. Here's your chance."

Sara overheard enough to get the gist of it. With an enormous display of willpower, she forced the corners of her mouth to keep from turning upwards in a wide smile. Jimmy certainly shared one trait with his father. He was indefatigable when going after what he wanted.

Ben cleared his throat, trying to curb his son's exuberant efforts at matchmaking. "What about all that stuff you 'borrowed'?"

"I'm making a robot for science class," Jimmy explained, giving him the details. "I came down here so I could get Ms Cahill's advice on a few things."

"A robot?" Ben repeated, looking quizzically at Sara. "What's this robot going to look like? Better yet, what's the worst it could do if it ran amuck?"

"Da-a-a-d!" Jimmy implored. How *could* he say something like that! He stared at the parts strewn over the desk, feeling totally stupid. Why did Dad always worry about the wrong things? He should have been working on the best way to get Ms Cahill to go out with him instead, and thanking him for trying to help!

"Jimmy—" Ben shook his head slowly "—maybe you should just come upstairs with me, and leave Ms Cahill alone."

Sara sat up quickly. "It's okay with me, Ben. I've already told Jimmy he can stick around. Professional courtesy, you know. However, don't let me interfere," she added as an afterthought. "It's your decision."

Ben smiled. "Are you sure? I wouldn't want to think that you're being taken advantage of." He gave his son a stern look. "Jimmy's quite a con artist when it comes to getting what he wants."

Jimmy stared at his father and blinked. How in the world was he ever going to help get these two together if Dad ruined it every time he was starting to get somewhere? Grown-ups could be so s-l-o-w sometimes!

"His project isn't as outlandish as you might think," Sara assured Ben. "It does have possibilities, and I believe Jimmy's got the ability to design what he wants. Providing it's all right with you, I don't mind if he comes to work here as often as he likes."

"I guess I'm outvoted," Ben said. He glanced over his son's shoulder, studying the drawing. "So tell me more about this project."

Sara stood to one side of Jimmy as he enthusiastically went over the details of his plan with Ben. The closeness between them was unmistakable. The love that each felt for the other was there in every word they spoke, and in their glances. Her heart melted when Ben reached out and gave his son's shoulder a reassuring squeeze. "Keep up the good work, Jimmy. This might be your best project yet."

Sara watched them both, wishing she'd shared the same type of closeness with her family. She still hoped to experience it, someday, when she married and had her own family to take care of.

Ben's eyes met Sara's. She held them for a moment, then glanced away. "I'd better be getting back to my own work," she ventured slowly.

Seeing his son busy with the sketches, Ben reached for Sara's hand, stopping her before she strolled back to her desk. "Thanks," he said in a quiet voice.

"No thanks necessary," she replied, trying to sound casual. His touch sent a fiery warmth coursing through her.

He brushed her cheek with his palm in a light, quick caress. "Jimmy's right. You are a very special lady."

Jimmy watched them out of the corner of his eye, a tiny grin spreading over his face. Way to go, Dad! There was hope for them yet!

THREE DAYS LATER, Ben made himself comfortable on one of the chairs in Sara's office. "Now before you start getting angry, let me tell you that I'm not here to check up on your progress." He stopped, then added, "Of course,

I'll listen to any news you might care to share with me."
He looked at her hopefully.

There had to be some good news somewhere today, Ben
thought. That morning he'd discovered the key to his file
cabinet resting on top of the cabinet itself. He never kept
it there, always returning it immediately to the hiding
place under his desktop pad.

Someone had obviously gained access to his private
records. But no sense in troubling Sara with the news. He
could handle the problem himself.

Sara leveled a blank stare at him. "So what does bring
you down here?" she challenged. She didn't really mind
the intrusion, but she'd never admit that to him. With the
exception of the times he'd come downstairs to check on
Jimmy, she'd scarcely seen him the last few days. His
phone calls had decreased considerably, too. He was
probably trying to please her. In any event, it was definitely not a case of Out of Sight, Out of Mind.

"I had a meeting with my maintenance and repair people, and they've advised me that the pipes down here and
the old boiler used for heating the building will have to be
checked out thoroughly and probably undergo some
minor repairs very soon. I honestly think you'd be better
off moving your offices upstairs."

Hadn't he figured out yet that it was useless for him to
try and run her life? She'd stay wherever she darned well
pleased. "Did they tell you it was *unsafe*?" she demanded.

"No, but it is an old boiler. Some of the pipes and
utilities that run the length of your office date back to the
time this building was built. You're not in any danger, or
I'd insist you move, but the fact remains that you're asking for trouble by staying down here. At the very least,

you're bound to be inconvenienced when the maintenance team starts its work.''

"I'll handle it. Besides, they probably won't find anything wrong with the pipes. I've been down here longer than you've been in the building. I know every square inch of this office. I'd spot signs of trouble long before it ever got started.'' She leaned back. "You know what really bothers me?'' Sara asked without waiting for his reply. "I think you've decided that you want me upstairs where you can keep an eye on me, and you're doing everything in your power to get me to comply.''

"That's not true,'' Ben countered, annoyed. He pursed his lips. "Not completely, anyway.''

A triumphant smile spread over her face. "You're still trying to regiment my business so it's in sync with yours. Don't you understand that to accomplish that you'd have to change *me*, and that won't work?''

He stood and walked to her door. "I'd like you upstairs,'' he admitted, "but the reasons I cited for your move are valid, whether or not you accept them.'' He stared across the room in pensive silence. She was driving him crazy, yet he couldn't make himself stop thinking about her. Maybe if her office was down the hall from his, where he could see her any time by just taking a short stroll, he'd be able to start concentrating on company matters again.

He met her eyes. "Sara, I wish I could get you to stop fighting me on everything. I'm not trying to take advantage of you—in business or otherwise.''

She walked over to where he stood. Should she explain about herself? Maybe if she did, he'd stop pushing her to do things she didn't want to. "Ben, I'm not a fighter by nature. But I have a natural aversion to having someone give me orders, no matter how they are couched. You're determined to rearrange my life to suit you, and I cannot allow that."

"There are sparks in the room every time we're close to each other, yet if it wasn't for Jimmy, I'd probably never even see you. Why are you determined to push me away? What are you afraid of?"

Her throat tightened. "I'm not afraid of anything, Ben," she replied flatly.

He shook his head slowly. "Yes, you are, but it looks like you're going to have to come to terms with that yourself. I can't help if you won't let me." He spoke slowly, from the heart. "Sara, something special is happening between us. You're a constant challenge to me. I know that just beneath the surface there's a special, intelligent and caring woman I'd like to know more about. Let's both take a chance, lady." He didn't wait for the response he sensed she couldn't give. Without another word, he turned and walked down the hall.

Sara watched him leave. He was right. She was afraid. Her attraction to Ben was much too strong for her to believe that their relationship could remain casual. Yet was she really ready to share her life, and get involved with his? What kind of compromises would she have to make, and would she be able to adapt to the demands a relationship would impose on her? He was a man used to getting his own way. If her feelings for him deepened, would it also lessen her ability to oppose him when he tried with his usual aggressiveness to assert his will?

What really worried her most was the fact that it might be too late for rationality. Her emotions were leading the way, overcoming the intellect that demanded caution.

Ben seldom spoke about himself, and when he did it was only in references to Jimmy. She'd glimpsed the tender, caring man beneath the cool business exterior, and had felt herself drawn to him by much more than just physical attraction. But where would it lead?

FOR THE NEXT FOUR DAYS, Sara forced her mind to stay on her work. Following a punishing schedule she'd deliberately set for herself, she'd arrive home too exhausted for anything except sleep, then go back for another twelve- to fourteen-hour stretch of work at the office. Jimmy had reached a point in his project that required him to spend a great deal of time at the library, so she didn't even have the boy to distract her.

She'd never spent a more miserable four days in her life. Still, every time Sara found herself contemplating the problems that had driven her to find solace in her work, she'd redouble her efforts and concentrate on the experiments.

On Thursday Sara came to work wearing a pullover sweater and a pair of jeans. It was unseasonably cold for late April. After turning up the temperature control in her office, she began to update her project file.

As she started to record the previous day's testing, she heard an odd, rumbling sound. She sat up and listened. There was a soft crackling noise, followed by what sounded like a long sigh.

Her eyebrows furrowed. Ben's warning about the pipes suddenly came back to her. Sara left her workshop and walked into her office. It was time to call maintenance. She dialed the number she'd received from Ben's staff shortly after they'd moved into the building. A machine answered and she left a message.

With a frown, she returned to her workshop and tried to concentrate on her project once more. Before long, one of the repairmen would stop by and check out the pipes.

It was probably nothing, but the tak-tak-tak noise sounded ominous.

She began to make new calculations, entering the data on the sheets before her. Today she'd try a new approach. She was on the right track with Ben's formula; it just wasn't there yet.

She'd been at the calculator for a half hour when she noticed the stifling heat.

Sara opened the door to the hall. For the first time since she'd moved into her basement offices, she found herself regretting the fact that she had no windows. She wiped the perspiration from her brow with a tissue, and took off her sweater. Sara rolled up the sleeves of her light blue oxford shirt, wishing she'd worn something cooler beneath her pullover. She stared at the rising thermometer in pensive silence. If the temperature went up much more, she'd have to get her computers and other heat-sensitive equipment out of the office. She couldn't risk damaging them.

Sara dialed the number to maintenance again, and left another message on the machine. Where in the world were they? She considered calling Ben, but decided against it. There would be nothing he could do personally, so why bother him?

She waited another ten minutes, then began to get really worried. The temperature had climbed to above ninety. If she didn't get her computer and disks out of the office, they'd be ruined, for sure.

It was quite a task, but slowly she managed to move everything that might be damaged by the heat into the hall. She called the maintenance people for the third time, then, after getting the machine yet again, slammed the receiver down hard.

Reluctantly she dialed Ben's number. "Are you having trouble with the heat?"

"It's a bit cold up here, but that's about it. Why do you ask?"

"Ben, I've got a problem," she admitted, exhaling softly. "I think something's wrong with the pipes."

"I told you that we were going to have to check them." He couldn't resist sounding smug. "What's happening? Have you called maintenance?"

"Three times, and all I can get is an answering machine. It might be cold up where you are, but it's hotter than an oven down here. I've moved most of the equipment that might be affected by the temperature out of the office, but I think you'd better get this boiler turned off."

"I'll see if I can track down Ralph and Dan for you. They must be around here someplace. It's unseasonably cold, and everyone was complaining about the lack of heat. Hang on, just a moment." He placed her on hold, then came back on the line a second or two later. "My secretary says that the repair guys went to pick up a new part for the boiler. With everyone turning the thermostat up, it was placing a lot of stress on it. They asked the staff to keep the office temperature at sixty until they could do some repairs down there."

She cringed. "I didn't know. It was cold in here when I came in, so I pushed it up to sixty-eight."

"How hot is it in your office now, do you think?"

"About ninety, give or take."

"I'm coming down."

"No, wait!" She was going to tell him that she would handle it, but he was off the line before she could.

Sara's hair lay against her face and neck, limp with perspiration. Her blouse clung to her as tiny rivulets ran down her body. It was bad enough that this had happened, but the thought of having Ben down here in a suit made her feel guilty. He'd roast for sure.

Tying her hair up into a ponytail, she began to move electrical equipment into the hall. A moment later, Ben arrived.

He gasped as the stifling heat engulfed him. "How long have you been battling this by yourself?" he demanded. "It's got to be over one hundred degrees in here!"

"Probably," she admitted, her spirits lowered by heat and exhaustion. "The pipes just started hissing real strangely, too. I think I'd better start moving my papers out."

Ben took off his jacket. "I'll give you a hand, but then we're getting out of here. Did you ever turn down your thermostat?"

She nodded.

"I've had everyone else in the building turn down their room temperatures. That should take the pressure off." He helped her carry a file cabinet drawer into the hall and placed it near the stairs.

As they started back toward her office, two men in overalls came rushing down the stairs. Ben stared at his maintenance crew. "It's about time. Get that boiler shut off, will you?"

The men started heading down the hall when a loud *whisst*, followed by a shrill hissing echoed around them. The tallest of the two dashed toward Sara's office, while the other disappeared behind the door to the boiler room.

"I got it shut off, Dan!" he yelled at his companion.

"Just in time, too," came the reply. He wiped his glasses with a handkerchief, then gestured for Sara and Ben to come take a look. "The soldered joint on one of the pipes broke. It's in one of those sections we were going to repair this morning. With everyone trying to turn the temperature up at once, I guess it overloaded the system.

I tried to warn you, Mr Lowell. This setup dates back to the horse-and-buggy days.''

Sara watched steam seep slowly into the room, enveloping her office and laboratory in a dense fog. She coughed, then backed up, and stood in the hall.

Ben placed an arm around her shoulders. "Come on, lady. You're soaked to the skin, and it's freezing outside. I'll get my coat so you can wrap it around you while I drive you home.''

"I can't leave!" Sara ran a soaked tissue over her forehead, wiping away the beads of perspiration that had formed there. "I've got to get all of my things out of that office. The steam's going to soak through my papers and damage all my document files.''

"I'll get some of my people to move your things upstairs. They'll take care of it.''

"Does everything always work out for you?" Sara asked angrily as she turned to face him. "You wanted me upstairs, now it looks like you're going to get your way. Even fate seems to be on your side.''

He grinned. "You're angry and you're tired, so I shouldn't kid you too much right now. However, there's something I want you to consider. If fate's on my side, then there's no use fighting me.'' His eyes met hers. "I like you, Sara. Trust me. I always watch out for my friends.''

"I don't have much of a choice now, do I?" she asked and sniffed. "This is the second time you've managed to get me to do precisely what you wanted.''

"The second time?''

"You wanted to start dating, and you wouldn't give up until I said yes,'' she explained. "Now it looks like my office is going to be relocated upstairs.''

"Have I asked you out since that time when you reluctantly agreed to see me?''

She frowned. "Well, no...."

"Would you honestly prefer staying down here in this office after what's happened? It's going to take some time for the maintenance crew to make their repairs and then get the place fixed up again."

"No," she replied candidly, "but..."

"Then what have you lost?" His eyes met hers in an intense gaze. "I haven't tried to force you into anything, Sara. I've tried to persuade you on occasion, but the final choice has always been yours to make. We both know that even if I wanted to, I could never talk you into doing anything you didn't want to do."

Her heart pounded against her ribs. "Maybe I have been overreacting to you, but you are rather aggressive, you know."

He laughed. "It's part of my nature, Sara. A man has to have the confidence to go after whatever he wants."

There was a quiet strength about him that hinted at a core of steel. Yet she knew he tempered that with the gentleness he reserved for those closest to him, like Jimmy. The combination was undeniably magnetic. "I must be very tired," she said and gave him a thin smile, "because I not only see what you mean, I think I agree with it."

He laughed. "On that note, I'll go get my coat upstairs, and take you home."

"I'll be okay," she assured him. "My car's right around the corner."

"Sara, you're soaked to the skin with perspiration. If you walk outside like that you'll catch pneumonia."

"What about you?" She pointed to his own shirt, which clung to his shoulders and back.

"I'll take my shirt off upstairs and slip on a sweater I keep in my office. I'll be fine. My clothes are a bit damp, but I'm not dripping wet like you are. I was only down here a few minutes, not all morning."

"Okay," she agreed, too tired to even think anymore. The heat had really worn her out. She cast a weary glance at the men in her office and nodded. "Okay. I'll wait for you in the lobby."

CHAPTER SIX

MINUTES LATER, BEN DROVE to the entrance and waited while Sara slipped into the car.

Shivering, his leather jacket wrapped around her tightly, Sara placed her hands in front of the heating vent on her side of the car.

"Where do you live?"

"It's less than ten minutes away," she said, giving him directions. She tried to remember what condition she'd left her home in that morning. Had she picked up at all? She couldn't remember.

By the time he pulled into the driveway of her adobe-style house, her teeth were chattering. "I can't seem to get warm," she said by way of explanation.

"Give me your keys," he ordered.

For the first time she didn't argue. Sara reached into her purse and extracted them.

"Stay here until I open your front door. Then get out of the car quickly and come into the house. I'll run a bath for you while you step out of those clothes."

She blinked owlishly. "Wait a minute...."

"Don't argue. You're in no shape for that," he growled.

He left the car in a hurry. The gust of cold air that hit her as he opened the car door made her gasp. Shaking, she waited as he had instructed, then dashed into the house.

"Hurry and get out of those clothes," he commanded, the minute she entered the living room. "Where's your bathroom?"

"Through the bedroom and to the left." Her voice was shaky as she huddled, trembling with cold.

"I'll run a hot bath for you." He stopped by her bedroom door and turned around. Seeing that she hadn't moved, he added, "Unless you want me to help you undress."

"No." She inhaled sharply. "In fact, you don't have to run the bath at all. I'm sure you need to get back to work."

"No, I don't. The business can do without me for an hour or two." He walked into her bedroom, then went directly to the bathroom. "I'll stay in here while you undress and slip into a bathrobe. It won't take long to get everything ready."

Ready for what? She might have been cold, but she certainly wasn't dead. Undressing with him just a few feet away made her head spin. Standing behind the closet door, she began to take off her wet garments.

"This is more difficult than I thought," he told her.

"What? Filling the tub?" she asked incredulously.

"Staying in here," he replied in a deep voice.

Her skin prickled at the sound of his words. "You said you would." Sara searched for her robe through the clump of garments on the hook behind the door.

"I know." He paused. "Care to renegotiate?"

"Absolutely not." She found her robe on the floor of the closet, where it had landed after slipping off the hook. Sara wrapped it tightly around herself and walked into the bathroom. "Thanks for running the bath for me," she said, her throat so tight she could barely breathe.

For a brief moment she felt the most irrational desire to ask him to get into the tub with her. Shaking her head, as if trying to rid herself of the temptation, she met his eyes. "Well? Are you going to stand there all day?"

"I'd like to," he drawled. "I don't suppose I can take that as an invitation...." He let the sentence hang purposely. He felt an innate need to pull her into his arms and kiss her until she no longer objected. He clenched and unclenched his fists, the heat inside him swelling and tightening his body.

Sara couldn't think. A palpable force that was as powerful as it was elemental in its nature was pulling them together. The intensity that shone in his eyes made her feel as if she were being consumed by a blazing, white-hot fire. Sara stood before him, trapped between wanting and not wanting.

He cupped her face in his hands, and bent his head toward hers. Twining one hand in her hair, he pulled back her head and penetrated her parted lips. He savored the sweet taste of her, plundering the moist recesses with a hunger he could barely disguise.

Need made his blood race, but he held back. If there was a chance that his instincts were correct and Sara was the woman for him, he would not cheat himself of the outcome. When he took her, it would be at a time when he could possess all of her, her heart and body. He wasn't interested in anything less, not with Sara.

He tore his mouth from hers. "Neither of us is ready for this, but make no mistake, Sara, I want you. There's nothing I want more than to feel myself inside you." He struggled to regulate his breathing. "If this doesn't convince you that I'm protective of your interests as well as mine, then I don't know what will."

She watched him leave, the warmth that enveloped her eradicating the chill she'd felt earlier. She knew it was too soon. The time was not right for them. Yet her flesh tingled as a mixture of impatience and anticipation washed over her. The feeling was one filled with promise, and she felt nourished by the hope of what might yet be.

She stepped into the bath, and relaxed as the warm water covered her naked body. She closed her eyes, and pictured what it would have been like to have him return and join her.

Enveloped in a pleasant cocoon of fantasies, her mind drifted. There was safety in being alone, but she needed something more in her life. Ben's tenderness, his strength and honesty, drew her to him. She wanted to know more about him, to understand him better. She had glimpsed the vast reservoir of love he freely shared with Jimmy, the person dearest to him. Perhaps that was part of the problem. She knew more about Ben, the father, than Ben, the man.

"Hey, are you okay?" a masculine voice asked.

She sat bolt upright in the tub. "Yes," she replied. "I'm sorry, I guess I lost track of time."

"That's fine. I was worried about you, that's all."

Reaching for the towel, she stood and stepped out of the tub.

She'd never been a romantic dreamer. Why did she have to acquire the habit now? She didn't need to fuel her feelings for Ben with X-rated fantasies. She had enough problems.

"I have to be getting back to the office too, Ben," she explained. "I'm sorry if I've kept you waiting. Let me get dressed and I'll meet you in the living room in a few minutes."

He didn't answer right away, fighting the impulse to throw open the door to the bathroom and carry her to the bed. He wanted to feel her against him, yielding and soft, crying out his name.

He muttered an oath. If he kept filling his mind with thoughts like that, there'd be no telling what would happen. He left her bedroom and strode into the kitchen.

He scoured her cabinets in search of something to drink, but the strongest thing the blasted woman had was milk. He paced around the house like a caged tiger. Her home seemed crowded with furniture, and it wasn't just his imagination. He studied the living room carefully. The furniture was all oversize, and made of roughly cut wood. Primitive, but the thick leather cushions on her sofa looked comfortable. There were bookcases filled with volumes ranging from textbooks to murder mysteries. "I can tell one thing about you," he told her. "You're definitely not claustrophobic."

"I'm a winter person. I like cozy rooms that sort of crowd in around me and make me feel bird-nest secure."

He would have liked to wrap his arms around her and give her all the feelings of security she needed. He forced himself to stop pacing. What kind of magic had this woman worked on him? He couldn't really explain his desire to make her want him with the same intensity and passion she showed for her work and her independence.

He stared out her living-room window. The temperature was in the high forties, yet the fire that coursed through him could have kept them both warm in the midst of a blizzard.

"Hi," she greeted him from behind. "I'm really sorry I made you wait so long."

His eyes raked over her figure. She was wearing jeans that fitted her just right, accentuating her slim figure, and a gray-blue turtleneck sweater that flowed over the gentle curves of her breasts. "No problem," he said roughly. "We'd better go."

"What's got you so upset? Have I kept you from a meeting or important business?"

He closed his eyes and opened them again. "Is that what you really think?" Ben's voice was low and sweet, like a lover's caress.

Her mouth went dry. She could lose herself in the mesmeric power of his gaze. "No," she admitted. "But you're right. We'd better get back to work."

SARA GLANCED AROUND her new office. Ben's people had been efficient. They'd moved all of her things, and rearranged them in approximately the same manner she'd had them downstairs.

This suite was much nicer, yet she couldn't quite rid herself of the feeling that her life was being subtly but pervasively changed under Ben's influence. She'd encountered aggressive men before, and had enjoyed matching her will against theirs, but with Ben it wasn't quite the same. In all honesty, she was fighting herself as much as him.

In some ways it would have been easy to place her life in the hands of a strong man who liked taking charge and making the important decisions. Being taken care of alleviated a lot of pressure. The trouble was that she wouldn't like herself very much if she allowed that to happen.

Was she asking for too much? She wanted a strong and assertive man who'd also respect those same qualities in her. It wouldn't be a relationship between two people who were less than whole without each other, but rather the union of a man and woman who were strong and capable in their own right. They'd blend their lives, neither over-ruling the other, in preparation for a lifetime of shared dreams and love.

"Daydreaming, huh?" she heard Jimmy say.

Feeling a warm flush spreading across her face, she turned around in her swivel chair. "Hiya Jimmy!"

"Don't you like your new office?" he asked as he glanced around. "Dad told me what happened. Maybe you should have moved when he asked you to," he added.

"P-lease," she replied, holding one hand up in protest.

Jimmy laughed and shrugged, pushing his glasses back up his nose. "I know, it freaks me out when I do something he's told me not to do, and it ends up he was right all along."

"That's different," she replied crossly.

"Maybe," Jimmy conceded. He was just about to get her really ticked off, he could tell. He shifted nervously, removing his cap and holding it in front of his chest. "Can I still come work with you here?"

She smiled. Sara had never seen him take off his cap for anyone before. "Yes, of course." The kid could thaw out an iceberg, she concluded. She felt the most inexplicable urge to hug him and apologize for being so crabby. Knowing she'd probably embarrass him, she remained in her chair. "It's nice to have company in my workshop."

"Am I interrupting?" Ben asked from the doorway. He glanced at his son and winked. "My secretary said you'd dropped by, Jimmy, and I saw your things by my computer. I figured you'd probably come here and visit until I was through with my meeting."

"She said it was okay, Dad. Really." Jimmy looked at Ben then at Sara. Rats! There had to be a way to get them going around together, he thought. But how did a kid make two grown-ups open their eyes and see what he already knew?

Ben looked at Sara and smiled. "Just remember, you asked for this."

"It's all right, Ben. As I told Jimmy, it's nice to have company in here."

Ben grinned slowly. "If I'd known that you were lonely, I'd have made an effort to keep dropping by, despite your protests."

Sara picked up some papers from her desk and filed them, refusing to look in his direction. "It's got nothing to do with being lonely. Jimmy's an inventor. We have a lot in common." Sara turned and gave Jimmy the thumbs-up sign.

Jimmy grinned, returning the gesture. Atta way, Ms Cahill! Make him keep trying. Dad always enjoyed a good battle.

"What is that all about?" Ben's eyes narrowed as he studied his son. "I've seen that look on your face whenever we're playing those board strategy games you like so much. You're up to something."

"Me?" Jimmy pointed at himself, a look of sheer innocence on his face. "I haven't said a word."

"Son, maybe you and I should have a talk."

"Can it wait until later, Dad? We'll have all evening, and I need Ms Cahill's help on my project."

Ben looked from Sara to his son, seeing the hopeful look on both their faces. He chuckled softly. "I give up. It'll wait."

Ben glanced around Sara's new offices. "Now that you're up here, do you see why I wanted you to move from the basement? This place is so much better. You'll love it."

Sara bristled at his tone. He hadn't even bothered to ask her how she felt about the whole thing. Why did he assume that he knew what was right for her? "I'm here only until my offices downstairs can be revamped, and the repairs made, Ben," she replied coldly. "These offices might be more plush, but they're also not in the rental range I'd like to keep. I don't want special favors. I can run my business and my life by myself, I assure you. I've been doing it for a long time."

Ben stared at her. Her words had been spoken in a quiet, soft tone, yet it was impossible to mistake her annoyance. He'd only been trying to help her, for heaven's sake! "Can we step into your lab for just a second or two?"

She nodded, knowing that he wanted to exchange a few words in private. That was fine with her. It was time to enlighten him on several matters. Glancing at Jimmy as she left, Sara noted that the boy carefully avoided looking up from what he was doing.

Ben closed the lab door, then faced her. "What is it with you? It wasn't my fault you chose to stay down there in the basement and almost ruined everything your company owns. This is a great office. I haven't asked you for a penny increase in rent. I don't need your money, Sara. Are you so uncertain about your independence that you're afraid to say thank-you? You won't owe me a thing, you know. There are no strings attached."

The anger that swelled inside her threatened to engulf her. She glared at him, trying to keep her temper from exploding. "I like making my own way. I don't need charity from you or anyone else. Ever since I met you, you haven't stopped making demands—more progress reports, let's go out, move upstairs! I feel like I'm trying to ride out a tidal wave. I don't want to be ordered around or manipulated, even if you believe that you are acting in my best interest. I have the right to be myself, and I feel you're trying to tamper with that.''

He stared at her, dumbfounded. "I had no idea that was how you saw it.'' He shook his head slowly. "Most of the women I've met didn't mind when I tried to help them out. I knew you were different, and perhaps that's what attracted me the most about you. I guess I did know that you weren't the sort to need anyone, but it's instinctive for me to protect those I care about. If I've offended you, then I'm sorry.'' He turned around and opened the door. Stopping in midstride, he glanced back and added, "I'll let you know when the basement repairs are finished and it's safe for you to move back in there.''

Sara stood immobile, too surprised to say another word. She watched him leave, unable to collect her wits in time to stop him. He *cared*. He wanted to *protect* her because he *cared*. She didn't need protection, but the fact that he wanted to provide it, and the reason for it, made her feel vibrantly alive. Her reaction was mindless and purely instinctive, and hard for her to define. Was this how love began? She banished the thought from her head, and walked out to where Jimmy still waited.

He seemed very quiet for some time. Finally, he glanced up and looked directly at her. "You and Dad had a fight, didn't you?'' The question was rhetorical. "When Dad's expression changes like it did, that usually means he's going to let someone have it.''

Sara looked at Jimmy, trying to figure out how much to tell him. "Don't worry about things. We'll work it out.''

"I'm not a little kid anymore, so you don't have to put me off like other people do,'' Jimmy said, his voice softly pleading.

Once again she let her chest tighten with an undefinable emotion. "I didn't mean to do that, Jimmy. It's just hard for me to know what to say to you right now."

"Dad really likes you. I can tell. Don't be too hard on him. He's kinda bossy, and I know you hate that. I could see you were getting angry with him before, but he really means well. He wants to take care of everything just to make sure nothing bad happens to the people he likes. He's a little scared or something, I think."

"Of what? Surely not of me," Sara commented, skeptical.

"No, not of you, not exactly." He fumbled for the right words. "Dad always tries to look out for the people who matter to him. He thinks that the best way to watch out for yourself or anyone else is to plan things out really carefully. That way you're always prepared and no matter what happens, you know what to do. I think it's on account of the way Grampa Robert was. Grampa liked to gamble and when Dad was a kid, he could never be sure if they'd have enough money to buy groceries and stuff. He went without a lot of things. Anyway, Dad likes to stay in charge because he thinks that if he knows what's going on all the time, the bad things that happen can't really hurt you."

Perhaps it was the way Jimmy had said the words, his tone not overly emotional, offering a simple explanation in hopes she'd understand. Her heart went out to Ben. She'd forgotten that everyone had hidden demons in their past, and part of life was learning how to come to terms with them, or if possible, defeat them.

She was about to reassure Jimmy, to let him know that they were all still friends, when Ben reappeared.

"Hello," Ben greeted them with a trace of a smile. "Jimmy, it's time for us to go home."

"Okay, Dad." He began to pick up his papers and put them into his backpack.

"Sara..."

"Ben," she said simultaneously.

They both laughed, a self-conscious sound that seemed like music to Jimmy's ears. That meant they were ready to make up. It was time for him to give them a hand. "Dad, Ms Cahill's been helping me a lot. Can she come to dinner tonight?"

Ben looked at his son in surprise.

"I'll even cook. In fact, it'll be my special treat. What do you say, Ms Cahill? Will you come over? I'll take care of everything—I'll even wash the dishes."

Sara glanced at Ben and saw him nod and smile his encouragement.

"Come on, Ms Cahill. What do you say? My dad's great company at dinner, and I make an outstanding pizza."

Sara laughed. "How could I possibly refuse an offer like that?"

JIMMY'S DINNER TURNED OUT to be a perfect example of an eleven-year-old boy's idea of a terrific meal. The salad was sparse, but the pizza he was making looked enormous. Sara tried not to laugh as she saw him place Ben's best china on the table, then bring out two silver candle holders.

"Are you sure I can't help you?" Sara asked.

"Naw, I got it covered. Why don't you and Dad relax in the living room, or maybe take a walk in the garden?" His eyes lit up mischievously.

"You wouldn't be matchmaking again, would you?"

"Me?" He tried to look as bewildered as possible.

"Never mind."

"So, go for a walk, or whatever," Jimmy said, grinning. "I'll take care of things here. I make the best combo pizza in the world. It's my own special recipe."

Sara met Ben in the living room. "He insists he doesn't need help."

Ben smiled. "I'm glad, because I need a chance to talk to you."

"If it's about this afternoon, Ben, there's something I want to say first." She walked around the room. Unlike hers, it seemed expansive, and the impression was accentuated by a large picture window and open spaces. Yet unlike the house she'd grown up in, Ben's home exuded a warmth that made her feel at ease. "All of my life I've had to fight to get my family to accept me as I am. Neither my mom nor my dad ever approved of me or my choice of career. It's been hard to establish myself in business, and I've had to struggle, but I made it on my own without anyone's help. The way I figure it, I took the risks, and I went through the bad times all by myself. No one has the right to come into my life now and tell me how to run things."

He nodded. "You're being protective of yourself and the life you've built. I can understand that."

She thought over his words. She would never have phrased it that way, but it was the truth. "Anyway, I guess I'm trying to make you understand. You see, I care, too."

"About what I think, or about me?" His eyes traveled over her lips, yet he stood immobile, making no attempt to narrow the distance between them.

The caressing quality in his voice excited Sara, making her want to touch him. It was as though a filmy curtain had descended, making everything except him seem hazy and unreal.

"Dinner's ready!" Jimmy announced. "Dad, you light the candles, okay?"

She tore her eyes from Ben's, confused by the crazy swirl of emotions that rampaged inside her mind and body. She didn't know if she was disappointed or relieved.

Disappointed, she concluded, as Ben offered her his arm. "My son, the chef, awaits us."

Sara looked at the table, puzzled. "There are only two place settings. Did you forget there's three of us?"

Jimmy's grin was slow and impish. "Nope, but candlelit dinners are only for two."

Sara grinned back. "So what should we do with Ben?"

Jimmy groaned. Did he have to draw them a diagram, for Pete's sake?

Seeing his son's expression, Ben laughed loudly. "Don't worry. We got the message, loud and clear." He paused, then continued. "A little too loud and a little too clear, I might add."

He was going to have to help them out a little more, that was all there was to it, Jimmy thought. "You sit here, Ms Cahill, next to Dad, and I'll get everything."

Ben smiled as his son left the room. "Sara, I know he's being a little obvious, but . . ."

She held up her hand, stemming his protest. "Ben, I'm crazy about your kid. The fact that he's trying to fix me up with you is, well . . . flattering. He wants to get us to start dating, and he's determined enough to show some initiative. He'll get a big kick out of getting us together like this. What harm is there in indulging a few of his fantasies?"

"I'd like it a lot more if you'd consider indulging mine," Ben said, changing the timbre of his voice to a low, seductive drawl.

His words pulled her into the realm of forbidden thoughts, sending tiny shivers coursing through her. Hoping that her expression hadn't betrayed her, she shifted nervously.

Jimmy sauntered out of the kitchen and placed a sliced pizza on the table in front of them. "Enjoy," he said, then turned out the lights, allowing only the flickering candlelight to illuminate the room.

"Where are you going?" Sara asked, almost too quickly.

"I'll be in my room," Jimmy told her. He smiled hesitantly. They looked made for each other. She'd make Dad the perfect wife. All Dad needed was a little encouragement. Dad was a smart man. He was bound to see it himself sooner or later. He switched on the stereo. "I found this music station that's perfect for people your age, Dad. You can dance your way."

"If the kid puts on something that sounds like a waltz, I'll strangle him," Ben muttered.

Sara chuckled softly, but quickly forced herself to look as serious as possible for Jimmy's benefit. "Thanks, Jimmy. Your dad and I will enjoy the meal."

"You're welcome. Oh, one more thing before I leave. I hope you like a lot of cheese. I cut it into strips and laid it on in real thick globs. I hate to use the cheese grater, it always skins my knuckles. The pizza dough is from refrigerator biscuit dough. You might try it sometime, saves mixing the flour and all that. And the mushrooms and stuff are those lumps under the mozzarella. I ran out of bacon so some of the meat chunks are baloney. Everybody likes baloney, I guess. Anyway, enjoy the meal and stuff; I gotta study now."

As soon as they heard Jimmy's bedroom door close, Ben started to laugh softly. "I don't believe this. I think he's ready to draft you as my girlfriend, whether you want to be or not."

"That kid's got remarkable taste," Sara countered with a smile.

Ben laughed. "He does at that."

"You know, I really do envy your relationship with Jimmy. You two are a team. You're always looking out for each other. I've never had that type of relationship with anyone—in or out of my family."

"I don't think you realize just how complicated it can get to raise a child nowadays," Ben replied thoughtfully. "I'm never sure if I'm giving Jimmy all the attention he needs. I try to be both mother and father to him, and that's hard. I believe a man should be strong, and I've tried to impart that to him by example. However, he also needs to know he's loved, and that he's the most important facet of my life, and that takes a gentler touch." He stared at his food and smiled. "But at times, like right now, I think I must have done all right."

She picked up a slice, not really hungry, yet not wanting to hurt Jimmy's feelings. "We'd better eat. We don't want him to think his efforts were wasted."

"Pizza is his favorite food. I think he could have it for breakfast, lunch and dinner."

She sampled the meal cautiously. "Hey, this isn't bad! For a while there I wasn't too sure about it."

"To be honest, I was also wondering if either of us would be able to stomach it. Baloney in pizza?" Shaking his head, Ben retrieved a bottle of wine from the cabinet. He filled her glass, then his. "How about a toast?"

Sara picked up her glass, and noticed that her hands were trembling. Great. So much for keeping her cool. Hoping he hadn't noticed, she braced her arm on the table.

"To what is yet to come," he said, a caressing note in his voice.

She clicked her glass against his, trying to appear calm. Her heart drummed wildly, and she felt besieged by so many different emotions that she didn't even try to sort them out. "To the present," she countered. "The future lies ahead, and the past is already done with. The present is the only part of our lives still within our grasp."

He smiled slowly. "Then we'll drink to moments made more special by the right companions."

The fiery liquid burned her throat. Or was it actually an internal fire she felt within her, separate from the sensations the wine left in its wake?

"Jimmy's choice of music isn't too bad. Shall we make my son very happy and dance?" He smiled, his eyes gentling as they studied her face. "You'd make Jimmy's dad very happy, too."

Sara saw the flicker of light in the depths of his eyes, like embers burning, waiting for just the right touch to explode into flames. To step into his arms... It didn't seem wise, yet something more compelling overrode her caution. She nodded wordlessly.

Ben took her hand and led her to the living room. His arms swept around her waist, and he pulled her toward him. She was aware of everything about him, from the way he held her hand, nestling it inside his, to the rough feel of his chin as it brushed against her forehead.

They seemed to fit perfectly against each other, her head reaching just to his shoulder. She felt the strength of his arms and the gentle way he guided her about the floor.

"So now you see the private side of me, and the home I've made for myself and my son. What do you think?"

She looked up at him. His gaze practically tore her breath away. "I...I think it's all very nice," she replied noncommittally.

"I'm not asking what you think about the decor, Sara," he chided quietly. "I want to know how you *feel* about what you've seen here tonight."

"Yes, I know what you mean." She sighed, resisting the impulse to bury her head against his neck and nestle it there. "I rather suspected that you were asking for a lot more than an opinion on the furnishings."

"Well?" he insisted.

She struggled between her reluctance to say too much and the urge to be candid. "I like being here, Ben. There's a lot of warmth and love between you and Jimmy, and that seems to spill over and affect anyone who comes into contact with you both."

The home he'd made for his son and himself was an integral part of his life, and he'd hoped her answer would go beyond what it had. She'd only skimmed the surface and he needed to delve deeper. Could she see herself as a part of it, or did she want to find a man without a past, one who would start a life anew with her? A child made demands that would invariably encroach on her independence. His feelings for her were growing. If there was no future for them, he'd have to protect himself and Jimmy. Letting her get too close to their hearts would end up hurting all of them.

"Ben, why do you ask me questions like that?" She sensed from his silence that he'd expected her answer to be different, or perhaps just more revealing.

"I want to know what you're thinking. I want to know everything about you." Sara's hair brushed against his cheek. The feather-light touch and the fresh smell of her impacted on his senses. It was hard to hold her close to him without demanding more. Her body was so soft against his. He forced air into his lungs.

"Yes, but you don't let me see inside you. You speak of Jimmy and your work, but not about yourself."

"Jimmy and my work are the two most important things in my life."

She pulled away from him. It was too hard to think in his arms. He was difficult enough to resist when there wasn't any physical contact between them. She stood by the glass door leading to his patio. "I'd like to get to know you, Ben, but I only see glimpses. You shield yourself very well."

He slid back the doors and led her outside. "Yes, maybe I do. I don't feel comfortable opening myself up to anyone. I will tell you one thing." He met her eyes, and held them. "You can trust me—" he paused, and added emphatically "—completely. I would never do anything to hurt or deceive you. You told me this afternoon that you can look out for yourself. I have no doubt that's true, but I watch out for the people who matter to me, Sara. I expect they watch out for me, too."

"You're right." Sara cared a great deal for him. That meant that without even thinking about it, she'd have his needs in mind. The hours she'd spent on his project were more than just a product of her dedication to the job. She wanted the results to be better than her best. So far that had been her only way of protecting his interests, but there was no doubt in her mind that had another opportunity come up, she would have been just as loyal. "You have the most disconcerting way of hitting on the simple truth."

"The truth usually is simple. What gets complicated is when we try to hide from it."

"Ben, would you have asked me here to your home, to share dinner with you and Jimmy, if Jimmy hadn't forced you into it?"

"Have you been worried about that?" He chuckled, then held her by the shoulders. "Yes, I would have. In fact, I had planned to ask you over next week. Only my son, with his usual flawless timing, beat me to the punch."

He drew her close, feeling her body fit itself against his. He held her for a moment, then wove his hand in the curtain of her hair. He traced soft patterns over the sensitive skin there. Feeling her shudder, he brought his hand back to her face and tilted it up. He kissed her tenderly, opening his lips against hers. He felt her yielding to him, and his control was shattered by her willingness.

He took what she offered, plunging his tongue deep into her mouth. A fierce possessiveness ripped through him. Yet, it transcended his desire to take the comfort she'd give his body.

He eased his hold on her and moved away. To take everything a woman like Sara had to give would mean giving all in return. Neither of them was ready to accept the vulnerability that would demand. He certainly wasn't, and he sensed that neither was she. Dammit all. If only his need for her were more basic, then he could desire her in a less complicated way. He had no doubt that they'd both find a great deal of pleasure in each other.

Sara stared at him, knowing instinctively why he'd released her. It had been too hot, too consuming. They were dancing in circles around a very dangerous fire, drifting close, then sidestepping the flames at the last possible minute.

"You felt it too, didn't you?" he observed after a moment's pause.

"Yes."

His eyes seemed to darken, filling with hooded shadows that shielded his thoughts from her. "I'd better go check on Jimmy and see how he's doing."

"Let's pick up the kitchen and do the dishes so he won't have to," she said lightly, hoping to shatter the tension between them.

Ben smiled. "He told us he'd do that himself."

"I know," she said, "but he did cook and go to a lot of trouble. How about it? I'd feel better."

"You don't want to spoil my kid, do you?"

"Just this once."

Ben chuckled. "Be careful. That boy will have you wrapped around his little finger."

"I'll risk it."

Ten minutes later they were in the kitchen side by side at the sink. Sara washed and Ben dried. "By the way, I hope you aren't going to think I'm a lousy dinner date, but I still have to go back to the office," Sara announced.

He nodded. "I figured that. I know you work late into the night." He dried the last plate, then set it in the cabinet. "I have to go back, too. There are a few files I forgot to bring home with me this afternoon. I've had some problems at the office lately, so I'm probably going to be bringing my work home with me, at least for a while."

"What's happened?"

"Oh, it's nothing. It's just the sort of thing that happens in business every now and then." He placed the dish towel on the hook. "Let me tell Jimmy we're going to the office, then we'll leave."

Sara watched Ben walk down the hall to his son's room. Although it was impossible to tell what was on his mind, she had a gut feeling that he was more worried than he was letting on. He valued his time with his son. He wouldn't have been going back to the office or bringing his work home, unless it was something really important.

Jimmy came out of his room. Hands jammed in his pockets, he stood before her. "I wanted to let you know that I'm glad you came."

She bent down and gave him a hug. "Thanks for inviting me."

Jimmy pushed his glasses back up his nose, not meeting her gaze. "Uh, sure. Um... We can do it again sometime, if you want."

"Anytime." Sara knew she'd embarrassed Jimmy, and for a moment tried to think of a way to make up to him. "I feel as if I had two terrific dates tonight, Jimmy. Not every lady gets to share her evening with a couple of great guys. Thanks." She saw his face turning a deep crimson and knew she'd only made things worse.

If he didn't think of a way to look up at her, she was going to think he was a real weenie. He tried, but didn't make it past her chin. "I hope you and Dad had a real good time."

Ben laughed loudly. "That's my boy! Never say die."

Jimmy glared at his dad. Buffalo chips! You'd think his father would give him a hand, rather than make it more difficult. Jeez!

"I'll see you tomorrow at my office?" Sara asked Jimmy gently.

"Sure!"

As she walked outside with Ben, she felt an odd oppressiveness settling around her. It took her a couple of minutes to realize that she hadn't wanted to leave. Ben's house was really a home. It had felt right to be there with Ben, knowing Jimmy was close by. It was as though she'd been part of their family. She'd enjoyed the feelings of warmth and the love she'd found with them.

"I had a great evening, Ben," she told him candidly.

"That settles it, then. You'll have to come back," he answered as they got into his car.

"I'd really like that."

"And maybe this time I'll even beat my son to the punch."

She laughed. "That would even be better."

He turned his head and held her eyes for a moment. "Jimmy's not the only one who wants you around."

She settled back in the cushions, relaxing. They rode along silently for several minutes, Sara glancing idly at the sparse evening traffic. As her eyes drifted back to Ben, she noticed that his expression had changed. His brows were furrowed and his lips were pursed. The frown etched deep lines across his forehead.

"Ben, what's wrong?" she asked softly.

"I'm sorry," he said, shaking his head. "My mind's drifted to work. There's a few things I have to figure out."

"I'm great when it comes to brainstorming."

"Sara, don't worry about me, all right?" His tone was tense. "I'm just under a great deal of pressure at work. I don't let it show around Jimmy, but when I'm not around him, I'm afraid my mind wanders back to it."

"Ben, it's obvious from your concern that this is more than just a little problem."

"It is, but I'll work it out," he replied as they pulled into the parking lot.

Sara remained quiet as they walked inside the building. Ben could be a puzzle at times. He acknowledged wanting to protect her, and had urged her to trust him, but it was apparent he didn't feel the same rules applied to him. Now that something was troubling him, he seemed determined to keep her at a distance.

She stepped into the doorway leading to her new offices. "I'll see you later. If you want to, stop by before you get ready to go."

He nodded, distracted. "I will." He leaned over and gave her a quick kiss. "Till later."

CHAPTER SEVEN

SARA SAT AT HER LABORATORY table, but she found it impossible to concentrate. Was Ben having financial difficulties? Was his mood linked to the needs for security he'd alluded to a couple of times in the past? Was he the target of industrial espionage?

She wanted to help him, but it was hard to know how. If only he wasn't so reluctant to share his thoughts with her. He'd admitted that confiding in others was very difficult for him. Even though she knew that it was simply his way of dealing with things, it sure didn't make it any easier for her to accept.

Setting her pen down, she stood up and walked to the door. She'd go to his office and then see what she could do. Sara went down the hall, her determination increasing with each step.

His door was open. She was about to say something when she saw him slam his fist against the desk, and heard him mutter a dark oath.

She stood immobile, not certain what to do.

Then he glanced up. His features relaxed, and the scowl slowly disappeared. "Sorry. I didn't mean to scare you," he managed to say.

"Ben, forgive me if I'm being too pushy, but I couldn't stop thinking about what you said. You don't have to tell me what's troubling you, but if it's financial, we could work out a more flexible payment schedule for the work

I'm doing for you. Or maybe I could help another way. If it's a matter of keeping your competitive edge, I could table all other projects and work exclusively on yours until I made a breakthrough. My other work is not under any severe time constraints. If finding the right chemical formula to suit your needs would be an advantage, I could double my time at the lab...."

His expression softened as his eyes traveled over her face. "The fact that you came here ready to do whatever you could to help me means more to me than you know." He walked around his desk and leaned back against it.

"You said it yourself. People who care watch out for each other." Sara sat down in the chair nearest his desk. "So what's the best way for me to help you?"

"Just keep doing what you're doing now. You don't have to take any special measures. I can handle what's happening," he told her in a soft voice. "This company will be just fine. I can maintain control over the situation."

Her offer had touched him deeply, she could sense that, yet he still wouldn't talk to her. "Ben, don't shut me out, please. You're worried. I can see it in your face."

He met her eyes, then glanced away. "What you're asking is hard for me," he said at length. "It's not my nature to talk about my problems, whether business or personal, with anyone. You know that."

His eyes were veiled, making it impossible for her to read anything beyond his words. "You won't let a friend be a friend, Ben." Perhaps it was just as well. Facing this trait in him would force her to accept the fact that the differences in their characters would forever stand in their way. Ben's need to control was stronger than his ability to really share his thoughts and feelings with someone who cared about him. Maybe now she'd stop thinking of the possibility of a future with him, and concentrate on her own life. This thought, however, gave her very little comfort.

She got up and started to walk out when he reached out for her. Grasping her arm, he forced her to turn around. "I've hurt your feelings, and that was the last thing I wanted to do. Why does this bother you so much?"

"I wanted you to trust me. I realize that there are degrees of friendship. Some people stay mere acquaintances all our lives, but others we allow closer, letting them see who and what we are without trying to hide behind the masks we wear all day long. That's what I want for us. I want our relationship to be truly special, to be more than superficial."

"Sara, you already have what you want. Can't you see that?" He held her eyes, trying to make her understand. "Did you expect me to be an open book just because my feelings for you lie below the surface? A man who can't stand on his own isn't much of a man at all."

"You know that you can stand on your own, Ben, just as I know I can do the same. It's not a matter of helpless inadequacy. What I'd hoped to do was share the load with you. In my book, that's what people who care for each other do."

He stared at an indeterminate point across the room. "I understand you, but what you're asking—" he paused "—is almost impossible."

Sara shrugged. "All right. I won't insist."

She turned to go, but once again he stopped her. "Sara, you mean a great deal to me, and I do trust you. Sit down, and let's talk for a bit. Maybe it'll help me sort everything out."

So she sat down again and watched him. Despite the difficulty it posed for him, he was still willing to try. At that moment she'd have done anything for him. Her heart filled with a rush of warm and intense emotions that left her feeling slightly disconcerted yet wonderful.

"You know that this company is my legacy to Jimmy. It's my way of making sure he'll always be provided for. It means a great deal to me to know that his financial future will be secure. I love that kid so much...." Ben stared pensively at the papers on his desk. "I don't ever want him to lack anything. Lately, all I own and have worked for has been threatened. Paul Tracht, one of the largest automobile parts wholesalers in this region, has started a campaign to edge me out of business. He wants to take over Classic Parts. With my company out of the way, Paul could corner the market. It's been a fight, but until just recently, it's been a clean, fair one. Now, I'm not so sure."

"What's happened?" she asked, leaning forward.

"A few days back I noticed that the keys to my file cabinet were not in the place I normally keep them. I believe someone has been looking through my private papers. Then I received Paul's latest offer. What made this one different was the information he'd managed to obtain about Classic Parts. He knew the exact financial state of the company as well as its strengths and weaknesses. That takes detailed inside information, more than what a casual glance through my files could have provided. I confronted Paul and accused him of industrial spying. It didn't do much good. He just told me to go ahead and try to prove it."

"Can he use what he's learned to actually pressure you into selling?"

"He could make it difficult for me, depending on how much influence he has with distributors and other people I do business with. I have to get my orders out on time, or I can't deliver. Expanding put a strain on our cash reserves. That's why I have to make sure nothing impedes the course of my regular business dealings. It's very important that Classic Parts continues to operate on the same level it always has.''

"Has Paul intimated that he can make things difficult for you if you don't agree to sell?''

Ben nodded. He was about to say more when Sara held up her hand.

"Did you hear that?'' she whispered quickly.

There was a muffled, padded sound in the hallway, then it seemed to fade.

"Someone's out there.'' Sara bolted out of her chair and dashed into the hall.

"Sara, no, wait!'' Ben bounded after her. "Get back in the office. I'll take a look.''

"Nothing doing! You go to the left and I'll take the right,'' she said, rushing off.

He swore softly. "We'll both go to the right,'' he answered, jogging to catch up to her.

They returned to Ben's office a few minutes later. Ben's lips were pursed in a thin, tight line. "Maybe we're both hearing things.''

"Not likely. It was footsteps, all right.''

"An old building always makes noises. We *thought* it sounded like footsteps, but maybe it was something in the pipes, or the heating system as it came on. For heaven's sake, you were out of that chair a split second after you heard the sound. Had someone been out there, we'd have found them.''

"Not necessarily.''

He shook his head. "Okay, but the fact remains we didn't see anybody.'' He picked up his telephone and dialed. "Charlie, this is Ben. Were you patrolling the upstairs floor during the last ten minutes or so?'' Ben paused. "You haven't seen anyone or anything suspicious, have you? I thought I heard something outside my office."

By the time he set down the receiver, Sara knew he hadn't made any discoveries. Frustration was etched too clearly on his features. "Nothing, right?"

"Charlie says we're the only people in the building, except for the two-man maintenance team. They're cleaning in the basement right now...." Ben leaned back in his chair, rubbing the back of his neck with one hand. "Charlie's part of Guardmark Systems Incorporated, but he's been contracted to work exclusively with Classic Parts for years. I've started to tighten up our security, so I've made arrangements to have him stay here full-time at nights from now on. In addition to that, we'll be taking on an ex-cop from Guardmark to be his backup. I've even had an electronics expert in here twice now, searching for hidden eavesdropping devices and microphones. He'll continue the work, but not on a set schedule. I have no intention of being an easy mark for Paul Tracht."

Sara nodded in agreement. "Ben, I'm still sure we heard someone out in the hall. Maybe we should keep looking."

"Charlie was downstairs at his post when I called him, Sara. No one could get into the building without him noticing. However, he's going to make a complete check right away, just to make sure."

"What about during the times he patrols the building, like now?"

"The front doors are locked and only two of my top executives have keys."

"Well, maybe someone else is in the building besides the maintenance crew, and he doesn't know about it."

"I think we're both getting paranoid," he said, forcing a smile. "Let me walk you back to your office. I need to be getting back home." After a moment, he added, "But just in case, Sara, start locking your door when you work here at night, okay?"

"I'll stay on my guard, Ben, but promise me you'll do the same."

They stopped by the door to her new offices. "I promise." He glanced at his watch. "I'd better be going. I don't like to leave Jimmy alone for any great length of time at night."

"I'll keep my eyes and ears open, Ben. Maybe together we can find some answers to what's been going on. If there is someone sabotaging your business, we'll find him."

His eyes darkened and his face grew serious. "Sara, I don't want you to even think of doing anything foolish. Dammit, woman, you scared the hell out of me. If someone had really been out there you could have been hurt!" He grasped her hard by the shoulders. "Do you realize the danger you could have put yourself in?"

"Ben, you don't have to worry about me. I can handle myself." She smiled and added, "I've seen lots of martial arts movies."

"Sara! I'm serious."

"So am I. Besides, if I had caught up to the person, between you and me he wouldn't have stood a chance."

"Sara—" his voice was gruff and his eyes sparkled with deadly intent "—I want your word that you'll never do anything like that again."

"I can't give you my word on that, Ben," she said quietly, "but I will promise you that I won't act on impulse. I'll make sure I know exactly what I'm doing."

"That's not good enough. I want your word that you won't go looking for trouble."

She thought it over. "Okay. I can promise you that. I won't go looking for trouble," she answered. However, if trouble found her, she wasn't going to run from it, either.

TEN DAYS HAD PASSED since the night Ben had told her about the information leaks that were plaguing his company. Then, a few days ago, she'd begun to notice some of her own materials were not where she'd left them. Granted, she'd never been one for maintaining a super-organized office, but she'd always known where to find everything she needed at a moment's notice. Not so, lately.

Sara scoured the office for the file containing the notes on her latest experiment. She could have sworn that she'd set it on top of her desk the night before. Had someone been in her office without her knowledge, or was she simply getting absentminded?

She plopped into her chair and stared angrily around the room. It had to be here. Somewhere. Unless the file had been stolen. But then, no thief would be stupid enough to take her incomplete notes. It would make far better sense to copy them and then come back periodically to check on her progress. And surely if an industrial spy had been clever enough to get into a building patrolled by security, he wouldn't be stupid enough to leave such an obvious indication of his activities.

"Hello," she heard a cheerful voice greet her. "You look positively furious. What's up?"

She glanced up and smiled. "Mike! What are you doing here?"

"I brought the computer analysis you wanted. Univax was able to predict what the results would be if you went ahead with your proposed changes for the formula. Our computer at the lab is fantastic working up those kinds of projections.''

"Great." She took the papers from his hand, then offered him a chair. "I can get you a cup of coffee too, if you'd like."

"No thanks. I remember tasting your coffee," he teased. "It should come with a warning label."

She laughed. "How did I know you'd help yourself to some that had been sitting in that coffeepot for a week?"

"It tasted really foul." He shuddered. "So tell me what's going on? Are you stuck on a problem? I gathered from your expression that things aren't exactly peachy."

"I've misplaced something, and it's driving me nuts."

"Can I help?"

She shrugged. "Only if you see a manila file folder with an orange label on it somewhere."

"Come on," he encouraged her. "I'll help you look."

"I've already searched the desk from top to bottom, and the lab. I've run out of places to look."

His eyes narrowed pensively. "Have you tried looking *behind* things? It might have slipped off a table."

"No, I haven't," she admitted. "I'll start with my workbench in the lab."

"I'll look behind the file cabinets in here."

She had just stepped into the lab when Mike called her. "There's something back here, but I can't tell what it is."

Sara returned to the outer office. "I'll take this side of the file cabinet, and you take the other. Let's slide it out from the wall a bit."

"Okay, we'll push on three," he told her. "One, two and three."

A few seconds later, Sara pulled out a folder from behind the cabinet. "That is it, but for the life of me I can't
figure out how it got there."

"You probably put in on the top, meaning to file it
later, and then brushed it off as you walked past."

"Mike," she said as she leafed through the file, "you've
just saved me hours of work. Redoing all the notes I have
in here would have taken me all afternoon."

"Great! In that case, you owe me lunch."

"It'll have to be next week sometime, okay?" she answered apologetically. "I've got too much work that needs
to get done at the moment."

"What's going on? You look as if you haven't slept too
well lately."

"Gee, thanks," she muttered sarcastically, then sighed.
"But you're right. I haven't. I've had a lot of things on my
mind."

"Like the owner of Classic Parts, who's obviously
given you these terrific offices?" He glanced around.
"I've got to admit, this is a vast improvement over your
previous digs."

"It's nice to know some things never change. You're as
blunt as ever."

"We're too close to have to mince words with each
other, Sara. All I know is that this office isn't your style
at all. You like closed-in places. Being in here is like living in a glass palace."

Sara laughed. It was hard to argue with a friend who
knew her so well. Perhaps that was why she'd always felt
comfortable around Mike. Neither one of them had ever
felt the need to pretend or keep up appearances. It was too
bad she'd never been able to fall in love with him, but the
chemistry hadn't been right between them. Their rela-

tionship would never go beyond the platonic, but she couldn't have asked for a better friend.

She gave him all the details behind her move, then continued. "I'll return downstairs, though, as soon as they repair everything."

"You hedged on my original question," he insisted patiently. "What's been causing you to lose sleep?"

"There are two people in my life right now, Mike, whose well-being and feelings mean as much to me as my own," she answered slowly. "This is all completely new to me. I'm usually very logical and guarded with my emotions, not the type who gets drawn into relationships very easily."

"If you've got *two* men in your life you care for that deeply, you've got bigger problems than I thought." His eyes widened in surprise.

Sara chuckled as she returned to her desk. "One of them is Ben's eleven-year-old son Jimmy. I'm absolutely crazy about that kid. If I ever had a son, I'd want him to be just like Jimmy."

"I said it once and I'll say it again. It sounds like you're in love, Sara," Mike said as he sat down on the other side of her desk.

"Well, I'm not ready to admit that yet," she replied, a little uncertainly. "I know I care a great deal for both those people, but love... I'm not sure."

"That's the old fighting spirit! Make him work to get you. He'll appreciate you much more."

Sara laughed. "I'll keep your advice in mind."

"So, is that why you haven't been able to get much sleep?"

"Partially. I've also been working on a project for Ben. He hasn't asked me to go double time on it, but I think it would really be a big help to him if I was able to find some answers quickly."

"Ben's a lucky man," he said, rising and starting toward the door. "I wish it had been in the cards for us. We get along so well."

"That's true," she admitted, "but the sparks were never there, you know that. That's why we were able to become such good friends. There was never anything else to interfere."

"I'm not so sure we couldn't have made those sparks happen in time," he said wistfully.

"That kind of magic can't be manufactured. It's either there, or it isn't," Sara replied quietly, accompanying him to the door.

"I still say Ben's a lucky man," Mike said as he gave her a quick kiss on the cheek.

"You're the best friend anyone could ever hope for. In my book that makes me a very lucky lady."

"I guess we've both got something to be thankful for. Girlfriends come and go in my life, but our friendship has always remained firm. It's nice to know you can always count on certain things." Mike moved down the hall toward the elevators. "Don't forget, you owe me lunch."

"You've got it."

Sara watched him walk to the elevators, then turned and went back to her desk. She still wasn't convinced that someone hadn't come into her office. It was possible that she'd brushed against that folder and sent it tumbling behind the file cabinet, but she had her doubts. From now on, she'd make a mental note of where her things were before she left the office each night. If it was just a case of absentmindedness, then no harm would be done. However, if it was more than that, the sooner she confirmed it, the better.

She stared at the computer printout Mike had brought her. So she'd been on the right track all along. Her instincts had paid off. She picked up the telephone and dialed Ben's number. "Hi! Have you got about ten minutes? I know you love progress reports, and I finally have something solid to report."

"Can you come to my office? I'm waiting for an important call."

"Sure. Shall I come down now?"

"Whenever you're ready," he answered.

Sara locked her door, though she felt that maybe she was becoming overly cautious. A few minutes later she walked into Ben's office.

Two men stood beside Ben, studying a set of graphs that were spread out on his desk.

Hearing Sara's knock, Ben glanced up. "Come in. Have you met Joe and Marc? They're my top executives."

Sara shook her head. "I've had calls from them, though."

"Which you effectively ducked," one said with a chuckle, then added, "I'm Joe McCallister."

"Pleased to meet you," Sara said as she shook his hand.

"I'm Marc Winger," the other man said as he introduced himself. "Boy, when you didn't want to be found, there was no way to get you out of that office of yours."

"Who'd have thought we'd end up working on the same team?" Sara noted ruefully, then glanced at Ben. "Is this a bad time? Do you want me to come back?"

"No, that's all right. We just had to take care of a few details. I'd like to hear what you have to say, and it would be better if Joe and Marc could get your report first-hand, too."

Joe sat down and leaned back. His enormous proportions seemed to put a strain on the construction of the chair. "We've got a lot of high hopes for this project of yours, Ms Cahill."

"Call me Sara," she said, then seated herself in the nearest chair. "I'm not through with all the tests yet, but I've made some very solid gains. I've spent a great deal of my time at National Laboratories, and using their equipment has really speeded up my work. It took longer than I'd hoped to come up with the exact formula I needed, but I believe I've found it. My progress should be fairly rapid from this point on."

Joe leaned forward and studied her. "Sara, how reliable are these laboratories you're using? We've got to keep your project under wraps for the time being."

Ben answered for her. "We've already covered that. Sara knows that it's got to remain secret."

Joe nodded, seemingly satisfied.

"If we could use this process of hers by the end of next month, our sales projections could increase dramatically," Marc commented.

"We still have to make sure our sealed bid beats out the competition this time and we win the Webley Motors account," Ben added. "That would insure that we could continue with our plans to expand at the present rate. Webley Motors is the number one chain of automobile repair shops in the country. They specialize in classic cars. We've got to get that contract."

Surprised, Sara noted their focus of attention had shifted quickly from her work to their financial dealings. Normally Ben would have wanted a detailed briefing, but as it was, he seemed too preoccupied for more than just the cursory report she'd given him.

She found the lapse annoying, but slowly another thought formed in her mind. His trust in her abilities must have grown significantly, if he was willing to accept the information she'd given him at face value. Consoling herself with that, she stood up. "I've got to get back to my office now, gentlemen."

"Thanks for the progress report, Sara. You're doing a great job for us." Ben walked around his desk and accompanied her into the hall. "We haven't had much time to spend with each other lately, have we?" he asked.

"No, but that's okay," she said, trying to reassure him. "We've both been very busy with our work. It *did* feel rather nice, though, to know we're working toward a common goal."

"Common goal?" he asked, puzzled.

She stared at him, surprised he didn't know exactly what she'd meant. "Classic Parts. I've decided to work on your project almost exclusively. I know you didn't ask me to, but I figured it might help."

"Sara," he told her gently, "I can take care of this company. I don't want you to jeopardize your business in order to give me preferential treatment."

"I'm not." She hesitated, then added, "Well, you are getting special treatment. However, there are no pressing deadlines on my other work right now, so it works out for everyone."

He nodded. "I appreciate it." His brow furrowed, and he stared off into the distance for a few moments. "There's something I've been meaning to ask you. How much does Mike know about the project you're working on for Classic Parts?"

"Enough to figure it out if he wanted to, but you don't have to worry. He's completely reliable. Even the government uses his labs from time to time. Mike has the highest security clearance given to anyone working on a federal contract. He's utterly trustworthy."

She paused, trying to figure out a way to quiet his suspicions concerning her friend. "Mike goes out of his way for me all the time, Ben. Do you realize that this morning he brought some data sheets he knew I'd need directly to my office? He didn't have to do that, you know. Then, while he was at my office, he even helped me find a file I'd misplaced containing all the notes of my experiment."

"He helped you? What do you mean?" There was an edge to Ben's voice.

"It had slipped behind the file cabinet," she explained. "To tell you the truth, I wondered whether someone had been inside my office the night before. I don't misplace things usually, though of course, there's always a first time. When Mike came over, I'd already searched the office once. If it hadn't been for Mike, I'd have probably still been looking for that file."

"Maybe he knew where to look," Ben muttered, then held up a hand, stemming her protest. "Either way, Sara, I want you to be extremely careful with the information you give out, okay?"

"You don't have to worry about Mike, or me," she told him flatly. "I know my business, Ben. Give me credit for that."

"I do trust you," he said and his expression softened. "I'm sorry I'm so preoccupied."

Joe came out into the hall. "Ben, you'd better get back to the office. That call we were waiting for just came through."

"I'll see you later," Ben told her, though from his expression she could see that his attention had already shifted to other matters.

Sara slowly walked back down the hall to her office. Ben was a businessman used to taking risks. She suspected that a part of him loved the challenge of pitting himself against the wiles of a business adversary. However, she honestly wished she might play a more active role in helping him solve his problem. She felt left out. More than anything she wanted to be at his side, shouldering the responsibility with him. Sadly, that seemed to be impossible.

CHAPTER EIGHT

ONCE INSIDE HER LABORATORY, Sara felt a little better. At least here, she could feel useful. Immersing herself in her work, she shut out all distractions and concentrated on the project.

Although it didn't seem as though a very long time had passed, almost three hours elapsed before she heard a knock at her door. With a frown, she walked out of the lab and answered it.

Jimmy's usually cheerful face seemed somber. A soulful, hurt look she'd never seen there before was mirrored in his eyes. "Hi!" Her voice softened instinctively. "You look as if you've just lost your best friend."

Jimmy stared at her, then at his shoes. "Can I visit for a while?"

"Sure," she stepped aside and gestured for him to come in. "What's up?" Seeing the report card sticking out of his front pocket, Sara pointed and added, "Is that part of the problem?"

Jimmy shook his head, then shrugged. "Maybe, but not in the way you think." He readjusted his baseball cap, then slipped off his backpack. "I've worked real hard this last quarter. I knew it would mean a lot to Dad if I managed to get straight A's. We talked about it once, and he said that he'd never been able to. He said that the only way he'd ever see a report card that looked that good was if I managed to do it. He made a joke out of it, but I knew he'd really be pleased if I did get straight *A*'s someday. Well, I did."

"Did you show the report card to him?"

Jimmy nodded. "He barely even saw it. He glanced at it for a second, then got busy with Mr. McCallister and Mr. Winger and forgot all about me." She was looking at him as if she understood, and somehow that made him feel better. "I guess I sound like I'm making a big deal out of nothing, but I really did work hard to get those grades."

"I know, and you have a right to be upset," Sara told him. She knew firsthand how hard it was when you tried to impress a parent, and your accomplishment was casually brushed aside. "On the other hand, I know your dad is really busy today, and under a lot of pressure. It happens that way when you own your own business."

Jimmy shrugged. "I suppose," he muttered, avoiding her eyes. He shouldn't have told her anything. All of a sudden he felt like a real horse's butt for bellyaching about his dad. He felt like a traitor, somehow. "That's okay, Ms Cahill. I know Dad didn't mean anything by it. It just hurt a bit, that's all."

"Has he signed your report card yet?"

Jimmy shook his head.

"This evening, when he's away from the office, he'll be more relaxed. I bet you anything, you'll be able to see just how proud he is of you and your grades then."

He smiled. She was such a neat-o lady. She was special, like a friend you wanted to be with because the friend liked you just the way you were. They'd build little places for themselves in your heart, and become a part of you in a way. Maybe she'd build a place for herself in Dad's heart, too, and she'd come and be part of their family someday.

"What are you thinking about?"

He pulled a candy bar from his backpack and offered her half. "Do you like Dad? I mean, *really* like him?"

She accepted the chocolate bar and tried not to smile. "Uh-huh," she replied with a nod.

"You know, Dad's lonely. He never talks about it, but I know he is."

She chuckled. "Jimmy, your dad could have an entire harem of lady friends if he chose to."

"Oh sure," he agreed quickly, "but it's hard for him to really relax in front of anyone else, like he does in front of me. People give up on him, I know. I've heard him fight with other ladies before. They think he doesn't care just because he doesn't talk much about himself. But I bet if someone had a lot of patience he would. And you know what? I bet he'd stop spending his free time all alone. He's got to be lonely, don't you think? He doesn't have any really close friends to talk to. I can always talk to him, but who does he go to? He can't always come to me. I'm a kid and a grown-up needs other grown-ups."

"You're fishing, Jimmy," she observed with a smile. "But just so you know, I'd always be there for him if he wanted to talk."

"Yea, but you've got to remind him of that, otherwise he forgets."

Sara laughed. "Jimmy, you little con artist, when you grow up you should go into business as a marriage broker. You're a natural."

"Does that mean you're actually *thinking* of someday marrying Dad?"

She almost choked on the candy bar. "It was just a manner of speaking, you devil, and you darn well know it. Now let's talk about something else, before I strangle you." She struggled to look serious, but figured he'd never be taken in by it. "Tell me about your design for the robot. How's it going?"

"I told my science teacher, Mr. McConnell, about it, and he really thought it was a great idea. He was a little concerned about safety, though. He wants to make sure I get some help with the electrical part of it. I told him I'd ask you, 'cause you'd know all about that." He looked at her hopefully. "Will you help me? I'd be glad to come by anytime you say. I know you're busy, but I'll stay out of your way and..."

"Whoa!" She laughed. "It's fine, I'll give you a hand and make sure you're not doing anything dangerous. Just let me take a look at the electrical components before you actually switch anything on."

"That's great! I've built the robot shell, and it looks really neat, but now it's time to attach the motor to it. I have to test it and make sure it's going to work."

"Have you got the robot here?"

"It's in the closet right outside Dad's office. I can go get it now, if you have time to take a look."

"Go ahead." Sara watched him dash down the hallway, then returned to her desk. She'd take her break now and help Jimmy. Being with that kid never failed to improve her spirits. There was something irresistible about the basic honesty of Jimmy's feelings. He was just the way he seemed to be and when he reached out to her, needing and wanting to be with her, he'd touched her very soul.

She would have given anything to have Ben treat her the same way. The problem was Ben liked taking charge too much. He felt more comfortable when he was the one in control. Opening up necessitated a sense of vulnerability she wasn't sure he'd ever be able to accept.

Jimmy returned only minutes later. "It doesn't weigh very much at all, but it sure looks neat. Wait until I take it out of the box. I've attached little red lights, like the ones inside the front panel of a car, for the eyes. That'll also let me know when it's on. The nose is an old gear-shift bar that Dad couldn't use, and the way I put the head on, it makes it appear that it's looking down. Actually, that lets the bar rest on the pages.''

Sara watched Jimmy extract his creation from the cardboard box. It looked a bit like a cutaway model of an electric can opener, with eyes. She forced herself to look completely serious. "It's certainly an original-looking robot. In fact, the entire idea is quite creative," she admitted.

"The problem is checking the connections between the motor and the power supply to make sure that everything will work properly. I've got a special sound-activated switch that I took from a burglar alarm kit hooked up between the motor and the power cord. That way when I give the voice command 'turn page' the switch will turn on the power and make the motor move the arms. At the same time the voice synthesizer will answer me, and say 'I'm turning the page now.'''

"Where did you get the voice synthesizer?"

"I got it from one of my old educational games that teaches children how to spell. I was just a little kid then, of course. With that, though, I could get my robot to talk back to me."

"Are you sure everything's been wired properly and it's all compatible?"

"That's what my science teacher and I aren't sure of. We need you to check it so we don't zap ourselves or short out everything."

Sara opened the back plate of the robot and examined all the printed electrical information on the various parts. "I'm glad you left the labels on all this stuff. We would have never been able to figure out anything about their voltage requirements without it.''

Sara took an electrical probe with a light and checked some of the circuits. ''All the soldered connections seem good and there shouldn't be any problems with compatibility. Fortunately, all your electrical equipment seems to be of the proper voltage. Nothing should burn out. Let me check and make sure it's all grounded properly.''

Visually tracing the wires of all the connections, she brought out her electrical tester one more time. After a few minutes she looked up. ''Looks good to me. Want to give it a try? The worst that can happen is that it won't work, but if all your equipment is sound, we should see some results.''

''Should I plug it in?'' Jimmy asked quickly, picking up the end of the cord.

''Let me do it this first time, just in case. We'll use the special outlet that will cut the power off if anything is wrong.''

''Can we test everything all at once? I want to see if it'll turn the pages of a book like it's supposed to,'' Jimmy asked. ''Oh, no, wait, I can't. All I have with me are my notebooks. I don't have any textbooks in my backpack today.''

''Take one of mine from the shelf,'' she offered.

''Great!'' Jimmy dashed across the lab quickly, then returned holding a large volume. ''Is this one okay? It's a manual for patents.''

''Sure. Just place it on the robot the way you planned, and let's give it a run-through.''

Jimmy set the book on the shelf attached to the robot's body. Lowering the trunk of the elephant's head over the middle of the book so that it was anchored in place, he sat back and looked at Sara. ''Now?''

"Go."

"Turn page."

"Turning page," the machine answered in an electrically supplied monotone.

The ex-windshield wiper arm reached across, fastening on to the bottom corner of the right-hand page. Almost faster than their eyes could follow, the arm whipped to the left, tearing the first page at the base, then returning to repeat the process with the next one. Torn pieces of paper started fluttering into the air.

"Unplug it, unplug it!" Jimmy yelled. "I forgot to program a 'Stop' command. It'll go through your entire book!"

Sara vaulted out of her chair and dived for the plug. "There! Did it quit?"

Jimmy stared at the ripped pages lying on the floor. "I blew it, Ms Cahill."

Sara looked at the paper scattered around, then at Jimmy's face. "Don't look so glum. It's okay. Some experiments need a bit of adjustment before they work. It's part of the business."

"You're not angry?" His spirits rose. Her attitude confirmed everything good he'd ever thought about her. "I thought you'd start yelling at me, and tell me to get out!"

"Jimmy," Sara said gently as she placed one hand on his shoulder, "we're friends, and friends stick by each other. So we blew the first round. We'll make it better the next time."

"Wow, that's great!" Everything was okay and it was going to stay that way. "You're really terrific."

"Thank you." She bowed slightly, then laughed. "Now are we going to sit here jabbering all day, or do you want to get some serious work done?"

He could have hugged her. "Let's get down to work."

It took another two hours before they had adjusted the pressure on the windshield wiper arms to Sara's satisfaction. "There's no way of knowing for sure, until we try it, that is, but I think it should work. What do you think about the glue? Shall we unwrap a bit of that tape so it doesn't stick quite so firmly?"

Jimmy stared at his robot, lost in thought. "Yea, I think we should." He unwrapped the first layer, then stopped. "Um...thanks for not just taking over. I'm glad that you know *how* to help. Do you know what I mean?"

She smiled and nodded. "Sure I do. It's your project. If I took over, it would be my project. That's not the way it's supposed to be."

"Okay, I think we've got this fixed. It's as ready as it'll ever get. Only I'm not sure we should use your book again. Maybe I should go to Dad's office and get one of his."

"Er, no," she answered quickly. She could just imagine Ben's expression if Jimmy brought back one of his books a page at a time. "Let's go ahead and use the same book we did before. I don't mind if I lose a few pages out of that."

"You sure?"

"When you're trying to isolate a problem, it's better to change only those things you think contributed to whatever went wrong. If you have too many variables, you throw off your own results."

"You're right," Jimmy agreed somberly. "I knew that, but I guess I forgot."

"I'm going to plug it in. Ready?"

"Go."

Jimmy saw the red lights that made up the eyes blink on. He adjusted the book, then sat back. "Turn page," he commanded.

The arms went to the upper right-hand corner and turned the page, at a slower pace this time. "Hey, it works!"

"Stop," he commanded.

The wiper blade ignored his command and continued. "Stop!" Jimmy repeated.

Sara stood behind Jimmy. "When we were adjusting the arms, did you remember to program it to understand the command 'Stop'?"

Jimmy felt his cheeks burn. "I guess I forgot," he mumbled, wishing the ground would open up and swallow him. His thinking was really starting to get fuzzy. "I guess I'll just pull the plug out."

Sara watched, sensing his embarrassment, her heart going out to him. "Well, after you get your programming straightened out, you'll have yourself a working robot. I think that's a great accomplishment."

He glanced up at her quickly. "I'm glad it stopped ripping pages. It shouldn't take me long to program it to recognize a 'Stop' command. I just got so worried about fixing the arms, I forgot about the rest."

"That's okay. The way I see it, you've got a versatile robot. It can turn pages or tear them out," Sara said very seriously. "Just think, with a bit of adjustment it could tear pages out and then feed them to a shredder, one at a time. You could destroy documents you wanted to keep private that way."

"Like they do with secret government stuff," Jimmy added excitedly.

"That's right."

"Thanks for everything," he said, meeting her eyes. Then, feeling his cheeks burning, Jimmy stared at the floor.

"Anytime."

"I should let you get back to work, huh?" Jimmy started picking up his papers. He didn't want to leave. He liked being with her and doing things like they were partners. It was fun at her lab.

"I have a few things to do, but I always have time for you if you want to talk."

He returned the robot to the box, then put his papers inside his backpack. "Ms Cahill..."

"Why don't you start calling me Sara?"

He looked up quickly. "Really?"

"That is, if you'd like."

"I'd like!" Out of habit, Jimmy pushed his glasses farther up his nose and readjusted his baseball cap. "Sara," he said quietly, "I don't remember my mom real well, but I hope that she was a lot like you."

Sara's heart swelled with love. "Jimmy, I hope I have a son like you someday."

He threw his arms around her neck and gave her a quick hug. "I'm going to figure out a way to get you together with my dad, forever, if it's the last thing I do."

The remark took her by surprise. Before Sara could think of a suitable reply, he grabbed his robot and backpack and dashed out of her office.

Sara slumped into her chair. She'd have to have a talk with Jimmy soon. He was determined to see Ben and herself get married and live happily ever after. Maybe she could explain to Jimmy that his friendship with her was not dependent on her relationship with Ben. Perhaps then he'd feel more secure. She sensed Jimmy's real problem was that he was afraid she'd suddenly disappear out of his life. Ben had told her that Jimmy had seriously tried to play matchmaker once before. What had happened to that relationship, and how had Jimmy been affected by it?

Her train of thought was interrupted as she heard footsteps approaching. Ben peered inside the doorway. "Is Jimmy still here?"

"No." She waved a hand, inviting him to come in. "You and I have to talk."

"Let me guess. He's driving you crazy and not letting you get your own work done." Ben exhaled loudly.

"No, that's not it. I really like him, Ben. Not just because he's your son, but because of the way he is. Do you understand?"

He pulled out a chair and straddled it. "I've already figured that." He chuckled softly. "I think you like him *almost* as much as he does you."

She glanced at her watch. "It's five-thirty, and I need something to eat. How about treating me to some junk food from your lunchroom?"

He laughed. "No wonder Jimmy's crazy about you. You have the same tastes."

He walked down the hall with her to the lunchroom. "What would you like?"

"Anything with lots of sugar. I have a long night ahead of me at the lab."

"So, Jimmy *did* keep you from getting your work done."

Sara munched on the candy bar he'd bought for her. "Yes, but I needed a break and he's fun."

"Then what's wrong?" They sat down.

She hesitated. "A couple of things, but I'm not sure how to begin."

He reached across the small circular table and covered her hand with his. "You said it yourself. We're friends. You shouldn't have to worry about being frank with me."

"Well, first of all, I know you were really busy when Jimmy came into your office today, but he was really crushed that you didn't say more about his report card."

"I didn't get much of a chance to look at it, but I'm sure they were good grades. I'll look at it more closely tonight."

"He got straight A's, and in my opinion the main reason he worked so hard to get them was so he could please you."

Ben leaned back against his chair and rubbed his chin with one hand. "I remember a conversation I had with him when he brought home the last report card. I think I know what you're referring to." His tense expression changed, and his gaze softened. "Thanks, Sara. I needed to know that. I'll make it up to him tonight."

She bit her bottom lip pensively, wondering how to bring up the other matters that had occupied her thoughts.

"There's more, isn't there. Is it his matchmaking? He finally drove you crazy?"

Sara laughed. "He hasn't. I think it's terribly flattering, really. He's so open and so affectionate. I'd have to be made out of stone not to respond to that."

"Then what is it?" He leaned forward and regarded her with a worried frown.

"It's partly something he said, and partly something I sense. I think that the reason he's trying so hard to fix you and me up is that he's afraid he'll lose me if it doesn't work out between us. I'm going to do everything I can to reassure him that his relationship with me is not dependent on mine with you. Is that okay?"

"Why are you worried about that?" His tone was guarded. Was she trying to tell him that she'd mistaken her feelings for him? Was this her way of pushing him out of her life? If she'd changed her mind about him, he'd coax her back. He'd always fought to get the things he wanted in life and Sara wouldn't be the exception. The strength of his resolve surprised him. Perhaps he'd been falling in love with her since the first day they'd met. "Are you worried that our relationship won't work out in the long run, and you might hurt Jimmy?" He forced his voice to remain even.

"No, that's not it at all. I just don't want Jimmy to feel insecure about his relationship with me. I'd like him to know that my feelings for him have no strings or contingencies attached to them. I like him, and I'll be there for him whenever he wants me, no matter what happens between us."

Ben leaned back and smiled, relief flooding over him. He couldn't fault her for loving his son, or for wanting to make Jimmy feel more secure. "I'm glad Jimmy and you have become close. He's needed someone like you for a long time. He's had a hard time of it. Jimmy's never quite fitted in with the other kids, at least not at the old school. I've tried to be there for him, to give him all the stability and love I could to build his self-confidence, but I knew he needed more than I could give. You've filled that gap for him."

"That's why I want to impress upon him that he and I can always remain as close as he wants us to be."

"I think your instincts are right." He reached for her hand once more. "I need to get out of this building for a while. Come take a break with me?" He pulled her gently out of her chair.

Sara thought he was going to take her into his arms, but instead he led her toward the door. "I can't go away for very long, Ben," she protested.

"Trust me. We're not going far." Leading her to the fire escape, he urged her on. "Come on. The climb will do you good."

"Climb where? We're already on the top floor."

They emerged on the roof a moment later. "We can watch the sunset from up here."

The view was breathtaking. Watermelon colors bathed the Sandia Mountains in a gentle pink glow. The sky above them was ablaze with brilliant streaks of fiery oranges, dazzling lavenders and blues. The skyline glittered with its palette of colors, encompassing the magical time when light and darkness blended in perfect balance.

"It's beautiful."

"If I have to stay here and work late, I try to take the time to come upstairs and watch the sunset. It helps me relax and put things into perspective." He turned and faced her, a grim set etched on his features. "I've had a hellish day. Paul Tracht undercut my last bid by a small margin, and beat me out of a very important contract. I know that he did that by getting inside information about my prices, but for the life of me I can't figure out who's getting the information for him and how that person is getting in."

He clenched his jaw, then forced himself to relax. "If I hadn't been so preoccupied I would have never brushed Jimmy off as I did. I'll apologize to him tonight, but I want you to know that it made me very happy to know you were there for my son. He's been the center of my life for so long, I wasn't sure if I'd ever have room for anyone else. Then I met you."

Ben hadn't mentioned love, but nonetheless she realized that it was there, woven into the meaning behind his words. Still, how could she make him understand that it wasn't enough, simply to be a part of Jimmy's life? She wanted to share in his, too. If there was a future for them, she'd have to be far more than a mother figure for Jimmy.

"What's wrong?" He'd expected her to be happy, yet the look on her face was far from that. Did she think him weak for explaining himself to her?

"I love Jimmy a great deal, Ben, but it's my relationship with you that I don't understand. You never talk to me about the way you feel, except when it pertains to Jimmy. For instance, this past week when you've had so many problems here at work, you never once came to me to talk, or to enjoy the comfort of being with a person who cared. You've faced this very much on your own. You shut me out. It's as if you want to hold me at arm's length; you'll let me come close, but not close enough."

"Sara, I'm more open with you than I've ever been with anyone, including Rosemary, my wife." If a man wasn't strong enough to handle his problems without leaning on someone else for support, he wasn't much use as a man. Couldn't she see that?

What she wanted was closeness, the type she'd never found within the circle of her own family. Couldn't he understand that? Such intimacy was the best foundation for a solid relationship.

"I've always promised myself," Sara explained, "that someday I'd have my own family and we'd all share that love and sense of belonging I never had as a kid. The only time my parents ever paid any attention to me was when I did something wrong. They were too wrapped up in their own lives and careers to notice anything else." She paused, trying to gather her composure. It still hurt to talk about her childhood. "I grew up with the dream that someday I'd share my life with a man who'd want me and need me. We'd be equal partners in life, depending on and standing by each other. But that takes openness, and the willingness to let another person see you with your guard down. You won't let me get that close, to see the private side of you and share your thoughts. I've felt as if I've hit a brick wall."

"There has to be a certain amount of separateness in our relationship, Sara. Emotionally, I believe it's healthier."

"Why?" she insisted.

Ben jammed his hands into his pockets and stared off into the sunset. "When I was a kid, my mom, my older brother and I were extremely close. I think we suffered more because of it. My dad had a problem gambling. We went through some really tough financial times. Having Mom, John and me sharing our thoughts and feelings seldom helped. For example, knowing John was scared that we would be evicted and wouldn't have a place to live scared me even more than I already was. His fear emphasized mine. After all he was older and knew more. Or, for instance, knowing Mom was always dreaming of better times and kidding herself made my brother and me feel really insecure. We knew Dad couldn't be trusted, and Mom's faith in him meant we couldn't trust her judgment, either."

He shook his head, as if trying to clear the painful memories from his mind. "I'm not telling you this to get your sympathy. As far as I'm concerned that part of my life is ancient history," he stated flatly. "But I want you to see my point and try to understand me better."

"I do," she conceded in a soft voice, "but only because you allowed me to see a part of you you've kept hidden until now. I'm not a child, and I don't need to be shielded from things. I can be there for you, to help you find solutions, or at times just to be supportive. Won't you let me through those barriers you've built between us?"

"You want me to open my heart and mind to you completely with the same childlike trust Jimmy's shown you." Ben met her eyes. "But I'm a man. My feelings don't heal as quickly as those of a child. The type of openness you want would leave me very little if things didn't work out between us." He brushed her cheek with his palm, then rested his hand at the base of her neck. His thumb made a lazy circle over the pulse point in her throat. "Besides, Sara, you're forgetting something very important. The type of openness you want is fostered over a period of time between adults. It's not something you can get on demand."

"I know that." His touch was sending tiny sparks racing through her. "But unless I ask, I'm afraid it'll never even start to happen."

He smiled tenderly. "I'll try, because I know how much it means to you." He pulled her closer, wanting to feel her against him. Maybe he could learn to be less guarded around her. "Are you always this impatient?"

"That depends on what you have in mind," she said, nestling in his arms.

His laugh was deep and dark. "Be careful. I may just do what you've asked and tell you exactly what I'm thinking," he teased roguishly.

"But you haven't hidden those thoughts from me, even if you haven't put them into words," she countered playfully. "Tell me something I don't know," she asked as she buried her head against his shoulder.

He tilted her chin upwards, his eyes meshing with hers. "You're stealing my heart, beautiful lady."

Ben filled his mouth with the taste of her. As she parted her lips for him, he felt his body grow tense. She was fire in his arms. He felt intensely male, and the primitive need to make her his surged through him.

Forcing himself to remain gentle, he kissed her softly. He drank in her sweetness, taking what he could without crossing the line that separated tenderness from passion. He shuddered, the effort eating at his will, making him crazy.

Sara pushed him away. Her hand, splayed against his chest, trembled. "I have to go back to work." She couldn't stay there with him much longer. Her need for him was becoming too powerful a force to deny. "And you have a young man waiting at home for you."

As he forced himself to concentrate on his son, his expression turned somber. "I have to make things up to him." He smiled slowly. "And I know just the way, too. For weeks he'd been begging me to enter the annual Rio Grande raft race with him. I've turned him down, because the problems I've had at work demanded my complete attention. In view of the situation, though, I'll tell him I've changed my mind. Straight *A*'s deserve a special reward."

"That's wonderful. He'll be thrilled."

"Come with us. We'll make it a family outing." Would she understand that this was his way of opening himself and allowing her into the very heart of his life? They'd be with his son, but more importantly, she'd be with him at a time when he was free to be himself. She'd be able to see him as a man, not simply a business associate.

A family outing. The significance of his words didn't escape her. "I'd really like that, Ben. I'd love to go."

CHAPTER NINE

AMID A BOISTEROUS, milling crowd of over two thousand, Sara, Ben and Jimmy watched and waited for their particular event to begin—the three-man raft division. Sara stared suspiciously at the bright orange, inflated rubber raft as it lay there beside them on the sandy beach. The water was calm. The Rio Grande for the most part was a shallow river, lacking rapids and swirling waters.

Still, she felt a bit apprehensive. Sporting events had never really appealed to her and she was particularly out of her element here among such an eclectic group of people. Some of the participants wore bathing suits, or cut-off jeans and T-shirts like Jimmy, Ben and herself. Other had come in costumes of a sort, like the group of college-aged boys who had dressed for fun in three-piece suits with ties.

Jimmy glanced around, checking out the competition, enjoying the smell of chili dogs and hamburgers many people were scarfing up. This was going to be so much fun. He looked at Sara and felt glad. They were like a real family now. Did Dad feel it, too?

Sara smiled at Jimmy, and he felt a large grin spread across his face. "Did you check out all those entries in the homemade craft category? Some even had boats they'd carved out of Styrofoam. One of them was shaped like a cup. It was really neat. Maybe next year we can enter in that class, huh, Dad?"

"No way," Ben replied flatly. "I refuse to compete against someone in a yellow Styrofoam duck." He glanced at Sara and gave her a wink.

"Sara, what about you? I bet we could invent the neatest craft. Did you see the adobe submarine? It looked like adobe but it was made out of painted foam. It really made good time."

"Let's concentrate on getting ready right now, Jimmy," she replied. "It's close to our starting time." Sara made a mental note of Ben's expression. Was he worried about work, or was it something else?

"Okay, team," Ben told them. "Let's haul our craft into the water and get to that starting point."

Nervous, Sara grabbed one side of the orange raft, while Ben took the other and Jimmy the rear. She'd never been able to participate in anything that was even remotely considered team sports. She'd tried to warn both Ben and Jimmy about her lack of experience, but they hadn't listened. She'd hoped to persuade them to let her stay at the beach and fix hot dogs for them or something, but they'd refused to even consider her offer.

Ben looked at her face and laughed. "Sara, stop looking so worried. Jimmy and I have both told you that it's just a fun race. It doesn't matter if we win or not. We probably won't, since none of us have trained together, but it's the perfect chance to get out and have fun."

"Sure," Jimmy piped up. "And if you get tired, we can just paddle to the shore and hike around the bosque along the riverbanks. There's some really nice spots. Dad's taken me hiking with him lots of times. We saw the neatest snake once."

"Are there a lot of rattlesnakes in this area?" She stared at her bare legs and sneakers. If only she'd worn long pants and boots!

Ben shook his head. "They're mostly bull or garter snakes. There are some rattlers, but they're not that common. If we do decide to take a hike and make our own detour, then we'll just make sure to keep our eyes open. There's no danger."

Pushing their raft before them, the group slowly entered the river. Sara trudged into the murky, knee-deep water, guiding their raft as she went along. "I wish you two had taken time to at least give me a trial run."

"Just watch me," Jimmy said. "I'll sit in front of you, and when I paddle, you paddle. It's easy."

Jimmy seemed eager to help her, and so intent on showing her a good time that she smiled. "I'll do my best, guys."

Jimmy took her hand and gave it a tiny squeeze. "Hey, you helped me with my robot. I can help you with this. It'll be fine."

Ben seemed uncharacteristically silent, Sara noted, wondering more and more about his mood. "Okay, let's get in," Ben instructed. The water was almost to Jimmy's waist, so he clambered in first. Then Sara and Ben slowly climbed in from opposite sides, careful not to tip over the light craft.

As they rose to their knees, Ben continued. "Everyone got a paddle?"

Sara stared at hers, wondering about the wisdom of agreeing to compete in something she knew absolutely nothing about. "Where would you like me to sit?"

Jimmy walked on his knees to the front of the large oval. "Dad and I will take both ends. He'll get the back, 'cause that's where most of the work is."

Sara laughed. "I like this son of yours, Ben."

Ben shrugged and smiled. "The kid's got brains. What can I say? He knows whom he can trust to take charge and shoulder the responsibility," he baited.

"Oh, spare me!" She scowled and feigned outrage.

"No, you two!" Jimmy wailed. "This isn't the time to fight. You're supposed to be falling..." He stopped and turned bright red. "I mean you're supposed to be thinking of the race."

"Right." Sara forced herself to look very serious. "So Ben has the rear. Where do I sit?"

Jimmy beamed. "In the middle, between Dad and me."

She tried not to laugh, but it was impossible to wipe the smile off her face. There was so much of Ben in Jimmy. He hadn't said it, but she could almost read his thoughts. She was to be in the middle, where they could both protect her.

Jimmy turned, setting his paddle aside and offering her a hand. "Can you make it?"

"Of course I can," she answered, scooting forward on her knees.

Ben watched his son and Sara. The interchange between them was disturbing. For the first time, he truly realized the depth of the relationship between her and Jimmy. Sara really didn't understand what was happening, but he knew his son well. Jimmy's heart and his love for Sara made him magnify the seriousness of Ben's relationship with Sara. To Jimmy, Sara already belonged to his dad and to him.

"Hey, Dad! Aren't you going to paddle too?"

Sara met Ben's eyes, a puzzled frown on her face. As Ben settled in the rear, she turned her head and whispered. "Something the matter?"

"We'll talk later."

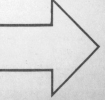

NO COST! NO OBLIGATION!
NO PURCHASE NECESSARY!

PLAY "LUCKY 7"
AND GET AS MANY AS SIX FREE GIFTS...

HOW TO PLAY:

1. With a coin, carefully scratch off the three silver boxes at the right. This makes you eligible to receive one or more free books, and possibly other gifts, depending on what is revealed beneath the scratch-off area.

2. You'll receive brand-new Harlequin Superromance® novels, never before published. When you return this card, we'll send you the books and gifts you qualify for absolutely free!

3. And, a month later, we'll send you 4 additional novels to read and enjoy. If you decide to keep them, you'll pay only $2.74 per book, a savings of 21¢ per book. There is no extra charge for postage and handling. There are no hidden extras.

4. We'll also send you additional free gifts from time to time, as well as our newsletter.

5. You must be completely satisfied, or you may return a shipment of books and cancel at any time.

She nodded. Taking her paddle firmly in hand, she waited for the signal that the race had started. Their raft drifted downstream toward the dozens of others that were jockeying for position. As the gun went off, she began paddling, matching her strokes to the pace of Jimmy's. Ben was paddling on the opposite side of the raft, so the raft wouldn't go in a circle.

It didn't take long before her arms began to ache. She was in reasonably good shape, but the unnatural pace, coupled with the water's resistance, took their toll.

She tried to divert her thoughts, concentrating on the other rafts and the bosque, or wooded area that surrounded the river. Everyone seemed to be having such a good time, splashing along.

"I think we have a problem," Ben said, after they'd gone about a mile downstream. "Sara, lean to your right and check out the valve. I think there should be a cap that sticks over that. See if you can find it."

She set the paddle across the raft and followed his instructions. "I don't see any cap, but when I hold my hand over the valve, I can feel a steady stream of air coming out. Does that mean that if we don't pull to the side soon, we're going to be swimming?"

"I don't think we'll make it to the finish line if we keep losing air at this rate. What called my attention to the valve was that the sides of the raft seem to be getting spongy. Block off the valve with your fingertip for now."

"Good idea," Sara agreed, following his suggestion to stop the air from escaping.

"Let's pull out of the race," Jimmy suggested. "We can let everyone go past us, then just paddle to the nearest bank."

"Agreed," Ben answered.

Rafts of all shapes and sizes raced past them, people laughing and shouting back and forth as they drifted along with the slow current. Sara glanced at the passing craft, then at Jimmy, who turned his head and beamed at her.

"Don't worry," he assured her. "We'll be fine. Dad'll fix it."

"I'm not worried," she told him. "I know I'm in good hands." Jimmy's love and attention, lavished so generously on her, made Sara feel wonderful. She'd never been so taken with a kid. She turned and smiled at Ben, basking in a sense of belonging.

His frown chilled her spirits. Something was definitely wrong. She'd sensed his somber mood right from the beginning. She remembered noticing it earlier that morning when they'd met the man who'd rented them the raft. They'd made arrangements to meet him near the finish line so Ben could park his car there. Then, leaving the inflated raft tied to the top of his four-wheel-drive vehicle, they'd shuttled to the starting line. Jimmy had sat in the back seat with her, encouraging her to feel less nervous about the race. Ben's speculative gaze had continually drifted over them, though he hadn't said much at all. He had seemed to be a million miles away.

Sara decided to talk to Ben as soon as she could. This was Jimmy's day, and no time to think of business. Or could something else be troubling him?

As they reached the nearer side of the riverbank that bordered the bosque, Ben jumped into the shallow water. Sara and Jimmy followed suit, and pulled up the raft onto the sandy shore. Sara moved carefully, making sure her fingers remained on top of the valve so that no more air could escape.

Ben leaned over and studied the raft, Jimmy by his shoulder. Sara watched both of them. She imagined herself as part of their family, her love for Ben and Jimmy enveloping her in a pleasant fantasy.

"Dad, we need to find the top of that valve. Maybe it just fell into the bottom of the raft somewhere."

"What we have to do right now, or as soon as possible, is figure out a way to stop that leak permanently."

Sara forced her thoughts back to the present and tried to think of an answer to their problem. Finding creative solutions was naturally one of the things she did best. She studied the valve, but without tools or patching materials, she couldn't think of a way to keep their raft from losing all its air, unless she kept blocking it with her hand all day. Maybe a stick could be wedged into the stem. She glanced around for a piece of driftwood.

"I've got it," Jimmy said quickly. "It's not a permanent solution, but it'll buy us time, and keep Sara from having to plug the leak with her fingertip."

"What have you got in mind, son?" Ben asked gently, a proud smile spreading over his face.

"Gum. I'll wad a piece or two around the top of the valve. It should hold. In the meantime, we can search the raft really carefully and see if we can find that valve top."

Sara smiled. "That's a terrific idea, Jimmy."

"You guys start looking in the raft. I'll take care of the valve," he told them, taking over for Sara. With one hand he unwrapped several pieces of gum, and stuck them inside his mouth.

"That valve cover is such a tiny thing," Ben mumbled, leaning over one edge of the raft. "Between the water that's splashed onto the bottom and all these folds the raft has as part of its construction, it's going to be tough to find it."

Sara leaned over and began searching the opposite side. "I'll take this side, and you take the other. I think we'll have better luck if we feel our way across the bottom instead of relying on sight, for the reasons you just mentioned."

Ben met her eyes and grinned. "I've always thought that it was more efficient to feel around at the same time as you do a visual search," he said, his eyes sparkling devilishly. "When searching for a small object, that is," he added for the benefit of his son.

Jimmy grinned. Grown-ups. They were worse than kids. If his dad wanted to flirt with her, he should! They didn't have to worry about him! He knew all about that sort of stuff already.

Sara averted her eyes and tried to ignore the pounding of her heart. Ben's sense of humor! He enjoyed making her squirm. "Wait. I think I've found something."

Ben came toward her. "The valve top?"

"I don't know," she said, reaching carefully. "It's stuck between the edge and the bottom of the raft." She stretched her fingers between the folds, then smiled. "I've got it." She extracted a tiny bit of white plastic. "Is this it?"

He took the plastic piece from her hand. "I think so. It looks like we'll be able to get back without swimming after all."

Jimmy cleared the gum out of the valve nozzle. "Hey, that's great!"

Ben snapped the valve cover over the exposed stem. "Sara, I'd say you've saved the day."

"Hey, Jimmy!" Hearing his name being called, Jimmy glanced at the seven boys paddling toward them in a large black, military-style raft. "Bobby! You managed to get your dad's stuff from the base! Looking good, guys!"

"There's room for one more!" the boys yelled. "Come on!"

Jimmy glanced back at his dad and Sara, then shook his head. "Can't," he yelled back.

"Aw, come on! You can meet your folks at the finish line later. We're going to assault the beachhead farther down, then go on in the rest of the way."

Ben placed his hand on Jimmy's shoulder. "It's okay to go ahead with your friends. Just be careful and keep your life vest on."

"Dad," Jimmy answered in a whisper. "I don't want to abandon you guys. I'd go in a second, though, if you'd promise to do one thing for me." He grinned slowly.

"Name it."

"Take her for a long walk along the shore with you, and hold her hand. I know women enjoy stuff like that. Penny loves it when we walk around the school grounds during lunch. It's kinda fun."

"Really?" Ben tried not to laugh. Now he was getting romantic advice from his son. Jimmy was certainly growing up fast.

"Oh yeah, Dad. Trust me, I know what I'm talking about. Go for it."

Sara watched them, wondering what was going on between father and son, but sensing that she shouldn't interfere.

"Hey, Jimmy! Hurry up!" the boys called from the raft.

He held up one hand. "Just a sec." He glanced back at Sara.

"Jimmy, I hope you're not hesitating on my account," she told him. "I don't mind meeting you at the finish line later. Go, and have a good time."

"Thanks!" He tugged on his father's arm.

Ben leaned down.

"Dad, don't forget. Just talk really sweet to her, and hold her hand and stuff. She'll love it."

"Right."

Ben watched Jimmy wade out into the shallow water, and saw him being helped into the raft with the rest of the boys. His son was growing up, and the inescapable knowledge was bittersweet.

"Hey!" Sara came up behind him. "What's a lady got to do to get your attention?"

Ben turned and put his arm around her shoulders. "If the lady is you, not very much at all." He stopped in midstride. "On second thought, maybe I should be harder to negotiate with. The question holds all sorts of possibilities."

Sara pushed him backward, sending him tumbling into the water. Seeing his expression as he sat up in the shallow river, she began to laugh. "You look positively silly sitting there." She held her sides, her body rocking with mirth.

"At least give me a hand up."

Sara took a step back. "No way. I don't trust you now."

Ben struggled to his feet, then stood before her, water running down his chest in rivulets.

Sara stared openly. His polo shirt clung to his body, revealing perfectly molded planes and muscular contours. The aura of raw virility he projected engulfed her and she felt weak at the knees.

He smiled, the intensity of his gaze letting her know he'd guessed the effect he'd had on her. In one fluid motion he scooped her up in his arms.

"Wait, no!" she protested. "What are you going to do, Ben?"

He didn't answer. Instead, he began to walk toward the middle of the river, stopping when the water reached the upper part of his thighs.

Sara felt his strength as he carried her easily against his chest, his arms holding her securely. The blatantly erotic pull he exerted over her senses left her completely at his mercy.

She didn't have time to dwell on the sensations, however. The next second, he opened his arms, dumping her into the waters of the Rio Grande.

She bobbed to the surface a moment later, thoroughly soaked. "You snake!"

"Careful, babe," he drawled. "Don't start battles you can't finish."

She struggled to her feet, pride not allowing her to back away from his challenge. Placing both her hands on his shoulders to distract him, she reached out with one foot and collapsed his legs from behind the knees.

With a resounding splash, he fell back into the river. "That's it, woman."

He stood up slowly.

Sara wasn't sure if he was calling an end to the game, or had just issued a promise as to its outcome.

His eyes glittered with an intensity of purpose that left her mesmerized as he came toward her. Before she could collect her thoughts, he folded her arms behind her back, holding her helpless, and took her mouth with his.

There was nothing Sara could do to stop him, but the truth was, she didn't want to. She could feel the warmth emanating from him, engulfing her, bathing her with its intoxicating heat.

He sensed her surrender before feeling her body relax against his. Primitively he forced her lips open, then penetrated her mouth with his tongue, seducing, taming and asserting his dominion. He stroked and loved the moist recesses, knowing that he was giving back as much as he was taking.

Sara was so pliant and soft in his arms. She was tempting his control, battering at his will. The heat that was engulfing his body was a constant reminder of what he really wanted. But Ben forced the thought from his mind, wishing he could blast that side of him straight to hell.

A moment later Sara stepped away, her body trembling. She'd wanted him to lose control, to give way to his need for her and take her. Yet the thought was an irrational one. This certainly wasn't the time or place. Besides, no commitment had been made between them. She wasn't being old-fashioned. It was more a matter of not settling for second best. To Sara, making love meant opening herself, body and soul, and sharing her very essence with him. She'd be giving Ben the most precious gift she had. Unless he was willing to accept what she offered, giving the same in return, the act would lose its meaning.

As she walked back with him to the shore, they both remained quiet. Restlessness rippled through Sara, making her tense and filling her with an acute longing that left her body aching.

In an attempt to divert her thoughts, she forced her mind back to the uneasiness she'd sensed in Ben earlier.

"Ben, what have you been so worried about today? Have you been thinking about work?" she asked as she sat on the sandy bank at the edge of the bosque, enjoying the warmth of the sun.

He lay sideways on the ground, propping himself up on one arm. "It's complicated."

Was he going to shut her out again? The thought made her stomach tighten. Was she asking too much of him by wanting him to take her more fully into his confidence?

"Sara," he began, measuring his words carefully. "Have you noticed how Jimmy treats you?"

"We're fond of each other," she admitted. "That's why I spoke to you about letting him know that my relationship with him was independent of the one between you and me."

He shook his head slowly. "You don't understand. It's much more than you suspected. I know my son very well. He already sees you as family, Sara. What he's feeling transcends friendship. He sees you as the mother he's wanted to complete our family circle. As far as he's concerned, you and I belong together, and he belongs with us."

Sara's mouth went dry. Had Jimmy somehow read too much into her words, or sensed her daydreams about Ben? Was she to blame? "Ben, I'm not sure what to say. I thought he just wanted me as his friend. Of course, I knew he hoped that our relationship would deepen, but I thought that was mostly because he and I get along so well."

"It's all tied together."

"Are you worried that we'll hurt Jimmy, or do you feel that the situation between the three of us is getting too complicated?" Did he want them to back away from each other? She wasn't sure she could. Her heart felt as if it were being constricted.

"Sara, I think I've been falling in love with you from the day we met, but I'm not sure that's good for either of us."

She blinked owlishly, trying to take in what he'd said. She'd wanted to hear those words so much, but not this way.

"Right now I need to concentrate on my work," he continued. "My business is under fire. I've got to keep my mind trained on that, yet I find myself constantly distracted by thoughts of you. Have you ever wondered what a relationship between us could be like? You want the type of togetherness I don't believe in. It's as much a part of your nature to need that, as it is mine to avoid it."

"I know. That's an obstacle we'll both have to work hard to surmount," she said quietly, wishing she could get the knot out of her throat. So there it was. He'd admitted the strength of his feelings for her, but instead of letting that draw them even closer, he was trying to pull away. "Yet there's so much between us that is right," she countered. "You're a tender, caring man. I saw that side of you right from the beginning. You're strong and confident, yet you can also be very vulnerable. Those are the qualities that made me love you. If what you're saying is that the negative outweighs all the good, then I'm not at all sure you're right."

So she'd said it. Hearing the words, knowing that his feelings were reciprocated completely made everything seem better. With that as a basis, maybe they could work out the rest. He chided himself for acting like a lovesick teenager, but it didn't help. He loved her independence and the saucy defiance she'd always shown around him. Had he really expected her to back down now? He chuckled softly.

"Come here," he ordered gruffly, pulling her onto the sand beside him. He lowered his mouth over hers, then kissed her deeply. He heard her moan softly and felt her straining against him. His kiss grew hard.

With a tiny cry of frustration, she pushed him away and sat up. She could hear the shouts of the crowd in the distance as the race continued. Seeking to occupy herself with something other than thoughts of him, she unfastened her ponytail and shook the sand from her hair.

"You're a handful, lady." He watched her speculatively. "Do you think the day will come when you'll accept *anything* I say at face value, just because it came from me?"

She pretended to consider the question at great length. "I doubt it." She glanced back up at him and smiled.

"That's what I thought," he acknowledged with a resigned sigh.

"Still, you did raise a very important question. We have to make sure Jimmy's protected. You know, there's something I've been wondering about. Perhaps you're mistaking how Jimmy perceives my relationship to both himself and to you. Maybe what you sensed was just wishful thinking. He's trying so hard to get us together! What if he's afraid I'll just disappear out of his life like your previous girlfriends? I remember you telling me once that Jimmy had tried some very serious matchmaking before. What happened to that relationship?"

Ben sat up slowly. "That ended about nine months ago," he admitted, "and Jimmy took it very hard. He liked Connie a great deal."

"Were you in love with her?"

He pursed his lips and thought in silence for a few moments. "For a while I thought I was, but then I realized that it wasn't love. I liked her, she was fun to be with and the type of woman I felt would be the perfect wife, but something was missing."

"You mean the sparks, that little extra that makes you more than friends, right?"

"Exactly." His eyes narrowed and he regarded her curiously. "You sound as if you've been through it."

"I have," she admitted. "With Mike. I believe he would have made a great husband, and he and I have a lot in common, but something basic was missing. All the logical reasons were there, but the right emotions were absent."

"Is this the same Mike who owns National Laboratories?"

She nodded. "He and I get along so well, but love has never been part of the relationship."

"That's what happened between Connie and me."

"You said that you thought she would have made the ideal wife. Why? What was it about her that made you come to that conclusion?"

He stood and offered her a hand. "Come on. Let's go for a walk," he suggested. They strolled in silence for a few moments, then he spoke again. "Connie came from a very traditional Italian family. To her, the most important thing in a woman's life was her home. She'd have dedicated her life to me, and done whatever she thought would make me happy."

"But?"

"I can't marry someone I don't love, no matter how logical the decision might seem."

"But what about the opposite? Falling in love with someone your intellect tells you is wrong?" Sara's voice was scarcely more than a whisper.

"I'm not sure." Ben kept her hand in his, not willing to let her go.

"What do you want from me?"

How could he answer that? To him, control was the one way of insuring that his life flowed smoothly. But he couldn't control Sara. Trying to do so was as futile as trying to capture a ray of sunlight. Only his need to maintain control was being replaced by the need to make her a part of his life. "It isn't that simple, and there are no easy answers. I've got to puzzle this out by myself. Do you understand?"

"Yes." How could she ask him for answers she didn't have herself?

"You want a man who'd share his soul with you, Sara, and I honestly don't know if I'm capable of that. It's such a risk, and in the long run, I'm not sure either of us would profit from it. There's an old saying about that. 'Bind two birds together and even though they've got four wings, they cannot fly.' Mature adults, like the pillars of a building, add strength to their relationship by standing apart from each other."

She followed him back to where they'd left the raft. "To me, closeness and love provide the security I need. To you, being in control and keeping a certain emotional distance from the people you care about is the answer. I would have to have blind faith to allow you to take over and completely run my life for me. Your kind of relationship demands that I give up a great deal in exchange for your love."

"I would cherish and provide for you. You'd never lack love, or the security of knowing that I'd take care of all your needs for as long as you live. Isn't that enough?"

It tore her heart out to admit it, but Sara steeled herself and forced her voice to remain even. "No. I want a partner to go through life with, not a loving caretaker." She kept her tone gentle, trying to make him understand, but the minute the words left her mouth, she knew he did not.

The blue of his eyes darkened like the skies in the center of a hurricane. "You ask a lot of me, Sara."

He helped her into the raft. "I'll paddle us down to the finish line. You don't have to wear yourself out."

"I'll paddle too," she insisted firmly, hoping to make a point.

He rolled his eyes. "Fine. Have it your way."

By the time they arrived at the finish line, they still hadn't spoken to each other again. They deflated the raft in silence, and were folding it up when Jimmy rushed toward them.

He dangled two large catfish from a small piece of rope. "Look! I just caught them. Dad, do you think we could have fresh fish for dinner?"

"Sure, son."

"Sara, will you join us? I'll split mine with you."

Sara smiled at him. "I can't, Jimmy. I have to get some work done tonight, but I'll take a rain check on that invitation."

Jimmy walked with them to the car. "This has been a great day. Did you guys have fun, too?"

Sara nodded, refusing to meet Ben's gaze.

Ben glanced at his son, then at Sara. He'd never seen Jimmy look happier. The knowledge wrenched at his guts. What the hell had he done by letting Sara get close to them? The woman had turned his life upside down! Would Jimmy be able to accept it if Sara and he stopped seeing each other? Ben pursed his lips. And what about his own feelings? Would he ever be able to forget her?

CHAPTER TEN

SARA STARED GRIMLY at her file cabinet. She was certain that she hadn't left any of the drawers partially open, for such an oversight had been one of her longstanding pet peeves. She'd always found it annoying to see drawers not completely shut. To her, it was a sign that the person didn't care enough to go a simple extra step. In an inventor's eyes, that was a particularly bad trait.

Hearing a light knock, she walked to the door and opened it. "Hi Ben," she greeted him somberly. "What can I do for you?"

"I wanted to discuss something with you. Can I come in for a few minutes, or are you in the middle of something?"

"No, come in and make yourself comfortable," she said as she stepped aside. "You'll have to forgive me. I've been puzzling something out, and I'm afraid I just don't like the answer."

"Something to do with your project?"

She shrugged. "The project's right on schedule, but I have some other news that's not quite so good. I'm certain someone has been getting into my office when I'm not here. One of my file cabinet drawers was open just slightly this morning when I came in. Now I realize that you'll probably think that's minor, but it's something I'm careful about. I can't stand to see anything partially opened.

To me, you either open something or shut it. It drives me crazy to see it hovering in midstream, so to speak.''

Ben nodded slowly. ''I don't doubt you for a second, Sara. I've had similar problems. For instance, I noticed that our costs for the copy paper and the machine we lease had gone up. I started keeping a closer watch on it, and I realize that although the feeder always looked full, the tally numbers were much too high. The machine keeps count of how many copies are made, you see. I started writing down the numbers before I left, and I discovered that someone must have been using the machine at night and making quite a few copies. Since my files have also been tampered with, I'm assuming they've been copying my papers. I've had the locks changed, but it hasn't stopped the intruder. My security guard says no one has been in the building after hours, except you and me and a handful of other people who've worked for me for years.''

''What are you going to do?''

''I've already made plans to make sure that it doesn't happen again. Don't worry,'' he assured her, then added quickly, ''but what I really came here to find out is how you're doing with the formula.'' He held up one hand, stemming her protests before they could start. ''I know you hate to give me progress reports, but I need this information. How close are you to finalizing the manufacturing process we need?''

Sara noted that he'd deliberately failed to take her into his confidence and share the nature of his plans. Just when it seemed he was starting to open up to her, the door had shut closed again. The realization stung. Once more he'd drawn a mental line, allowing her just so close, but no closer. ''By the end of this afternoon, I'm hoping to have some very concrete results to share with you. First, though, I want to go over to Mike's lab and check out a theory. I believe I'm close to the end, but I won't be certain until I investigate further."

"Will Mike be helping you?"

"He usually does when I'm in a rush." Sara gave Ben a level glance. "Trust me. I'm not wrong about Mike."

He rubbed his chin with one hand. "Sara, you said that your relationship with Mike had never developed past a friendship, but is that the way *he* wanted it?"

Sara pursed her lips. She wouldn't lie to him, but despite her assurances earlier, the answer to his question was bound to cause him even more worry. "Mike has said on occasion that he wished it could have been different, but it's not because he was in love with me. It's because we're so compatible."

Ben narrowed his eyes and clenched his jaw. "Does he know about our relationship?"

"Yes," Sara admitted, "but honestly, I wish you'd believe me about this. If you're thinking that the problems you've been having are somehow connected to him, you're wrong. Mike is not a jealous suitor."

"You just told me he wished that it could have been different between you two. What else does the guy have to do to get through to you?"

"You're deliberately misconstruing what I said. Mike and I make great friends because we're alike in a lot of ways. We both realize that it would have been the ideal match, but logic and emotions don't always go hand in hand."

He gave her a rueful smile. "That much I already know." He sat down and stretched out his legs. He wasn't going to argue with her, but what if Mike's feelings for Sara went deeper than she thought? There had been no physical evidence of industrial espionage until he'd hired

Sara to develop the formula. Sara was blameless, but what if someone connected to her business were not?

He still didn't trust Mike, in spite of Sara's faith in him. If Mike were harboring strong feelings for Sara, he might strike out at the man he perceived as his only competition. Mike was working with Sara frequently, and could be piecing together a lot of information. If he had teamed up with Tracht, it was possible he had knowledge of the break-ins. He remembered the file Mike had conveniently found for Sara. The possibility of Mike's involvement was certainly worth thinking about.

"You look tired," she observed.

"I am."

"Do you want to talk about it?"

He rubbed the back of his neck with one hand. "I think this whole business of industrial spying is taking its toll on me. I hate having to run security checks on my own people, and knowing that someone in my employ can't be trusted. I go out of my way to make sure all the salaries are competitive and that our employees know that I think of them, not just my profit margin. It's bothered me a great deal to know that someone has betrayed me."

"It must be very difficult not to know whom you can trust."

He nodded slowly and pursed his lips. "I think that's the worst part of all."

"Well, I hope you know that there are two people you can count on and trust, no matter how tangled things become."

"Two?"

"Jimmy and me." Sara walked into her lab, reached into the small refrigerator and picked out a can of soda. "Want one? I forgot to get some coffee, so this is the closest to caffeine I have."

"No thanks." Ben followed her into the work area, and stood by a long bench. His eyes caressed her. He hadn't been able to stop thinking of her. Her face appeared before him at the oddest moments, like when he was shaving or trying to go over the accounts. "Sara, you said I never really share what I'm thinking with you. Well, there's something I want to say to you now."

Ben stared absently around the lab, then joined her by the window. "I've been under a lot of pressure, but knowing that I could count on you to deliver the process I hired you to find has been a very big help. You've given me your best, and even though I didn't ask you to, you placed me at the top of your list of priorities. You were there, and proved you could be counted on when the going got tough. And the fact that you did it because you cared about me made it even more special. I've wanted to get you out of my thoughts, Sara, but I haven't been able to. Logical or not, you're in my heart."

"I can't think of any place I'd rather be, except one." She wrapped her arms around his neck and pulled her body close to his.

Entwining his arms around her waist, he held her for a moment.

Sara felt Ben's body tighten as he pressed against her. With a heavy sigh, she moved away. "Right now, you need to concentrate on what's happening at Classic Parts and I'm going to help you the best way I know how. If this manufacturing process will give you the advantage over your competition, I'm going to do everything in my power to see you get it as soon as possible."

"I have complete faith in you, Sara. In the meantime, I've got to find the person responsible for that leak, and make sure I put a stop to it. Until I do, will you exercise discretion with Mike, too? I doubt if he's the one breaking into our offices, but he could be one of the many players involved."

She exhaled softly. "Take my advice and forget about Mike. Concentrate on your own people, because I'm certain that the answer is there."

He walked to the door, then stopped. "Let me know how your lab session goes. I'm eager to hear how your tests turn out."

"I'll do that."

Sara watched him leave and close the door behind him. She stared across the room. It couldn't be easy for Ben to fight a matter as serious as industrial espionage completely on his own, yet that was exactly what he seemed determined to do. In truth, she admired his courage. Had it been her own company under attack, she felt certain she wouldn't have handled it with such aplomb.

If only she could be of more help to him. Espionage was strictly out of her league, however. She walked into her office and gathered up her notes. Well, for now she'd concentrate on the work at hand. Sara picked up the notebook and her purse, and walked to the door. She'd go straight to National Labs and test her theories. It was time to find out if the formula was compatible with the molding process.

The afternoon passed quickly. Even though she hated not asking Mike for his help, she isolated herself in one of the smaller labs and worked alone. It was close to five by the time she had found her answers and was ready to leave. She couldn't wait to give Ben the news.

Sara practically collided with Mike in the hall.

"Whoa, Sara!" he said as he regained his balance and regarded her with surprise. "I didn't even know you were here. Why didn't you stop by the office and say hi?"

"I didn't even have a second to spare, Mike. I have to meet with a client this afternoon. The man expects some answers."

"Ben?"

She nodded. "I gave him my word I'd have something definite to tell him by today."

"I can't believe this. He's got *you* giving progress reports. This guy must be a magician," he goaded her playfully.

"Let's just say he wore me down," Sara admitted with a chuckle.

"Are you on your way back to your office?"

She nodded. "Why don't you walk me to the car?"

"Sure." He fell into step beside her. "I have a feeling you didn't ask me along just for company, though. Is there something you want to talk to me about?"

"Mike, you run one of the most successful labs in the state. You've got government contracts, industrial contracts and all sorts of highly classified projects going on. How do you keep your security so tight? As far as I know, you've never had any problems with leaks or thefts here."

He raised one eyebrow and regarded her thoughtfully. "If you believe you're the target of something like that, don't try to handle it yourself, Sara. That's a high stakes game."

"Tell me how you handle security here at the labs," she insisted.

"First of all, since I own the building, I can control access to it. That's why everyone from staff to visitors is required to go through security before entering the building, and why everyone is required to wear badges. Also, my employees are thoroughly checked out. I've heard them kid around, saying that it would be easier to get a job working in a top secret section of the government. The reason I don't have problems is because I prevent them before they ever start.''

''Well, that certainly wouldn't work for me.''

''What's happening, Sara? Tell me, otherwise I'm never going to be able to stop worrying about you.''

''If I tell you, you'll probably worry more.''

''That settles it. Either let me help, or move into National Laboratories until you solve whatever's going on.''

She laughed. ''What is it about me lately? Everyone wants to dictate where my offices are going to be!''

''Are you still using that upstairs suite in Ben Lowell's building?''

''Yes, the basement was in bad shape with the water and steam damage. I know they've been working on it, but Classic Parts hasn't got around to refurbishing my old offices yet. It's not exactly top priority for them.''

''Not to mention that Ben probably wants to keep you accessible to him.''

She laughed. ''Mike, will you be nice?''

''It's the truth, but let's not confuse the issue. What's all this business about security?''

''I think someone's been breaking into my office when I'm not there, probably late night or early morning. I'm certain of it, in fact. I just don't know what to do besides the obvious, which is to have the locks changed.''

''How many people have access to your keys?''

''The security guard and maintenance, no one else.''

''Think! How about Ben or his people? That suite belonged to someone else prior to you taking it over.''

''True,'' she admitted. ''In that case, the entire world could have a duplicate set of keys.''

"Change the locks, and don't let anyone have a set," he advised. "If they still break in, they'll have to make it plain and that means they'll leave a trail."

"The problem is that I have to give the maintenance people a key, and the security people another. It's part of the lease."

"Then have that agreement changed, if you can. If not, then you're going to have to lock up everything you consider sensitive in a secure vault before you leave at night. I don't see any other way." He started to say more, then stopped.

"What were you just about to say?" Sara asked, instantly alert.

"I don't know what you're involved with, and how high the stakes are, but keep in mind that you run a risk by making it harder for the thieves to break in. Depending on how badly they want what they're after, they may decide not to wait until you're gone."

She considered Mike's words. "Naw, I don't think they want anything that badly. That's a whole new ball game. They'd have to be willing to risk harming me, not to mention the fact that a move like that would take the security right out of their strategy."

"True, but do keep it in mind, all right?"

SARA COULDN'T HELP IT. As she drove back, she couldn't shake the uneasiness that crept through her. How persistent were these intruders prepared to be? She'd brushed the matter aside in front of Mike; after all, she couldn't really give him any of the details. But the matter was very much alive in her mind.

It was five-thirty when she walked through the front doors of the Classic Parts building. A security guard met her.

"Ma'am, could I see some identification, please? I need to check your name against our list."

She blinked in surprise, then stared. "I beg your pardon?" Had she walked into the wrong building? "I've never seen you here before. Who are you?"

"I'm part of the new security team Classic Parts has hired to watch the building after hours."

She took out her driver's license. The man checked her photograph, then matched her name to the list on the clipboard before him. "You're cleared, Ms Cahill. Go ahead. Sorry for the inconvenience."

As she walked to the elevator, Sara noticed a television camera mounted in the lobby. She'd only been gone a few hours, but everything had changed. It was like stepping into the twilight zone. Had something else happened, or was it all part of Ben's plans to combat his security leak?

She didn't even stop by her own office. As the elevator hit the top floor, she strode directly to Ben's. If he was still there, she was going to find out exactly what was going on.

She was almost at his door when Ben stepped into the hall.

"Hello. I was hoping it was you. I tried to get a hold of you before, but I figured you were still at National Laboratories."

"I was. What's been going on?"

"Up to now I had locks changed, done level one security checks on my staff, and tried just about everything I could think of, but obviously someone was still getting in."

He walked to his desk and sat back in his chair. "So I called Guardmark, our security service, and asked them for suggestions on how to make the building and our offices even more secure. The owner of the security company, Rick Taylor, is a man I've worked with for nine years. In fact, he's the one who recommended we use Charlie as our night watchman. Rick's also the one who found the ex-cop we took on as Charlie's backup. Between both of us, we came up with a plan that I believe will work.''

"I must say it took me by surprise. I wasn't sure if I'd walked into the right building or not."

"I've also had your locks changed, Sara.'' Ben was prepared to have her lose her temper and tell him that if it was her office she had the right to make those decisions herself. Like it or not, however, he was going to make sure she was safe. It had worried him a great deal to learn that someone had been breaking into her office, too, particularly in view of the strange work hours she kept. He handed her a new set of keys.

Sara nodded. "Yes, I think you're right about this. I spoke to Mike in very general terms about security, and he made me realize that almost anyone could have keys to that suite.''

"Sara, you didn't tell him about our problem here at Classic Parts, did you?''

"No, of course not. He figured I was speaking about a security problem at my own lab. That's why he suggested I move permanently to his labs. He was worried that I might get involved in something dangerous, and he believes that National Labs are as safe as a vault.''

He would. Ben scowled. "You're not moving there, are you?''

"No, of course not.''

"Good.'' So Mike had wanted Sara right there in his own building. Ben began to feel very uneasy about Mike's so-called friendship with Sara.

Sara noted his silence. Until Ben found his spy, he'd never stop suspecting Mike. She exhaled softly. "Anyway, I'm glad you changed my locks. We wouldn't want just anyone walking through my labs." She paused and added, "Now that I've found that the formula is perfectly suited to the molding process."

"You're finished?" Ben's voice rose in surprise.

"Well, no, but now I've proven that the formula will work more than just theoretically, since it can be molded properly. From this point on, I can concentrate on the casting process itself. The test ovens are too small and the industrial ovens are too expensive to run. I need to create one that is suitable for your needs. We're almost there. Soon you'll be able to manufacture all the car parts you can sell."

He wrapped his arms around her waist and swung her around in a small circle. "You couldn't have told me at a better time. I really needed good news for a change." Relief flooded over him. And he wouldn't even have to fight with her over changing the locks without her permission. Apparently she'd arrived at the same conclusion.

"Next time," Sara chided gently as he set her down, "talk to me about changing my locks before you do it, okay? It could have been awkward." She didn't want to spoil his great mood.

"I will," he said, grinning.

"Thanks."

Ben walked around the office in pensive silence. His expression grew serious once more. "Sara, I want you to listen and consider what I'm about to tell you very carefully. I know that you don't like anyone to interfere with your life, but right now I'm in the midst of playing a very dangerous game. My business opponent has shown me that he can't be trusted, and that he's completely unethical. I've taken security precautions, but I'm not at all sure they'll be adequate in the long run. Working strange hours as you do, you're in the building at a time when most people are gone. You're fairly isolated. The security people can't be everywhere at once, and the cleaning crew isn't much help in that respect, either. They work from floor to floor until they finish, and then they leave. Why don't you make an effort to keep regular business hours?''

"I've never run from anything in my life, Ben, and I have no intention of starting now. I'll keep alert, and make sure my door's locked. However, I refuse to alter my life-style out of fear of what might happen," she replied flatly.

"I just knew you'd say that." The hands he'd rested atop his desk clenched into tight fists. With effort, Ben controlled his temper. "Sara, use your common sense. There are times when the only logical thing to do is to back away from a situation."

"Don't you talk to me about logic. We're both walking testimony to the fact that logic doesn't always win out, nor should it. There are other factors involved here."

"Like what, for instance?" he asked.

"Standing on principle when you know what you're doing is right, and having the courage not to run from a problem. You know, all those virtues you practice in your daily life, both business and personal, but refuse to allow me to practice freely on my own."

With a groan he left his chair and began to pace around the office like a caged tiger. "Woman, for heaven's sake, I'm trying to keep someone from hurting you! I'm not sure how far my competitor's people are willing to go. You could get that stubborn head of yours bashed in."

"I can take care of myself."

He glared at her, torn between the urge to lock her in the closet and keep her safely out of the way, and the desire to take her into his arms.

"So now what?" she challenged, wondering about the peculiar gleam in his eye. "Will I ever be able to convince you that I'm not the helpless sort?"

"It's not a matter of being helpless or not, Sara. Anyone can be termed helpless, depending on the degree of opposition they face. I would be helpless, for instance, against a squad of armed men."

"You?" She smiled. "I doubt it. In fact, I do believe those odds would appeal to you immensely. In a scenario like that, my money would be on you. By the time you finished, they would have sold their guns to you in exchange for stock in your company. No one would get killed, but everyone would come out making a profit."

For a moment he just stared at her, then suddenly he began to laugh. "You're outrageous. I'm not going to persuade you to play it safe, am I?" He had to admire Sara. She knew the risks, yet refused to bow down to anyone, including himself. Not many people had ever openly challenged him this way, and won.

"Nope," she answered candidly. "What I worry the most about is your opinion of me. Do you honestly see me as someone who's unable to handle herself? That's not very flattering, you know."

Ben returned to his desk and took a deep breath. "That's not it at all." He stared across the room. "Being a businessman gives me all the uncertainty and risk taking I want out of life. I don't have to look for excitement; it's there. What I *can* do is protect myself and those I care about. Taking chances is part of my business, but I won't gamble with the safety of the people who matter to me most. Can you understand that?'' He met her eyes in a direct gaze.

"Yes, but remember that even though you and I share a personal relationship, I am also a businesswoman. I run my own company and I love doing it. Taking risks is part of my professional life, too. It suits me as much as it does you. Why deny me the same things you admittedly enjoy?''

"Because I've had enough pain in my life, Sara. I don't need any more.'' He pulled off his sport coat and slipped off his tie, hanging both on the rack behind the door. "Rosemary was never very organized, but she was a good wife and mother,'' he said, returning to his desk. "I'm sorry to say I wasn't a very good husband to her. To this day, that fact still haunts me. I was so preoccupied with work, trying to get my company off the ground, that I didn't look after her the way I should have.

"You see, Rosemary had suffered from rheumatic fever as a child, and her health was always fragile. I normally made sure she didn't overdo the housework or get too involved with projects involving Jimmy. Then Classic Parts started growing, and it began to demand more of my time. It was just temporary, I kept telling myself, so I didn't give it much thought. I got so involved with company business, I wasn't aware of what was going on at home most of the time. Finally, one day I came home late, and found Rosemary dead. She'd had a heart attack and collapsed on the kitchen floor.''

His face was etched with deep lines, his muscles taut as the memories assailed him. "I found out later from her sister that Rosemary had felt neglected. Wanting to get my attention, she'd embarked on a campaign to become the model wife. She worked for two days on plans for a perfect evening with me. She shopped for all my favorite foods, made preparations for a gourmet meal, and cleaned the house until it was spotless. She even made plans to have Jimmy off at her sister's for the night. She was trying so hard to please me, she pushed herself too hard." His voice was raw and tortured. Ben walked to the window and faced away from her, staring at the gathering twilight outside.

"I'm sorry, Ben." Sara stayed in her seat, sensing that to go to him would be the wrong thing to do. Had he wanted her comfort, he wouldn't have turned away. "But don't you see? She did what she wanted to do. It wasn't your fault, or hers. She made plans and had fun carrying them out. In my eyes, she died happy. She knew you loved her. Rosemary was only doing what any woman would have done when her husband got too busy to pay attention to her—she was campaigning for equal time."

"Don't you understand?" Ben asked the question without turning around. "I wasn't even there to help her when she needed me the most." He squared his shoulders and forced himself to face her. "At nights I'm at home with Jimmy, at least as much as I can. I can't be there to watch over you, too, should something go wrong." He took a deep breath, his eyes never leaving hers. "I couldn't stand it if something happened to you when I wasn't there."

Sara couldn't spend her life hiding from trouble just to ease his mind. "Then let's work on the problem itself." She stood and faced him. "You've already taken steps to prevent any unauthorized people from entering the building. Let's see what else we can do."

She considered the problem silently for a few moments. "We need to let your competitors know that you've stepped up security, and that entry to the building is going to be really tough without credentials. If the intruder still manages to get in, then he won't be able to avoid leaving a trail. By checking with the guards, you'll be able to track him down.''

"And what about you?'' he insisted. "I can't keep you safe if you refuse to help yourself. If I make matters more difficult for my competitors, I'm also going to be testing their determination. The stakes are high. If Paul Tracht can run me out of business, he stands to make quite a large profit for himself. Classic Parts is a very solid company, despite its current problems. The reason I decided to take our profits and reinvest them in an expansion program was that we were getting a great deal of business. With your formula, I intend to capture an even greater share of the market. I'm not sure how rough they're prepared to play.''

"Are you saying that I might be in physical danger?''

"I'm not sure, that's my point. I don't believe they'd purposely go after you or anyone else. What they want is information. However, when they discover how difficult it's going to be for them to gain access to these offices, they're sure to come up with a countermove. I have no idea what that's going to be. If you're here after hours, you're putting yourself in a position where you may end up seeing too much, or perhaps getting in their way. I don't want you hurt.''

"I agree with you. I don't want to get hurt either. My problem is that I'm at my most productive at night. That's when I get my best ideas, and that's when I'm at my peak efficiency. If I hear, or even think I hear someone on this floor, I'll call the guards downstairs and have them check it out. I won't take chances or get complacent, I promise. I'll even call them when I'm on my way down from the office. That way they'll watch for me.''

"You won't try to handle any trouble that might come up by yourself?"

"No, absolutely not. That's why you hired the guards. It's their job to face an intruder, not mine."

Ben regarded her with a worried frown. "All right. I guess that's the best we'll be able to negotiate." The calm, the order that had ruled his life was dissolving right before his eyes, yet he could do nothing to prevent it. If only he could get it through her head that he needed to know she'd be safe. It was natural for a man to protect a woman. Why couldn't she see that instead of fighting him?

"I know you're worried about me, but if I give in to fear and allow it to dictate how I run my life, I wouldn't have much respect for myself. It's like giving in to a blackmailer or a terrorist. The way I see it, you fight the best way you can, and take your chances."

"Dammit, don't you see that's precisely what I'm trying to get you to avoid? I don't want you to take chances. If I can't keep the woman I love safe, then that doesn't say much about me as a man! I failed Rosemary. I don't want to fail you, too!" Ben's hands trembled with pain and anger. He shoved them into his pocket so that she wouldn't see. How could she say she loved him, and not show the slightest glimmer of understanding?

"Ben . . ." Sara paused, searching for just the right words. "Every woman fantasizes about the knight in shining armor who'll stay at her side and fight to protect her. In a way, what you offer me is very seductive. I need you to care about me, and I want you to watch out for me, but not if it means that I have to withdraw from life. I would be very safe in a gilded cage, but I wouldn't be very happy. If you love me for the way I am, then you've got to let me be myself."

"You are the most aggravating woman I've ever met." Ben wanted to hold her, told himself not to do it, but finally he couldn't help himself. "Aw hell, come here," he said gruffly as he pulled her to him. "I can't control you, I can't get you out of my mind. I feel as if I've let a tornado of devastating proportions into my life."

She laughed, lacing her fingers at the back of his neck. "I've believed the same about you for a long time. I thought you should have come with directions and a warning label."

"You want a warning? I'll give you one." He bent his head and roughly took her mouth. He molded her tightly against his body, enjoying the gasp that was torn from her throat as he pressed her into the cradle of his thighs. He forced her lips to part, then pulled back her head, his fingers tangled deeply in her hair.

Sara couldn't will herself to step out of his arms. Her body throbbed with a longing so potent it made her feel weak. He filled her mouth completely, taking his time, branding her senses with the need for him.

When at last he released her, each stood trembling before the other. Sara understood. The message had been clearly given. Neither of them would be able to continue ignoring the primitive needs that made their bodies turn white-hot.

Ben brushed her face with his palm. That kiss would haunt his dreams tonight. He met her eyes, trying to tell her with a look what he couldn't put into words. *Sara, help me! You want me to share my life with you, to let you come as close to me as I am to myself, but how can I take that kind of risk when I can't control anything about you?*

CHAPTER ELEVEN

TWO DAYS PASSED. Sara concentrated on the task of designing a casting furnace that would enable her to make use of the formula. After that, it would be a matter of creating her first prototype, and field-testing the part. If her results met Ben's requirements, then Classic Parts could start exploiting the process.

Though the steps that remained were important, it would all be downhill from here. Sara searched her office, then the adjacent lab. She'd left the set of specifications and drawings for the furnace on top of her desk. She was certain of that, only what had happened to them since last night?

Had the intruder defeated them once again by circumventing all of Ben's security precautions? But how could anyone have obtained enough detailed information about Ben's new security plans to be able to do that?

She was trying to come up with plausible answers when she heard a knock at her door. "One second," she said loudly. Sara took her notes from the top of her desk and shoved them into the first drawer.

"Hi Ben," she greeted him, opening the door.

"We have to talk. Can I come in for a while? Something very important has just come up."

"Sure," she said as she waved him inside. "What's going on?"

"I've spent thousands on the new security system we have in this building now, and someone still managed to get into my office last night. The security guard downstairs swears that it's impossible. No one came into the building last night, and he had a record of when everyone checked out for the day. Nonetheless, two files are missing. One on a new corporation whose business I'm hoping to win, and the other on your project, and my projections of its impact on our financial picture."

"You can add something else to that. I can't find the design blueprints and specifications I've made for the casting furnace."

Ben paced around her office like a lion on the prowl. He jammed his hands into his pockets and held his shoulders rigid. He hated anger; it blocked his ability to think clearly, yet right now it was the controlling force in his brain.

Ben glanced at Sara, then relaxed. Well, perhaps it wasn't just anger. "What really worries me is that they're growing even bolder. They're not worried about disguising the fact that they've been inside my office. They're practically flaunting the fact in my face. Of course, with all the security, maybe they don't have the time to cover their tracks." He pursed his lips into a thin, white line. "I'll tell you something. When I finally find whoever's responsible for this, I'm going to shove his teeth down his throat."

The sense of outrage and pent-up frustration he felt spread to Sara. "Let's try to figure this out," she said calmly. "You know ultimately that Paul Tracht is behind this, since he's trying to take over Classic Parts. If his spy is getting around security, then your leak must be someone in security, perhaps someone on the maintenance crews, or maybe even one of your executives who has access to your plans."

"You're right," he conceded. "Only I can't imagine anyone from Rick Taylor's security agency being the culprit. Rick's a tough old bird, and he handpicks his men. Besides, since the leaks started prior to my heightening our security, that means Charlie would have to be our suspect. I find that very difficult to believe. He's had plenty of opportunity to do something similar in the past, and he's never been anything but loyal. In fact, he and his wife even offered to take care of Jimmy for me after Rosemary died, so I'd have time to make all the final arrangements. I think you can take Charlie off your list," he stated flatly.

"Well, let's explore the other possibilities. The new locks haven't been on the doors for more than forty-eight hours. Besides you and me, who else has a copy of the new key to my office?"

He considered her question. "The maintenance people and the security guards."

"Where do the security guards keep their keys? Is it someplace where they'd be accessible to anyone else, or subject to theft?"

"They hang them from their belts," Ben replied, "but the maintenance people may or may not have the same system. I remember seeing a pegboard down in their office once. I'll have to check. I really doubt that either of those men is involved with industrial spying, though. As I said before, I don't think Paul would be able to buy off two of my people, and these men work in two-man teams. They're never out of each other's sight when they're here. I've checked on that by talking to the guard and others on my staff, and they've verified that they use a buddy system."

"Well, until we find some answers, we'd better come up with a contingency plan. If we assume this intruder can continue to search through our offices, then we have only one other option. We have to make sure that he doesn't find anything worthwhile."

"By now, my competitors know that we're very close to having the process we need to manufacture our own parts at a low cost. That means the game's bound to get a great deal rougher. I'm not sure how to stop them without putting you in more danger than you already are. They're obviously breaking in at night, sometime after you leave. They must be monitoring you. If they think you're taking files home with you, they might just follow you there," Ben warned.

"Fine. In that case, I'll just sleep here tonight."

"Then they could find you here at a time when you're alone on this floor. You can't do that either," he replied emphatically.

"How about if I leave misinformation behind? I could doctor a few files, making them look like the real thing, and write out a report stating that the process failed."

"That's a good idea," he conceded. "It'll buy us some more time." His eyebrows furrowed as he lapsed into a thoughtful silence. "Is there any chance that they've already managed to steal your formula?"

Sara shook her head. "No way. I usually take the notebook pertaining to my experiments home with me. Then, if I wake up at an odd hour with an idea, I always have the information I need right on hand. The most they could have learned from my files is my rate of progress and some generalities."

"That's something to be grateful for, at least. It's my guess they'd rather steal the formula and the process together. They're probably biding their time. Sooner or later, they know they'll find all your notes, but until you complete your work they won't do them much good anyway."

"Agreed. That makes my idea of leaving false information behind even more useful to us."

"You're right." His shoulders slumped slightly. "Whether I like it or not, it looks like we're in the thick of this together."

"Cheer up. You couldn't have teamed up with a better ally," she assured him, placing a hand on his arm.

"Sara, I'm going to have to go out of town to a conference for the rest of the day, so I won't be seeing you until tomorrow." Ben placed his hand over hers. "If you insist on working this evening when I won't even be in town, please be very careful."

At least he hadn't asked her not to work. They were making progress. "I will." She gave him a quick hug. "Thanks for not asking me to stay at home."

"I would have, if I had thought it would do any good," he said, wrapping his arms around her waist and gathering her close to him. He brushed her forehead with a kiss.

"Well, whatever the reason, you didn't, and I want you to know that I really appreciate that." Sara stepped out of his arms. The sexual tension between them had grown to a level where even light contact could spark the hunger that lay smoldering just beneath the surface. "Now I have a favor to ask, and hopefully it's something that will work out to everyone's benefit."

"What's that?" Ben regarded her warily. With this woman, one never knew. It could be anything from wanting to become their new head of security to conducting an experiment with projectiles down his hall.

"You said you were going to be out of town until late."

"That's right."

"I thought it would be nice if Jimmy and I could spend some time together this evening. He could do his homework here while I finish up a few things, then we could both go out for dinner."

Ben smiled, his expression softening. "He'd like that a whole lot better than spending the evening with the housekeeper."

"So, is that a yes?"

"That would mean you'd be leaving the office early, then after dinner you'd stay home with Jimmy until I got there?"

"Actually, I thought I'd take him to my place, if it's all right with you. I have some terrific computer games that I know would appeal to him. I use them to unwind after work."

Ben nodded slowly. "That's fine. I'll tell the housekeeper not to expect him for dinner. He usually comes over here after school on the bus, but just in case, I'll leave a message telling him to meet you here."

"That's great."

"I should be back at ten or ten-thirty. I'll pick him up at your place then. Is that okay?"

"Sure, take your time. Jimmy and I will get along fine."

He laughed. "That I don't doubt for a minute."

SARA FOUND HER BACKUP COPY of the casting furnace specifications and then spent the day working on them. Tomorrow she'd contract Techtronics, a firm she worked with frequently, and have them make a prototype. She couldn't wait to try out the formula and process by field-testing the actual product. They were nearing the finish line.

Time passed quickly. She never even stopped for lunch, unaware of the hour until she heard someone knocking. Sara glanced at her watch. Where had today gone? She'd hoped to get a few things ready for Jimmy before he arrived from school, but it was too late now.

She greeted the boy with a smile. "Hi. I hope you don't mind. I asked your dad if we could have some time together while he went out of town."

Jimmy knew he was grinning like a jerk, but he couldn't help himself. Dad had told him that she'd *asked* if he could visit this evening. He'd get to do some of his work here, then go to her house, have dinner and play computer games. "I'm so-o-o glad you asked Dad. Our housekeeper, Florence, is a nice lady, but she's incredibly boring to be with. She doesn't talk much, and when she does, it's usually to ask me to straighten up my room, or something like that."

"Well, here's what I have planned. We both get our work done—you can do your homework while I finish up this project. Then we'll go home and see what we can hunt up for dinner. If nothing looks good, we'll go out and get some hamburgers or something. Afterward, I've got a terrific computer game I think you'd like. It's one of those role-playing games where your character can advance to higher power levels the better you get at it."

"I love those." He walked to the table and slipped his backpack onto it. "Can I use your computer here to do some of my work?"

"No problem. I won't be needing it. Is there anything I can get for you?"

He shook his head. "You don't have to entertain me or anything. I can take care of myself while you get your work done."

"Okay. If you need help with anything, just let me know. I'm going to be in the next room, going over some figures."

Jimmy watched Sara. It was not something he could have spoken about to his dad; the words just weren't that easy to come by. Yet ever since Sara had come into their lives, he hadn't felt like going through his dad's scrapbook showing Mom, Dad, and him all together at Christmas or Thanksgiving, or times that were special because they'd made them that way. Even though he couldn't quite remember Mom, he could remember loving her. His thoughts were jumbled, but in his heart he knew. Sara had helped him accept the fact that Mom wouldn't be coming back, and that it was okay if he didn't think of her all the time. Sara made everything seem better. Did Dad feel the same way? Sara showed both of them that they could love someone besides each other without feeling like traitors.

He opened his notebook and tried to concentrate on the words, but his mind just drifted. Sara was completely gorgeous. If Dad didn't hurry, he would probably lose her to some other guy.

Sara peered out of the doorway. "You do know that the power switch on that model of computer is on the left side, not above the cord, don't you?"

Jimmy felt his face burning. "I'd have found it, but I'm not ready to start on that part yet."

"Oh, I *knew* you'd find it. I was only trying to save you some time looking." She saw his face turn crimson. Had he been daydreaming? Was he embarrassed to be caught dallying? She could remember the same thing happening to her when she'd been his age. "By the way, if you want to read or just goof off for a while, it's okay. Just make sure you give yourself enough time to get your homework done. We'll be here for another ninety minutes or so.''

''Thanks, Sara.'' She trusted him enough to let him set his own pace. Jimmy watched her duck back into her lab, and felt the same kind of love for her he had for his dad. The best part of Sara was that she accepted him exactly as he was. He couldn't ask for more.

Jimmy opened his notebook, and this time he started studying the notes he'd made for himself. His favorite invention, the automatic pencil dispenser, had a few flaws in it. He'd been trying to figure them out for weeks.

Sara glanced up an hour later, her neck sore from leaning over. She was ready for a break, and was looking forward to sharing it with Jimmy. Having Jimmy there made the lab seem even more special. It was as if she could see her work area through his eyes, as they darted to and fro, always inquisitive, always alert.

Knowing his penchant for junk food, one she also shared, Sara pulled two cream-filled cakes from the drawer. She glanced out her open doorway and saw Jimmy hard at work. With a smile, she walked toward him and placed the snack wordlessly beside him on the table. As she started to pull back her hand, a sharp projectile skewered the cake, going through the cellophane wrapper and all.

''Aw, fungus! It did it again!'' He gave her a horrified look. ''Sara, I'm sorry. Did I ruin your food?'' He extracted the pencil from the cake, then added, not waiting for an answer, ''I guess I must have, unless you like chipped pencil paint and lead in your goodies.''

She blinked, then gathered her wits and began to laugh. ''What in heaven's name was that?''

''My automatic pencil dispenser,'' Jimmy said, looking dejected. He rolled up his sleeve, and showed her a spring apparatus he'd attached to his wrist by small leather straps. "The idea is for me to be able to bend my wrist just so, then have it shoot the pencil into my hand." He stared at the device and shook his head. "So far it's missed my hand every time. At first it would just sort of drop from the dispenser, more out of gravity than from pressure, and fall to the floor. I knew I had to adjust that first."

"Well, it's certainly stronger now. I've heard of impaling vampires with a wooden stake, but I never saw anyone try to ward off a snack cake by spearing it with a pencil."

Jimmy laughed. Count on Sara not to be ticked off.

"Can I help?" she asked.

"I'm not sure." He didn't want to always come to her for help. She was going to think he was a complete wasteoid. "I know that I've got to fix the spring pressure. Before, it was so weak it would just fall out of my sleeve. Now I've turned it into a missile."

Sara studied the apparatus for a moment. "Have you tried playing with it using a screwdriver and a pair of pliers? Maybe a twist here and there is all you need." She glanced at the drawings and equations in front of him. He was trying too hard.

"I'll give it a shot."

"No, please don't," she teased him.

He laughed. "Did you come in here to tell me that you were ready to go?"

"No, actually I was going to share one of the snack cakes with you."

Jimmy opened the cellophane wrapper. "Hey, that's great! I don't mind eating something that had my pencil through it. I chew on the pencil half the time anyway."

Sara began to stop him, but by the time she opened her mouth it was too late. With a sigh, she walked back to her lab.

She stared at her work, spread over the lab table. Now all she had to do, providing the casting furnace worked, was figure out which engine part she should cast. She considered her options. A drawing from one of the textbooks she'd managed to find at a bookstore showed detailed diagrams of all the mechanical parts inside a working automobile engine.

She leaned back in her chair and tried to make her selection. She wanted the test to be fair, but demanding. She needed something that she could have installed in her own car, a part that would endure a great deal of stress. Twenty minutes passed.

With a sigh, she closed the book. She'd need more information before she could make the best choice. Sara leaned back again in her chair and stretched. Her work could wait until tomorrow.

She stared at the materials in front of her, wondering about the intruder. Ben had not been willing to consider the possibility that his security guard might be involved in the incidents. Yet Charlie was undoubtedly the man with the greatest opportunity to spy. In her own mind that placed him at the top of the list of suspects. Of course, the maintenance men were also a possibility, no matter how unlikely.

She pursed her lips, lost in thought. Then again, perhaps she'd been too hasty in her conclusions. The building had many doors and windows. It was probably fairly easy for someone to pretend to leave the building and then sneak back in. There were many possible methods of entry a really motivated person could use.

She packed most of her papers into her attaché case, then stepped out of the lab. "Jimmy, how would you like to help me prove a theory?" she asked, strolling into her office.

"Sure!" He felt right on top of the world. To think she was asking for *his* help. At that moment, he'd have helped her do just about anything.

"I have this theory, you see, that no matter how many guards there are in a building, it's still possible to get in and out without anyone knowing. And I don't mean having someone use extraordinary means. I think all it would take would be a little ingenuity. It's just a game, really, but how would you like to help me prove my theory?"

"Sure, it sounds like fun. What would you like me to do? Want me to be your backup?"

"In a way," she answered with a chuckle. "We'll both go downstairs to the guard's station, and go through the process of checking out. I'll pretend to leave the building when you do, but actually, I'll stay behind. I'm going to duck into the lobby bathroom, then I'm going to make my way back up here. I'll time it so the TV camera is pointing the other way when I scramble for the stairs. Then I'll sneak back down. If I'm right, I'll never be caught. If I'm wrong, then I'm going to have to do a great deal of explaining. However, just in case anyone thinks I'm serious, I have to take a few precautions. First of all, I'd like you to take my briefcase and my keys. If my things are already outside, no one will think I'm trying to steal anything."

"You want me to distract them so you can sneak back in, is that it?"

"No, all I want you to do in fact is to follow my lead. If I appear to take my time going through the doors, don't worry. And of course, go to my car. It's the white sedan in the last parking space by the side of the building. Wait for me there. Be sure and lock the car doors after you get in, okay?''

"Sure." This sounded like she'd made a bet with his dad. Dad had hired so many guards lately, it was really a pain to come and visit. She'd probably told Dad that it wasn't really doing much good, and now had decided to prove it. She was such a change from Dad's other girlfriends. They'd gone along with anything Dad said, just to keep him happy. This time Dad would freak out, but it would be funny, and in the end, he'd probably like her more because she'd shown she wasn't afraid of him. "It'll be lots of fun to go into a cloak-and-dagger operation with you."

She laughed loudly. "Yes, that's exactly what it is. Now, are you ready?"

He gave her a snappy salute. "Lead the way, general."

Sara and Jimmy took the elevator downstairs, then approached the guard, who sat behind a desk near the entrance. Sara picked up the pen and signed the sheet, indicating the time she was leaving. As they neared the door, however, she slowed down and gave Jimmy a wink. "Here, Jimmy. Let me fix your backpack. I think you left it open."

With a conspiratorial smile Jimmy turned around, facing in the direction of the guard. "The flaps don't always shut the way they're supposed to," he complained.

Sara stooped over and pretended to adjust and readjust the straps. Taking advantage of the first moment the guard turned away, she whispered, "Okay, go for the door."

Quickly she moved in the opposite direction. Ducking behind a plant and staying in the shadows, she angled toward the far side of the hall and furtively slipped around the corner as the guard leaned back in his chair and placed both feet on the desk.

It seemed forever before the telephone rang and he turned to pick up the receiver. Taking advantage of the fact that his back was to her, Sara waited for the camera to turn away, then scrambled for the stairs.

It was a long climb, but gathering her courage, she continued. By the time she arrived at the top floor, she felt a curious sense of excitement—and disappointment. She'd made it this far. Surely Ben's new security system was much more fallible than he'd thought! Even the TV cameras had missed her. As she opened the door leading to her office entrance, she heard footsteps. Ducking back inside the stairwell, she waited for a moment, then decided to investigate.

Sara crept noiselessly into the hall. Flattening her back against the wall, she peered around the corner. The oldest security guard, Charlie, seemed to be coming out of her office. Afraid to get caught, she edged away and started down the stairs. Could she have been right? Despite Ben's confidence in Charlie, was he their culprit?

The more she pondered the question, the less sure she became. After all, she couldn't have sworn that Charlie had actually been in her office. She hadn't been able to get a good enough look. Lingering around hadn't exactly been advisable either, under the circumstances.

Slowly she made her way down the steps vowing that there would be no more carelessness. Perhaps actually testing the security system in this way had not been as good an idea as she'd originally thought.

By the time she arrived at the ground floor and peered into the lobby, Sara knew she'd never make it through the front doors. The system, as far as she could tell, involved having a three-man team; one patrolling the building at all times, one dividing his time between making rounds and the desk, and a third who would monitor the entrance and the cameras.

Unfortunately, two of the guards were now at the desk, and from the looks of it, neither was about to leave anytime soon. She watched them make themselves comfortable at their posts, cups of steaming coffee in their hands. For a brief second, Sara thought the game was up, but then she had an idea. She could sneak back up to the first floor, open a window, and slide down the outside drainpipe.

She crept noiselessly up the stairs. Remembering that all the offices would be locked, she headed for the only room she could escape from.

As she entered the ladies' rest room, she glanced about, verifying that she was alone. Sara opened a window that faced the parking lot and waved at Jimmy. Holding her index finger to her lips, she indicated that he should remain quiet.

She stared at the drainpipe, noting that the blasted thing was at least twelve feet from the bathroom. Worst of all, the ledge leading to it wasn't very wide. She was still trying to figure out the best way to get down, when she heard loud footsteps coming in her direction. *The guard!* She could hear him trying the doors, making sure each was locked.

Hesitating only briefly, she stepped out onto the ledge. She could always duck back into the bathroom as soon as he was gone. If Charlie really was responsible for the industrial espionage that had been going on, he was the last person she wanted to catch her. His actions couldn't be predicted, particularly if he thought she might have spotted him engaging in something illegal.

Keeping her back to the wall, she edged sideways on the ledge and waited, praying. At least she wasn't too far up. Still, the ground did look quite far away. She might break a bone if she fell, she told herself, but she probably wasn't high enough to seriously injure herself.

Just then Sara heard the bathroom window being slammed shut and locked. She closed her eyes for a second, then opened them. He'd unwittingly cut her off. There was no other alternative now, except to slide over slowly until she reached the pipe, then climb down.

CHAPTER TWELVE

SARA MOVED WITH EXCRUCIATING care. The ledge was barely the width of her shoes. It seemed to take an eternity before she reached the pipe. Turning carefully, she gripped the pipe tightly with her hands, then wrapped her legs around it. Slowly she slid to the ground.

"Wow!" Jimmy greeted her at the parking lot as he got out of her car. "That was terrific! It was like watching a superspy at work. Weren't you scared?"

Sara considered trying to impress him by lying, then decided against it. She gave him a sheepish smile. "Let me put it this way. I'll *never* do that again. I think I aged twenty years."

He laughed. "But you did it! And you didn't get caught. Are you going to tell Dad? I bet he'll freak."

"Yes, I'll tell him, but I hope he'll understand and think it's as neat as you did."

"My dad? No way! He'll go berserk, for sure!"

Sara slipped into the driver's seat as Jimmy walked around and jumped into the passenger's side. "Yes, you're probably right," she conceded.

"Now what? Do we get to have a celebration dinner at your place?"

"Sure." Sara was eager to get home. By the time she pulled into her driveway ten minutes later, she'd managed to calm down somewhat. Her nerves were still a bit frazzled and her hands shook when she took them off the steering wheel. "Let's go. I'll kick off my shoes, and we can see what I've got in the cupboards and the refrigerator."

"Don't worry about me," Jimmy said. "I eat almost anything. In fact, I might even be able to cook, depending on what you want."

Sara led him into the house, and watched him study his new surroundings. "I love places like this, with lots of books and stuff. It's cozy."

"That's exactly the way I feel, too." She shed her shoes and left them beside the door. "Make yourself at home. There are very few rules here."

Following her lead, he pulled off his sneakers and padded around in his socks. He went from room to room, peering into each one. "Wow, this is some house! You've got bookcases in every room. And it looks like a woman's place too, with all that frilly junk."

"What frilly junk?" she countered, feigning outrage.

His eyes widened. "Rats! I did it again, didn't I? I didn't mean anything by what I said, honest!"

She laughed. "Neither did I."

"I just mean you have the type of bedspreads and curtains that girls like, with the ruffles and stuff."

She glanced over his shoulder, following his gaze. "*Two* ruffles," she corrected, "one on each pillow sham. Jeez!" She exhaled loudly. "It's just a normal bedroom."

"Normal for a girl," he baited, enjoying the teasing now that he knew that she wasn't mad.

"Or a guy."

"Not unless he's weird. You wouldn't catch my dad or me picking that type of bedspread."

"Okay. Since you're such an expert, what would you consider a man's style?"

"Oh, something like mine. I have a bedspread with Komputer Kong on it." He saw the puzzled look on her face and added, "You know, like King Kong, only better."

"You know what you are, Jimmy? You're a miniature sexist."

"Maybe." He grinned sheepishly. "Hey, I'll tell you what. Let's go see what you have in your refrigerator. I found a great recipe in an old Boy Scout manual I bought at a garage sale. It's really simple. All we need is aluminum foil, hamburger, a couple of potatoes and some carrots. And some marshmallows," he added.

"Wait a sec." She gave him a wary look. "How do the marshmallows fit into that?"

"You'll see," he said as he bounded off through the living room into the kitchen. "Do you have all the stuff we'll need?"

She nodded. "Yes, as a matter of fact, I do." She pulled out the carrots from the crisper, and a package of hamburger meat from the freezer.

"Here, give me the hamburger and I'll nuke it in the microwave. It'll defrost quickly that way."

She tossed it over to him, wondering if she was going to regret this evening later on. One look at Jimmy's exuberant face, however, quieted her misgivings. He was having fun, and in all honesty, so was she. "Okay. The potatoes are right below you in the cupboard. What's next?"

"We'll make big, thick hamburger patties, then cut up chunks of carrots and potatoes. We'll stick the marshmallows on top of the carrots, so they'll get nice and gooey in the oven. That's about it." He frowned. "Except I forgot to tell you that we stick it all in tinfoil, and bundle it up, and that's how we cook it in a regular oven."

"Uh-huh," she agreed hesitantly. "You sure about this recipe?"

"I tried it before. Hamburger à la foil is really good, even if you don't cook it over camp fire coals. You're really supposed to put celery in it too, but celery's gross. The little strings always get stuck in your teeth, then you end up looking like a geek."

Forty-five minutes later they sat down at the table. "The best part is not having to scrub any pans. I hate washing a bunch of dirty dishes, particularly when it's my turn to clean up the kitchen."

"Your turn?" Sara sampled Jimmy's recipe and she was surprised at how good the food tasted.

"Dad and I take turns." Hungry, he took large bites. "By the way, Sara, be careful how you tell Dad about what you did tonight. It's better if you can wait until he's in a good mood."

She smiled. "What makes you say that?"

"Experience." He bundled up the foil that he'd insisted should also be used as their dish, and tossed it into the trash. "See how simple that was?"

Sara followed his lead. "Do you think your dad will be very angry?" She wasn't so much afraid of Ben's reaction; rather it was Jimmy's point of view that concerned her. Sara could still remember Ben's warning that day at the Rio Grande that Jimmy already saw her as a part of their family. Her relationship with Ben was filled with risk. Both Ben and she had accepted that from the start. If things didn't work out, well, they'd both understood the chance they were taking right from the beginning. But things weren't so simple when it came to Jimmy. He'd given her his love, not thinking of risks, not knowing enough to hold back.

"Are you kidding? Dad will hit the ceiling when he finds out what you did." He met her eyes. "At first I thought that you and Dad had made a bet of sorts, and you were just trying to beat him." He shook his head slowly. "But then, when I saw you coming out onto the ledge and shinnying down the pipe, I knew there was more to what you were doing. You were really scared there for a bit. I saw the way you kept looking back at the window, and how relieved you were when no one came out of the building. If it had been just a game, you wouldn't have reacted that way."

She'd underestimated Jimmy. He'd been able to put a lot together. "I see."

"I don't know what you were up to, but I know it was dangerous. Or maybe it just turned out that way." He jammed his hands into his blue jeans pockets and stared at his socks for a minute. "Dad won't like it when he realizes that you were taking chances without his being there to protect you. You two sort of belong to each other."

She exhaled softly. "That's just it, Jimmy. Ben and I are more than friends, true, but we're not that serious about our relationship yet."

His expression went from alertness to a look of total dejection. "You mean you've decided that you don't want each other after all?"

"No, that's not it." Sara took him by the hand, and led him into the living room. "Okay, kiddo. You and I have to have a talk."

"That's what Dad usually says when I'm about to get really chewed out. Are you angry with me?"

"I'm not in the least bit angry. However, I do want to talk to you about a few things." She paused, searching for the best way to convey what she wanted to say. "What happens or doesn't happen between your dad and me is completely independent of our friendship, Jimmy. You see, I like you a lot. You're very important to me. I'd hate to think that you wouldn't want to be my friend anymore if your dad and I didn't date."

"Oh no, I'd still want us to be friends," he said slowly.

"Talk to me, Jimmy," she coaxed gently. "Tell me what you're thinking. By now you should know you can trust me."

He glanced up sharply, his gaze cold. "It's just that I've heard all this before. Connie promised me we'd be friends, too. Then, once Dad and she broke up, I saw her a couple of times and that was it."

So that's what had worried him so much. She'd guessed right all along. "Jimmy, I can't speak for Connie, but I do know how close you and I are. We spend time together and we have fun, whether or not your dad's with us. True?"

He nodded. Everything that had happened between Sara and him was fixed brightly in his mind. "I think I know what you're getting at. You'd like me no matter whose kid I was."

She smiled broadly. "That's it," she answered.

"I believe you, Sara."

The words touched her. Impulsively, she pulled Jimmy to her and gave him a hug. "I always knew you were a bright kid."

Grinning, he pulled away. "But that doesn't mean I don't think you and Dad belong together, because I do. And I'm not going to stop trying to make you both see that." He tugged nervously at his T-shirt. "You know, it's funny. We kids can sometimes spot things it takes you adults months to realize."

Sara laughed. She'd made her point, but Jimmy's ir-repressible nature had taken everything in stride. "All right. I give up for the time being."

"Hey, let's go back into the kitchen and have some dessert."

She followed, and stood behind him as he scoured the refrigerator and freezer. "You've got vanilla ice cream," he said enthusiastically. "Let's make sundaes."

"I'm not sure I have all the ingredients."

Jimmy grabbed a box of cookies from the shelf. "You've got chocolate cookies. We can smash them and sprinkle the crumbs over the ice cream." He opened the cupboards and began rummaging around. "You don't have chocolate syrup, but you do have maple. I think it'll do. And you know what? We can melt some of your marshmallows and make our own marshmallow crème."

"I've never tried to do that." Sara stared at the marsh-mallow bag. "I think you'd need to be very careful, otherwise the marshmallows wouldn't melt. They'd just stick to the bottom of the pan."

"Naw, you're getting too complicated." Jimmy took one from the bag, then glanced around. "Hey, can I use some of these toothpicks?"

"Sure. They're leftovers from the last time I had com-pany and served some canapés. Help yourself."

"They're wood instead of plastic, so it should work." He turned on the burner of her gas stove, then browned the marshmallow, holding it by the toothpick end. "Now we could smear it all over the top. We'll stick the cookies on it, then add just a tiny bit of maple syrup."

A few minutes later, they stared at the two massive ice cream plates. Sara had had a sweet tooth all her life, and the thought of polishing off their makeshift dessert ap-pealed to her.

"Now all we need are cherries," Jimmy said.

"Sorry. I'm afraid we're completely out of luck there."

Jimmy held up one hand. "I've got it. I saw a can of fruit cocktail in the cupboard. We'll fish the cherries out of that."

A few minutes later they were seated at the table once more. "Not bad, huh?"

"Great meal," she answered, wondering what Ben would say if he could see them. Well, she wasn't spoiling Jimmy. He had eaten meat and vegetables first. And their sundae really was scrumptious.

"Sara, be sure and remember what I told you about Dad. Wait until he's in a good mood before you tell him you played secret agent today."

"I know. He'll freak," she said, using Jimmy's words.

"You got it. But I've got good news."

"What's that?" She scraped the bottom of her bowl clean.

"If he wasn't nuts about you, he wouldn't care."

"Nuts," she said, avoiding the issue. "We should have added nuts to the topping."

By the time Ben arrived, Sara and Jimmy were both on the couch. Jimmy had fallen asleep with his head on her shoulder, and she'd dozed off with her face against the soft side cushions.

Hearing the doorbell, she struggled awake. Jimmy shifted, but remained asleep. Sara positioned his head on the pillow, then answered the door.

Ben smiled, but before he could say anything, she signaled him to keep his voice down.

"We both fell asleep, I'm afraid. We were going to watch his favorite cop show, then play computer games, but I think having a really heavy dinner made us both too sleepy."

Ben glanced at his son, then back at Sara. Her hair was disheveled, and she had a rumpled look about her. Instead of being put off, however, he found her totally irresistible. She'd be beautiful in the mornings, waking up in his arms.

"What did you guys eat for dinner?" Ben asked, trying to redirect his thoughts.

"Jimmy fixed dinner for both of us." She stretched lazily. "It was good, then we had a wonderful makeshift sundae for dessert."

Ben chuckled softly, his eyes running over her as the material of her pullover, following the lead of her arms revealed the satin-smooth flesh around her stomach.

He watched her for a moment. She was completely unaware of the effect she was having on him.

He shifted his gaze to his son's peaceful, sleeping face. Maybe Jimmy was right. They all did belong together, differences be damned.

"I'll wake him up," Sara offered, a trace of hesitation in her voice. "Unless you think it's okay for him to spend the night. He could sleep right where he is. You could bring some clothes for him tomorrow and drop him off at school on your way to work."

Ben took a deep breath. "I might as well. He looks so darn comfortable." He envied his son. He'd also like to spend the night. "I've got a cab waiting outside. I'll go home and drive over here tomorrow."

"What happened to your car?"

"I usually take a cab when I go to the airport. I hate to leave my car there with all the construction that's been going on. It's quite a hike to the terminal. The cab, on the other hand, leaves you right in front."

"Tell the cab to go," she told him.

For a second he could scarcely breathe. Was she asking him to stay? His body ached with need as he contemplated taking her into the bedroom and making love to her.

"You can take my car, then bring it back tomorrow when you pick up Jimmy and me. After we drop him off at school, we can swing by your house and pick up your car. No sense in paying for a cab. It's the least I can do for you in exchange for letting me take care of Jimmy while you were out of town."

"The thought of having Jimmy and you together, looking out for each other, made me feel good." What was he saying? Was he more tired than he'd thought?

"I never knew you felt that way."

Ben glanced away. "I didn't either, until now," he muttered. "I'll get rid of the cab," he added quickly, wanting to end the conversation.

Sara smiled broadly as he left. His words had warmed her. She felt content, but sensed at the same time that something was missing. As he walked back indoors, her eyes met his. She knew then. She needed the comfort of his arms, needed his love.

He took her hand and pulled her to him. He cupped her face in his hands, then brushed his mouth across hers. He had intended the kiss to be light, no more than a casual caress, but something in him snapped. Groaning, Ben clamped his mouth over Sara's, his tongue meeting hers.

They were both shaking as she tore her lips from his. Sara clung to him, unwilling to leave the circle of his arms just yet.

"I need you, Sara," he breathed.

Her eyes traveled to Jimmy. If only... She stepped out of Ben's arms, trying to regain a measure of restraint.

Ben's eyes drifted over his son, then captured Sara's once again. He nodded, letting her know he understood.

Sara walked to her purse and took out her keys. "See you tomorrow," she said, handing them to him.

Leaving her house was the hardest thing he'd ever done. Everyone he loved was inside, Ben realized with acute longing. And here he was going home to an empty house, devoid of warmth. Wondering about his sanity, he slipped behind the wheel and drove off.

Sara kissed Jimmy's forehead lightly, so as not to wake him, then spread a blanket over him. Noiselessly she crept out and walked into her bedroom.

Sensing he was alone, Jimmy opened his eyes and smiled. That had sounded like some kiss. His dad did pretty good for an old guy. Still grinning, he shifted to his side and drifted off to sleep again.

Sara paced around the bedroom. Just looking at her empty bed made her body throb. Powerful forces were drawing Ben and herself together, despite their protests, demanding they find solutions to the obstacles that stood between them. She loved Ben, and dear heaven, she needed him. Nothing else seemed to matter.

With a frustrated sigh, she settled between the cold sheets. She'd been sleepy before, when Ben had first come in, but not now. This was going to be a long night. Sara lay on her back, staring at the ceiling, and thought about him. Would the relentless burning she felt also plague Ben and keep him from sleeping tonight? She shifted irritably, staring at the curtains. Seven more hours to go.

BEN ARRIVED AT SARA'S HOME shortly after six-thirty the next morning, carrying a change of clean clothes for Jimmy. While his son got ready for school, he shared a cup of coffee with Sara in the kitchen.

"Did you sleep well?" he asked, waiting intently for her response.

Sara's eyes narrowed with suspicion. Did she look as weary as she felt? Her best estimate was that she'd slept less than two hours. "Wonderfully," she replied with a straight face. "How about you?"

His eyes twinkled roguishly. "Same as you."

Trying not to laugh, she turned around and pretended to get something out of the refrigerator. "Toast?"

"No, thanks. For some reason, I'm just not very hungry. I'm just restless. Do you know what I mean?"

She knew precisely what he meant, but wasn't about to admit it. "I get periods of restlessness myself," she hedged.

"Like right now?"

"No, I feel calm at the moment."

"Is that why you've put eight teaspoons of sugar in your coffee?" He grinned. "I kept count."

Sara gasped and looked down at what would have become the ninth. "I just wasn't paying attention." She poured her coffee down the sink, and started again with a fresh cup.

"Did Jimmy have breakfast already?"

"Yes. He finished eating right before you got here."

Jimmy bounded into the kitchen. "Come on you two, I have to catch up with the other guys. Dad, you did remember to bring me the backpack full of clothes I had ready, didn't you? This is the day we go on our trip to the mountain observatory. I'll be gone overnight."

"Your hiking pack is in the car, son. I can go get it for you if you need it."

"No, I just wanted to make sure you had it with you." He glanced at their coffee cups. "Come on, you guys are done. Hurry, okay?"

Sara laughed. "What's your rush? There's plenty of time."

"I know, but I want to make sure I get a good seat on the bus. The school chartered one for us, and all the top science students get to go on this field trip. It's going to be really neat."

"Well," Ben said as he stood, "just remember, if you need anything just call me. I'll either be home or at the office."

"Da-a-a-d! I'm not a little kid. In a few weeks I'll be twelve. Besides, I'm going to be with a bunch of other guys. I *can't* call you."

Sara grabbed her purse and met Ben by the front door. "Do you go on these field trips often, Jimmy?" she asked.

"This is my first time."

"Do you think you'll get homesick?" Sara glanced at Jimmy. She'd never seen him so excited. He could barely stand still.

"Naw," he said, brushing aside her concern. "I mean, Dad will be here tomorrow when I come back." He glanced at his dad, then back at Sara. "There is one thing you can do for me, though," he added slowly.

Ben watched his son carefully. He knew that tone. When Jimmy became that humble and hesitant, something was afoot.

Sara brightened. She liked knowing that Jimmy would turn to her if he wanted something. "Name it."

"Well, when Dad went out of town, we looked after each other. Now that I'm going out of town, will you keep an eye on Dad for me, so that I don't have to worry?"

Ben choked.

Sara bit her lip, not knowing whether to take the request seriously or not.

Ben grasped his son by the shoulder and led him toward the car. "One of these days, son, I'm going to kill you," he whispered.

Jimmy glanced back at Sara as they walked. "Will you? It would really help, you know."

"I most certainly will."

"Son," Ben growled. "I'm your father. I don't need anyone to look after me."

"Oh, I know, Dad, but just think. It'll be nice to have someone to have dinner with, and make sure you get enough to eat, and go to bed on time. I worry about you."

Ben held open the door of Sara's car and glared at his son. "Get in."

"Do you prefer to drive, Ben?" Sara offered him the keys.

"No, you go ahead. I'm going to be busy murdering my kid."

Sara didn't want to interfere, but trying not to laugh took a great deal of willpower. Make sure Ben got to bed on time? She smiled. What a creative mind like hers couldn't do with a simple idea like that!

Sara followed Ben's direction and soon they arrived at Dewey Middle School's congested parking lot. Parents and students alike crowded around a chartered bus. Sara and Ben helped Jimmy get his pack and jacket out of the car.

"Oh, Sara, I forgot to remind you that our school's Career Day Fair is coming up in a couple of weeks. Remember when you said you'd come?"

"Sure. I'll be there. Just let me know the time and the date."

"Great!" He glanced around quickly. "Well, I guess it's time to say goodbye," Jimmy ventured.

"Son, you behave yourself." Ben pulled out his wallet and gave Jimmy a few bills. "That should take care of anything you might need if you stop somewhere on the way."

"Thanks, Dad!" Jimmy gave Ben a solemn hand-shake, then, with an enormous grin, he gave Sara a hug and a kiss. "Take care of Dad," he whispered.

Sara burst out laughing as Ben gave his son a scathing look.

"See you tomorrow, Dad. You guys probably have to get to work right away, so you don't have to walk me to the bus. Goodbye."

Realizing that Jimmy was saying goodbye out of sight of the other kids gave Ben some idea just how fast his son was growing up. His birthday was about three weeks away. Time was passing by much too quickly. As soon as Jimmy had disappeared, Ben started to laugh. "He's impossible, but what can I say? I still love him."

"When exactly is his birthday, Ben? I heard him mention it, but I didn't get a chance to ask him."

"The twenty-ninth of this month. I can't believe that in another year he'll be a teenager."

"Then girlfriends and dating," Sara commented. "Think you're ready for all that?"

"No, and I probably never will be," Ben replied with a wry smile.

With Jimmy gone, the atmosphere in the car seemed charged. Sara was aware of everything about Ben as she drove along. His virility was a powerful force that made the air between them vibrate with tension.

He shifted and faced her. "So, are you going to?"

"To what?" she asked, puzzled.

"Watch over me tonight?"

"And make sure you go to bed on time?" Sara couldn't help adding. She started laughing so hard, she had to pull over to the side of the road.

Ben joined her, and for a minute or two, neither could say much. "Jimmy's something else."

Sara pulled out and rejoined the flow of traffic. "You know, we don't need to go pick up your car," she told him. "I can drop you off after work today."

"In that case, let's go straight to the office." His mood changed, and he became quiet.

"Have you managed to make any progress finding out who the person responsible for the leaks is?"

"No, not really." Ben's frown deepened.

"Ben, please talk to me," she pleaded softly.

He took a deep breath. "I'm in a real bind with this, Sara. Unless I can catch the person who's been spying on my company and giving Paul inside information, I may have to consider selling the business. The company can't continue taking the reverses it's suffered lately. Even the process you've discovered won't be enough to keep Classic Parts in the black if we keep losing customers. If I'm forced to sell, I know that I won't get as much as I want for the company, and that will be the biggest blow of all. I wanted to give Jimmy a secure financial future. Facing the fact that I might end up failing my own son is tearing my guts out."

Her heart went out to him. She reached for his hand. "Ben, let me tell you what I did last night, right before I left the building." Sara proceeded to give him a detailed account of the events. As she finished, she glanced at him and noticed that his face had turned white. His fists were clenched into tight balls.

"How could you have been so foolish! You could have been killed! Woman, what in the world am I going to do with you? I can't trust you to stay out of trouble from one second to the next!"

"I wasn't in trouble," she answered calmly, "and I did manage to prove two things. One—a person could circumvent your security and sneak back in and out of the building. Two—that security guard is most definitely not above suspicion."

"Pull over," he ordered gruffly.

"What?"

"Pull over!"

She did. "Now what? If we keep pulling over, we'll never get to work."

Looking at her earnestly, Ben cupped her face in his hands. "I want your solid word of honor you'll never do something like that again."

"I won't have to. I've already proven what I set out to."

He closed his eyes, counted to ten and reworded his statement. "Sara, promise me that you won't do *any* investigating without telling me first. Do this one thing for me."

"Okay," she said, relenting. He looked so worried! No one had ever shown this much concern for her safety before. His love, a palpable presence, washed over her in gentle waves.

He leaned back and exhaled softly. "All right. Let's get to the office."

"Ben, there's something I want to say. You're afraid that if something happened to your company, you'll have failed Jimmy, but that's just not so. Jimmy adores you. Money isn't important to him. You are. As long as he has you, he's on top of the world. And when Jimmy grows up, he'll make his own way through life, using all the values you've taught him. Even if you didn't have Classic Parts, he would never start off at a disadvantage. What you've already given him puts Jimmy way ahead of the crowd."

He took her hand and put it to his lips. "I'll never forget what you've just said, Sara. Those words mean the world to me."

When they arrived at the office fifteen minutes later, Ben seemed lost in thought.

"Have you thought any more about what I told you concerning the guard? I think you should have him watched, Ben."

"Charlie? You misconstrued what you saw. I'm sure of it. As you said yourself, you couldn't swear he'd been in your office. He was probably just checking the door to make sure it was locked, which is part of his job."

"Well, if you don't believe your security people are to blame, then you can't really think I was in danger. If that's the case, why were you so upset with me?"

"You could have ended up being shot. You were out on a ledge, for Pete's sake, trying to avoid the guards! If that didn't look suspicious, I don't know what else would! Not to mention the fact that you could have broken your neck trying to make your getaway." He kept his voice down as they passed the guards' station.

"I still say you should have Charlie watched," she insisted stubbornly as they entered the elevator. "I trust my instincts, and that's exactly what they're telling me."

"I've had another thought. Tell me about National Laboratories. Do you work in an area set aside for your use only?"

She rolled her eyes. "Back to poor Mike, are we?" she asked. "Yes, as a matter of fact, I do work in an area that's private."

"Tell me exactly what you do when you go there."

"I check in past their guard, show my identification card, and go down the hall to the last laboratory facility on the right. It's small, but it has everything I need."

"Do you lock the door behind you?"

"No, of course not. Mike usually comes in and helps me, though he hasn't done so the last couple of times."

His eyes lit up watching her dangle her keys from one hand. He stopped in midstride. "Your purse, Sara. Where do you leave your purse?"

"There's a small office adjacent to the lab. Much like the setup I have here." She stopped by her office door. "I keep it beside the desk."

"Out in the open, unattended? And with the door unlocked?"

"Yes," she admitted. "But you don't understand. Mike's labs are so tightly guarded that the chances of anyone stealing my purse are almost nil."

"Not stealing, Sara, but how about taking the keys out of your purse long enough to make copies? You wouldn't have noticed if you were busy working, and that would explain how the intruder managed to get the new keys two days after I changed the locks."

"Another possibility is that the intruder is one of your own security guards." She shook her head and forced herself to remain patient. "Ben, I really believe you're letting your personal feelings blind you on this."

From Ben's point of view, it was simply a matter of common sense. He knew Charlie far better than she did. He wasn't exactly accusing her friend Mike, but he was dead certain that at least some of the answers would be found at the labs. He couldn't quite forget how Sara's missing file had mysteriously reappeared with Mike's help. The most incriminating fact of all, as far as he was concerned, was that his serious break-in problems hadn't started until Sara had begun to work for Classic Parts. If Mike were more interested in Sara than she realized, then that would clear up a great many questions. Jealousy was the oldest motive of all.

With Mike helping Paul Tracht, his opposition was formidable. Sara, after all, spent a lot of her time at National Labs, and her project was of the utmost importance to Classic Parts.

Now the trick would be trying to keep Sara safely out of the way while he investigated Mike and National Labs. He formulated a plan quickly. "We're less likely to miss something pertinent if we each investigate the other's work environment. For example, if you looked into things over at National Labs, you might automatically dismiss something important because you're used to it, and you'd consider it routine. The same applies for me here at Classic Parts."

Ben paused, knowing that he either sold her on the idea now, or he'd never be able to keep her from venturing into areas where the real danger lay. "I'll handle the investigation concerning National Labs, and you study the situation here at Classic Parts. Look into Charlie's background or his routines, whatever you feel is necessary. I'll talk to Mike, and see who would have had access to your purse and so on. I'll also have a level two check done on all my employees, including the maintenance crew, office staff and Charlie. That will include a detailed check of their financial status and any family problems they may be having."

She nodded slowly. "All right. I think that's a sound plan."

Ben breathed a silent sigh of relief. She'd be safe around his people. He'd tell the guards that she was to come and go as she pleased, and that they were not to be surprised if they found her wandering about the building. He'd just say that as an inventor, she often strolled around as she tried to think of new ideas.

Poor Charlie, though! The man had probably just been making his rounds, and all of a sudden he'd become the number one suspect on Sara's hit list. Charlie was the kindest person Ben had ever met. Sara couldn't have picked a more unlikely target as the target of her investigations.

Sara walked into her office and placed her purse in the bottom drawer of her file cabinet. "Let me know when you're ready to go home. I'll take you back, then maybe return to work after my dinner break."

"How about having dinner with me?"

"You mean you really do want me to watch over you and make sure you eat right, like Jimmy said?" she teased.

His eyes shone with a peculiar light. "Oh, I don't know. Let's just see what happens. I have a feeling it'll be much more interesting that way."

His words left her feeling light-headed and tingling all over. She watched Ben leave, then forced herself to think about the tasks she had to accomplish. What in the world was wrong with her? All he'd really done was ask her to dinner. The rest? Well, she'd teased him, so he'd teased her back. Or maybe not.

She didn't get a whole lot done that day. Coming in early in the morning had thrown Sara off her stride, though she wasn't sleepy. She felt impatient and frustrated. Time seemed to drag but she couldn't get anything done. It was almost impossible to concentrate. No matter how hard she tried, her thoughts continually drifted back to Ben, to Jimmy, and then back to Ben, in an endless circle.

CHAPTER THIRTEEN

IT WAS LATE AFTERNOON by the time Sara finally settled on the car part she wanted to fabricate as a prototype. She made final plans for the last phase of Ben's project, then decided to call it a day.

She was starting to close the lab, when Ben stepped inside her office.

"Hi. Are you almost ready to quit?"

"As a matter of fact I am. I came in early, so I'm going to take the rest of the night off."

"How did you like keeping regular hours?"

"Well, I'm not a morning person, as I told you. I didn't really get anything worth talking about done until after 1:00 p.m., but after that it was okay."

"Do you have any ideas on where you'd like to go for dinner tonight?"

"Not really. I'm open to suggestion." She locked the door to her office, and walked to the elevator with him.

"I do have an idea. It's going to be a clear night, and it's nice weather. How about a picnic in my backyard? We could pick up some fried chicken and fixings and a great bottle of wine, and just relax."

"That sounds heavenly." The thought of kicking off her shoes and relaxing, away from waiters and prying eyes, really appealed to her tonight.

"Okay, then it's settled." He led the way outside.

An hour later they were at his home with all the provisions for their picnic. Ben brought out paper plates while she spread a blanket over the lawn. "You know," she told him candidly, "I'm glad you thought of this. It sure beats going to a restaurant."

"To tell you the truth, I'm rather glad you agreed. I wanted to bring you here for two reasons. First, it's more private and we'll get a chance to talk. Also, I don't like coming home alone when Jimmy's not here. Without him, it seems colder somehow; less like a home and more like a house. You know what I mean?"

She sat down in front of him as he opened a bottle of wine. "Yes, I do. It's perfectly natural. You love him and he fills a place in your thoughts and your heart. You feel his absence in more than one way."

They sat in the gathering twilight, sheltered by the large pines that surrounded Ben's yard. "That's exactly the way it is." His expression grew pensive and a faraway look came over his features. "I'll tell you something. The worst kind of hell is the emptiness you feel when you lose someone forever. A part of you turns cold, and you feel numb for a long time. You miss that person so much, it's hard to accept. After Rosemary died I found it almost impossible to sleep once I got into bed. So I moved, sold the furniture that held so many memories, and bought this house for Jimmy and myself. It was easier to make the adjustment then." He took a deep breath. "I've become used to being a bachelor, and I really thought I liked it . . . that is, until I met you. Then I started questioning everything."

"Yes, I understand precisely what you mean."

"Do you?"

"Oh, yes. I've had quite a struggle, you know. You're quite different in many ways from the type of man I thought I'd end up falling in love with. Then again, in other ways you're not."

"What were you looking for in a man?"

Sara placed the chicken on two plates, then handed him one. "I wanted someone who'd accept me precisely as I was, and adapt to me."

Ben nodded. "I can understand that. I wanted the same thing, a woman who'd accept me just the way I was, and not require me to change anything about my life." He toyed with his food, his mind drifting. "I thought I wanted the kind of woman who'd depend completely on me to fill all her needs. Only these problems I've had with Classic Parts have taught me something."

He paused, his face pensive. "I still want the woman I love to need me, make no mistake, but you've taught me something else, too. Sharing my thoughts with you has made me feel vulnerable, but in the end it's helped ease some of the pressure I've been under."

"That's what I was hoping to do," she answered. "To my way of thinking, that's what people who love each other do for one another."

"You know, I always thought that if I stayed firmly in control of Classic Parts, never letting my guard down or allowing myself to get complacent, nothing could ever threaten me or my company. But as hard as I've tried, my efforts haven't been enough."

She touched his arm gently. "You haven't lost yet, Ben. You've got me as an ally, the love of your son, and your own skills as a businessman. That's quite a triad of assets. I have a feeling you'll come out on top. I believe in you and in the team we make together."

He met her eyes, and brought his wineglass to his lips. "You know something? You're right. We do make quite a team. Let's toast to us."

She touched her glass to his. "To the best combination since the Three Musketeers."

He watched Sara sip her wine. The woman had woven a spell around his heart. The love he felt for her was deep and full. Like the currents of a great river, it could carry them to places beyond the cares of an ordinary world.

She held her breath. Love burned in Ben's eyes. Her throat constricted as his gaze drifted gently over her face, lingering on her mouth, and trailing down her body.

"Last chance," he whispered, in a raw voice. "To paraphrase a familiar saying: 'leave now or forever hold your peace.'"

Sara couldn't have moved if her life had depended on it. She'd fantasized how it would be to make love to him, she'd vividly pictured every detail in her mind, but nothing could have prepared her for the intoxicating fire seeping through her. And he hadn't even touched her yet. "I'm not running away."

"That's good, because I'm not sure I would have let you go, had you tried." He drew her close and took her mouth in an explosive kiss that seemed to go on forever. She parted her lips so that his tongue could enter, exploring, filling her. When he eased his hold, she felt bereft.

Ben stood slowly, then pulled her up. In one fluid motion he scooped her off her feet and into his arms. Wordlessly he carried her to his room.

He set her down gently a few feet from his bed, and slowly began to undress her. With deliberate slowness, he brushed aside the layers of cloth that separated her from his gaze. He wanted to hold back, for her sake, for his own.

Sara stood before him, trembling, naked. His eyes ran over her, not sparing any part, then he took her hand and led her to his bed. She lay back on his pillow, expectant, languorous. Her hair cascaded around her face, flowing across his pillow.

He didn't let go of her hand. Still clothed, he stood by the side of the bed, his eyes drifting possessively over her. "I've pictured you there so many times, on my pillow, waiting for me."

"I've wanted you to love me, and to see you as you see me," she said softly.

He stripped off his shirt. "And you will. Tonight there'll be no secrets, no barriers."

Sara watched him. Her eyes consumed him greedily as he removed his clothing and at last stood naked by the side of the bed. The sight practically tore her breath away. His body was perfectly sculpted and so intensely male. Instinctively she opened her arms and held them out in silent invitation.

Ben lowered himself onto the mattress, lying by her side. "Show me what pleases you," he murmured, kissing her, then trailing a moist path downward until his lips closed over her breast.

She arched, and gasped as he filled his mouth, sucking the sensitive nipple into aching submission.

"Do you like that?" he muttered against her in a raw voice.

"Yes," she managed to say, gasping, trying to breathe despite the inescapable pleasures that ripped the air from her lungs.

His hand stroked dancing fires over her as he touched her everywhere, yet lingered nowhere.

She moaned softly, writhing against him. "I can't stand too much of this. Please make love to me."

"I will, and tonight you'll see that there's no end to how much you stand and still want." He nuzzled the curve of her waist, then tasted the concavity of her stomach, tracing a line with his tongue that drew ever downward.

She gasped as he settled over the area he sought.

She arched again in a frenzy, in need, and wild with a passion that promised to make the night explode into a million fiery stars.

"Open yourself to me," he coaxed, "then let go, let go."

His words echoed as if from a distance. Nothing mattered, only the mind-rending sensations that left her quivering helplessly. When at last Sara settled back onto his pillow, she didn't move. Scarcely breathing, she drifted back to earth like a feather trailing in the wind.

She opened her eyes slowly. Ben held her against him, his lips brushing against her sweat-dampened forehead. For a moment, she was content to nestle in his embrace.

Several minutes later, she shifted in his arms. Sara felt the hardness of his manhood pressing against her. Some ancient and compelling instinct made her want to touch him, to excite him as he'd excited her. She needed to make him feel the same fierce swell of passion.

She moved away from him slightly, but remained facing him. She pressed a kiss against his mouth and trailed her hand down, exploring the length of him as far as her hand could reach. His flesh quivered beneath her fingertips.

Ben inhaled sharply. "No, don't. You'll make me crazy," he whispered harshly. He could feel his body tighten with a need that made his blood burn. Her fingers continued to tease, running delicately light caresses over his rigid flesh. He took her nipple in his mouth to keep from crying out.

Relentlessly she continued to stroke him, inciting him further. With a groan, he took her hands in his and pressed her back onto the mattress. Easing himself between her legs, he entered her with a slow driving force that robbed her of sanity. She gasped his name, her body arching yet again in submission.

He drove into her, the moistness and warmth of her body dissolving all rational thoughts. He wanted to lose himself in her.

He held her tightly, capturing her tiny cries of pleasure with his mouth. He urged her on, wanting to feel the delicate shivering before his control shattered.

She cried out his name, wild beneath him, then with a sigh lay still.

He allowed her only a moment, then began to ease himself deeply into her again. To his surprise, she moved with him, encouraging him to take what he so desperately needed.

"Show me that you want me," she begged. "Don't hold back."

Her words drove him mad. The intoxicating sweetness of her body engulfed him, inviting him to take all she could give. He plunged into her, his mouth closing fiercely over hers as a shudder of relief rocked his body.

Moments later, he held himself over her, his upper body resting on his forearms. "I'm sorry, sweetheart. I didn't mean to take you so roughly. I just lost control." Would she see the love in his eyes and understand? "I didn't hurt you, did I?"

"No," she whispered in a passion-drugged voice. "You made me feel so wonderful, so loved."

"You are loved," he said as he kissed her tenderly. He enjoyed feeling her naked beneath him. With a trace of reluctance he started to move away.

Her arms tightened around him. "Please don't," she murmured.

"But I'm too heavy for you."

"No, it feels good." He was heavy, yet she needed to feel the damp warmth of his body pressing against her. It felt right somehow.

Lazily he kissed her nipples and nuzzled the underside of her breasts.

Sara sighed softly, her hand reaching down to where their bodies were joined.

Ben sucked in his breath and kissed her savagely. "What you do to me...."

Joyfully she discovered that what they had shared before could be made better and better. There was much to learn about each other, and about the many faces of love.

SARA WOKE UP SHORTLY AFTER midnight to the feel of Ben's mouth over hers.

"Wake up," he murmured. He liked having her beside him, warm and pliable. Would he ever get enough of her? She'd challenged everything in his life and now she was disputing his last shred of control. "You're probably going to be the death of me," he told her, pulling her over him.

"Such romantic words," she teased, her drowsiness replaced with a vibrant awareness.

"What would you have me say?" He guided her movements, forcing her to keep the pace slow. "That I love you...that I like needing you and having you show me you need me? All that is the truth."

She gasped, losing herself again in the slow, burning fire that was building within her.

His muscles quivered as she wove her fingers into the rough hair that covered his chest. Wrapping his arms about her, he rolled her back against the mattress and lowered himself between her parted thighs.

With a gasp, she welcomed him inside her once more. "More," she begged in a ragged voice.

"Like this?"

She inhaled sharply and clung to him. "Yes, oh yes!"

"Sara! Oh Sara!" He groaned her name over and over.

BEN HAD COFFEE READY by the time Sara emerged from the bedroom the following morning. "Here you go," he said, handing her a cup.

"Do you always get up this early?" she asked, peering at him, her eyes heavy with sleep.

"Actually today I slept thirty minutes more than I normally do. I couldn't quite make myself leave the bed." He gave her a lazy grin. "That means I've got to get going. I have to pick up Jimmy at school and bring him back home. He's returning this morning and doesn't have classes today since his teachers are having what they call an in-service day. That means they'll have planning sessions but they won't teach." He finished his coffee while standing.

"I'd better leave right now," he added, glancing at his watch, "or he'll be waiting there, thinking I've forgotten all about him."

Sara put her cup down. "I'm going to head home for now. I need to shower and change, then I'll catch up to you at the office later."

"Today I'm going to pursue the investigation we discussed. Do you think you can set up a meeting for me with Mike?"

"I can set up a meeting," she said grudgingly, "but I think you'd better let me have a talk with him first. He's liable to just have you thrown out if you go in there asking the type of questions you have in mind."

"I intend to be tactful, Sara. You don't have to be overprotective of your friend."

"I wasn't worried about Mike," she said and smiled slowly. "I was thinking about you. I wouldn't want you to approach him wrong, and end up getting nowhere. I know how important this is to you."

Ben pulled her close. With a playful growl, he took her mouth in a deep and searing kiss that left them both shaking. "If my son wasn't coming home, I'd make love to you right now against the nearest flat surface."

"Oh, how romantic," she teased. "Love against the kitchen sink."

"Careful. If you challenge me, I may feel compelled to change your mind." He kissed her lightly once again, then headed quickly to the door. "I've got to get going, so I'll see you later at work."

Sara drove home slowly. The traffic was light since the early morning rush wouldn't begin for another hour. The sun was just rising in a cloudless sky. At the stoplight she turned down the rearview mirror and studied her reflection. How long had it been since she'd had a full night's sleep? She'd need a gallon of makeup or plastic surgery to hide the bags under her eyes. With a grimace she repositioned the mirror, and continued driving after the light turned green.

Two hours later, after she'd showered and dressed, Sara left her home, ready for work. Life seemed brighter today. There were colors and sounds in the world she'd never noticed before. As she drove to National Labs, she was amazed at the variety and sparkle of everything around her. People rushed by in cars or hurried down the sidewalks. It was like watching everything through a finely focused camera lens.

As she arrived at the lab and made her way through the complex security checks, she wondered about Ben's suspicions. It seemed absurd to think anyone at National Labs was responsible. Perhaps once he saw how elaborate and thorough Mike's precautions were, Ben would realize that he was on the wrong track.

Sara knocked lightly on Mike's open office door, and smiled as he glanced up from his desk. "What happened to your secretary? Did she finally tell you that you're an impossible boss, and quit?"

"You must be joking," he countered playfully. "She thinks I'm wonderful. Most women do, you know."

She rolled her eyes. "You must do something about these delusions of yours, dear friend. They're starting to get away from you."

He waved her into a chair. "What brings you here so early?"

"It is early for me, isn't it?" She glanced at her wristwatch, and noticed it was a little after eight. She sighed. "I think love's changing me. Normally I wouldn't be up for another two hours."

He laughed. "I don't believe it. Did this guy manage to change your night owl schedule?"

"Only for the last two days. The way I figure it, I've done my share. Now let him try my schedule for a change."

"That's why I like you. You're as docile as a bear." He gave her a speculative look. "Now are you going to tell me what's really on your mind? I have a real problem believing you stopped by my office at this hour just to chat."

She exhaled softly. "You're right. I've just been trying to gather enough courage to tell you."

"What's up?" He leaned forward, resting his elbows on the desk.

"Mike, I want you to keep whatever I tell you this morning strictly confidential, all right?"

He nodded. "No problem."

"Ben has been victimized by industrial spying. He knows who's ultimately behind it, but he can't find the person who is actually doing the dirty work, coming into his building to steal information. He's done just about everything he can to find the spy, but he keeps coming up empty-handed. At one point he changed all the locks, but within forty-eight hours he had another break-in. Ben ran out of leads to follow, so he came to me. Since my lab was also broken into, we went over everything we'd both done after receiving the new keys. To make a long story short, he discovered that sometimes when I'm here I leave my purse in the outer office of the lab I use, and that I never lock the doors. I don't have to, I know that," she added, heading off Mike's protests. "The problem is he doesn't. He thinks that his competitor might have managed to get someone here to duplicate my keys while I was busy working."

"He's out of his mind," Mike snapped, pursing his lips into a thin line. "My lab has an excellent reputation. The people who work here are checked and double-checked. Even the government doesn't have any complaints about the way I run this operation. You might suggest to Ben, and very strongly, that he look for suspects elsewhere."

She'd known Mike would react this way. "I realize that Ben's wrong, but he's really under a lot of pressure. He's checking all the avenues, believe me. Although he wants to talk to you about the possibility that one of your employees might have copied my keys, he's also investigating his own staff. If the situation was reversed, you'd check everything out, too."

He took a deep breath. "Sara, he has no right to insinuate that one of my people is mixed up in his problems. He has no real evidence to support that."

"True," she answered in a conciliatory tone, "but Mike, he has to investigate all the leads he gets. That's the only way he'll be certain that he's not missing anything."

Mike leaned back and regarded Sara thoughtfully. "What do you think about this?"

"I don't agree with Ben's theory that someone here duplicated my keys." She stood and began to pace. "I honestly believe that the answers to his problems are right inside his own building. On the other hand, I think Ben's correct not to draw any conclusions until he gathers the facts for himself."

"All right. I'll have my people cooperate with him. I imagine he'll want to come over and speak to my staff."

She returned to her seat. "First, let's set up a meeting between you two. How soon can you get together with him?"

Mike glanced at his calendar. "I don't want this to drag on any longer than it has to. How about if we schedule it for this morning, say at eleven?"

"Can I use your telephone?" Seeing Mike nod, she dialed Ben's office and verified that he could make the appointment. "Okay. It's all set. Now, I'm going to the lab down the hall to get some work done. I have to prepare a set of blueprints, and I'd like to use your computer to help me speed things up."

Mike walked her to the door. "You know, the only reason I'm agreeing to meet Ben is because of you. His evidence for suspecting the people who work here is so flimsy, it borders on ridiculous."

"Maybe, but I think that eventually you'd have agreed to meet him, anyway. You'd never fault anyone for doing what you yourself would do under similar circumstances."

Mike laughed. "At least let me pretend I'm a tough guy," he said.

With a wave she walked down the hall. Sara stopped automatically at the security checkpoints, then continued to the lab. She wasn't at all sure about the meeting she'd just arranged. Mike and Ben were both businessmen with a lot on the line; Mike was determined to protect the reputation of his labs, and for Ben the future of Classic Parts was at stake. The situation made them natural adversaries. Would she get caught in the middle of a very unpleasant confrontation?

Sara made herself comfortable in front of the computer terminal and began to finalize the blueprints for the casting furnace. There were so many requirements that needed to be taken into account that the task was turning out to be harder than she'd originally thought.

The furnace had to be transportable and able to hold one or several molds. It needed the ability to generate enough heat to cure the epoxy ceramic material and maintain the constant temperature until the material hardened. Commercial furnaces were just too big, too expensive to run, and she wouldn't need half the heat those provided. She had to find a way to keep Ben's costs down.

Sara sat by the worktable and concentrated on the job. The closer she got to finding the answer, the more excited she became. It took her completely by surprise when Ben and Mike knocked at her office door.

Sara smiled hesitantly. "How did the meeting go?" she asked, almost afraid of the answer.

"I explained our security system to Ben, then let him have a look at our daily traffic logs," Mike explained. "I showed him that to even walk down the length of this hallway a person has to have a badge and sign in at two different checkpoints. Ben understood then that it wasn't likely anyone could steal your keys, make duplicates and put them back in your purse without leaving a written record of his coming and going. Even I have to sign in with the guards. There are no exceptions."

Ben nodded. "I'll be taking another look at those logs and studying them in greater detail later, but I doubt I'll find any answers there." At least Ben had managed to find out one thing for sure—his suspicions of Mike had been wrong. He'd focused on the forty-eight hours between the time when Sara had received her new keys and when the break-in occurred. In the course of their conversation Ben had discovered that the other man had been in Los Angeles at a four-day conference that had spanned the entire period. Mike couldn't have known the locks had been changed, or been involved in taking the keys. Unless a closer inspection of the logs uncovered something new, it looked as though he'd reached another dead end, Ben concluded.

He glanced over Sara's shoulder at the clock behind her. "Are you almost ready to call it a morning? I thought I'd treat you to lunch."

"Sounds good."

Ben nodded to Mike. "Why don't you join us?"

"I'd love to, but I've already got a lunch date." Mike refused in a polite, but cold tone. "Let me know when you want to come over and take a closer look at those logs, Ben." His gaze shifted to Sara and he smiled. "I'll be seeing you soon, sweetheart."

Sara noted how Ben stiffened in response to Mike's term of endearment. She managed to keep from laughing, but was unable to suppress a smile. "Ready?" She grabbed her purse and stood.

"Let's go." Ben walked out of the office with her. "How about going to Casey's?"

"That's fine, but since I've already got my car, let me follow you there."

Ten minutes later, Sara parked her car next to Ben's and walked into the restaurant with him. Casey's was the businessmen's favorite spot in town. Although she'd been there before, she'd always been forced to wait a long time before getting a table. Today, despite the fact that it was as crowded as usual, they were seated shortly after they arrived.

"How did you do it?" Sara questioned as soon as the maître d' departed.

"How did I do what?" Ben asked as he looked up from his menu.

"Get a table for us that fast? It usually takes a half hour for me to be seated when I come here."

"I guess people recognize authority. Anytime you want to get served right away, just bring me along." He winked.

"I can't stand it," she replied, with a long, exasperated sigh.

Sara examined the menu. She hadn't eaten breakfast and by now she was ravenous. "What are you having, Ben?" He seemed intent on something across the room. "Ben?" she repeated.

"Oh, sorry." When he turned to face her, an unabashed grin spread over his face.

"What are you so pleased about?" she asked curiously. She glanced across the room, following the direction of his gaze.

"Take a look over there in the corner. I'd say your friend Mike is in love, or darn close to it."

Sara studied the stunning blonde sitting with Mike. "That's great. He does look rather serious about the whole thing, doesn't he?" She noted how the other couple's hands were intertwined over the table. Oblivious to Ben and Sara, Mike and his date stared into each other's eyes. Sara smiled, pleased for her friend.

"Did you know he had a girlfriend?" Ben asked.

Sara laughed. "Mike always has a girlfriend, Ben."

He scowled. "Well, it looks like he's really taken with this one."

Immediately aware of Ben's change of mood, she started to laugh again. "You wanted him to have a lady friend, didn't you?" she observed. "I don't believe it! You were jealous!"

"Me? Jealous? Of whom?" Ben exclaimed.

"I kept telling you Mike and I were only friends," she added, ignoring his pleas of innocence.

"I wasn't jealous of him, Sara. I was afraid that he'd somehow be connected to the industrial spying incidents I've had at Classic Parts." He shrugged, as if dismissing the matter. "I thought he might have been in love with you, but after talking to him and now seeing him here, I believe you were right all along. He sees you as a good friend, that's all."

"You could have saved yourself a lot of that time you spent worrying if you'd just listened to me." Sara couldn't resist the tiny barb.

"Keep handing out jabs like that," he countered good-naturedly, "and I'm going to be too wounded to pick up the tab."

Smiling contentedly, Sara turned her attention to the menu once more, intent on enjoying lunch.

CHAPTER FOURTEEN

Two days later, Sara sat in her office staring at the blueprints for the casting furnace. She'd hoped to start field-testing the car part she'd manufactured using her special process. But her plans had gone very wrong.

The night before she'd cast the prototype engine component, using a conventional duplicate as a form in the molding process. This morning, full of confidence, Sara had taken the new part to her mechanic. She'd instructed him to install it in her own car in place of the factory original. However, when they began to bolt the engine part into place, a large piece had broken off.

She stared at the fragment in front of her. From its appearance it was obvious that although the outer shell had hardened, the interior had not completely set. It had remained in a gooey, semiviscous state.

Now she'd have to figure out a way to cure the parts at a higher temperature without completely redesigning her furnace, if possible. In addition, she'd have to make sure that the heat inside the casting furnace remained at a constant level, but the design modifications that would have to be made promised to be extremely complicated. She sighed loudly.

"That sounded forlorn." Ben's voice interrupted her musings.

Sara glanced up and smiled. "Come in," she greeted him. "Don't worry about me. I'm always this way when

I start testing my inventions. That's usually about the time when problems that need to be corrected begin cropping up."

"What happened?"

"Oh, it's the casting furnace. It's not working quite right. Don't worry, though. It's nothing major, just a setback." Seeing the worried frown still etched on his features, she added, "How about you? How are you doing?"

"Not so good. I've been trying to work up a bid for a specialty car dealership that's supposed to be relocating to this area. This contract could mean a lot of revenue for whoever wins the account. Classic Parts needs to get a fair shot, so I've had to take extra precautions." He pursed his lips and shook his head. "I hated doing this, but I've decided to keep all the details to myself this time. I'm not even letting my two top executives see the figures. There's a great deal at stake, and I can't take the risk of having any of my prices leak out. I dislike having to treat my own employees as suspects, but there's nothing else I can do. The problem is, I'm damning the innocent along with the guilty, and that's just not right."

"I'm sure everyone understands, Ben. It's purely a business decision. You're not trying to malign anyone."

"My people do understand, and they're being very supportive. In a way that makes me feel even worse, though." He sat down and stretched out his legs. "Anyway, enough of that. I'm here on a mission for my son."

She smiled. "You are?"

"Jimmy wants me to tell you that the Career Day Fair is this coming Monday evening, from five-thirty to seven-thirty. That's a little less than a week away. Do you still want to go, or shall I politely tell my son to find himself another victim?"

Sara laughed. "I'll go, but I do have one question. What is it, exactly, that I'm supposed to do?"

"Talk about your work, your qualifications and that sort of thing, in general terms. I've done it before, and it's not that complicated, really. Besides, I'll be there to give you moral support. What more could you ask for?"

"I'm not sure yet," she teased. "I'm still new at this. Give me some time to think it over."

Ben grinned at her. "You're a tough lady to deal with." Following Sara's gaze as her eyes drifted back to the blueprints on the table, Ben grew serious. "Now tell me about the casting furnace. What went wrong?"

"My design will have to be modified a bit, that's all. The results of the first engine prototype I cast turned out to be less than spectacular. Actually, I shouldn't be surprised. In my work, it's extremely rare to get everything right on the first try. It's usually a matter of trial and error and a lot of hard work. With each failure I learn, then eventually I get it right."

"That's the way it is in any business. Hard work and determination are the only things that make a difference in the long run."

"Well, I've got plenty of both, Ben, so don't you worry. You'll have the process you hired me to find before too much longer."

"I don't doubt that for a second." He stood up slowly. "I'm going to be working long hours both at the office and at home for the next few days. I probably won't be seeing much of you during that time. There's one thing I want you to remember, though. If you need me for any reason, all you have to do is let me know. I'll always have time for you."

A pleasant warmth coursed through her. "I hope you realize that the same applies to you, Ben. I'm always here for you, too."

He brushed his palm against her face in a gentle caress. "Thanks."

Ben started toward the door, then stopped in midstride and turned around. "Oh, by the way, don't make plans for after the Career Fair at Jimmy's school. I thought we could all get together afterward. Nothing special, just maybe go get some doughnuts or something."

"Okay. Sounds good to me."

As he left her office, Sara pursed her lips in pensive silence. Ben was going through a very rough time, and the strain was mirrored plainly on his face. If only her experiment had gone better. Ben looked as if he could have used some good news.

Sara shifted her attention back to her work. Maybe, with a bit of extra effort on her part, she could fix the problem with the casting furnace and at least have some encouraging news to give him by next Monday. With that goal clearly in mind, she began to rework her designs.

The next few days passed quickly. Sara scarcely took breaks, and worked twelve- to fourteen-hour stretches at a time. She had to enlarge the furnace slightly, then install more powerful heating elements. Finally, she planned to attach some sort of ventilation system that would create a uniform convection current inside the oven itself. The temperature would then be even throughout. She was so close to her goal! Knowing that gave her the extra energy she needed to keep up the frantic pace.

Except for an occasional visit or brief telephone call, Ben and she scarcely spoke to each other until the following week. It was close to two one afternoon when Ben walked into her office.

"I thought I'd stop by and remind you that tonight's the Career Day Fair at Jimmy's school. Would you like to drive over there with me after work?"

"I was planning to leave a little early, and stop by my house first." She placed several folders in her file cabinet.

"I could pick you up there, if you want," Ben offered.

"That would be fine. I want a chance to shower, change and maybe relax a bit. I'm a little nervous about tonight."

"What are you nervous about?" He straddled the chair nearest her desk and rested his chin on his arms. "You'll just be talking to a bunch of kids. I've done this sort of thing for him before, though not at this particular school, and it's simple."

"It's easy for you to face a room full of people. You have dozens of employees, but it's not the same for me. Remember, I work mostly on my own. I deal with clients, sure, but it's on a one-to-one basis the majority of the time." Sara wandered around the office, too restless to sit.

"Why didn't you just tell Jimmy that you preferred not to take part in something like this?"

She gave him a sheepish smile. "It seemed important to him. I couldn't say no."

He shook his head in amazement. "I'm going to have to have a long talk with my kid. I've got to figure out what sort of magic he's worked on you. You can't say no to him, but I've noticed you don't have the same problem with me."

She leaned back against her desk and gave him a playful look. "Jealous?"

"Yeah," he admitted with a chuckle.

"By the way, I've got some good news for you. I've redesigned the casting furnace. Until I finish my tests, I won't know for sure, but I believe this time it'll work the way it's supposed to. Techtronics has already started building the new model for me, and in a few days I should have everything ready for a trial run.''

"You sound very confident."

"I am." Before she could elaborate, Sara's telephone rang. "It's for you," she said, handing him the receiver.

"This is Ben," he answered. He listened for a few minutes, then handed the receiver back to Sara. "I've got to get going. That was Marc. There's a problem down at shipping and receiving I've got to attend to." He walked to the door. "I'll pick you up at home this evening at five. Is that all right?"

"Sure. I'll be ready."

Sara spent the rest of the afternoon preparing for the tests she'd be running on the new casting furnace. At four o'clock she left the office and drove home.

A long hot bath, one of her favorite methods of relaxing, failed to help her this time. Bracing herself for the evening ahead, she dressed slowly. Sara decided that a white, notch collared shirt with French cuffs, and a kick-pleated navy skirt would help her look professional. She rather suspected that the kids' mental image of an inventor would be straight out of a Walt Disney movie. Maybe if she managed to convey the seriousness of her profession, they'd view Jimmy's wish to be an inventor as a more credible goal. Imagining herself in a room filled with active twelve-year-olds sent a tiny shudder up her spine.

The shrill peal of the doorbell disturbed the silence. Sara took a deep breath and went to answer it. At least she would be spared having too much time to dwell on what lay ahead of her tonight. Ben was right on time.

Jimmy, standing by his father's side, smiled up at her. "You look great!"

"That's supposed to be my line, son," Ben said good-naturedly.

"Are you ready?" Jimmy asked, excited and eager to go. "I can fill you in on the details while Dad drives."

"What details?" she asked quickly. "You're not about to spring a little surprise on me, are you? Like maybe I'm supposed to give a forty-minute speech or something like that?"

Jimmy laughed. Dad had been right. Sara was scared. "It's okay, Sara. It's nothing like that. I just thought you might want to find out what's supposed to happen before you get there."

Sara nodded. "That might help."

She slipped into the front passenger seat of Ben's car, while Jimmy made himself comfortable in the back. "The fair's going to take place in the gym. It's got a tile floor so the coach said it was okay. There's a whole bunch of tables set up in there, and everybody in my class has a career we're supposed to tell about. I've got a display all set up. I've managed to get pictures and posters of some famous inventors, like Edison and Robert Goddard, and I've put some of my own inventions on the display table for the other kids to see. The page turner robot you helped me with is the main display."

"Are you telling me that I'm part of your display?" Sara joked nervously.

"Actually, yes," he admitted.

Ben and Sara exchanged quick glances. Ben broke into a wide grin, and Sara shot him an icy look.

"Kids will be coming to our table," Jimmy continued, undaunted, "and asking questions about what it's like to be an inventor, how to get started and that kind of stuff. Instead of me just telling them, I thought it would be really great to bring in a real live inventor so they could get to meet you themselves." Jimmy leaned forward, trying to see her expression. "It won't be hard at all, really. And Dad and I will be right there if you get scared."

She chuckled softly. Jimmy and Ben. What a combination they made. "With both of you there to take care of me, how can I *possibly* go wrong?" She'd meant the question as a tiny, teasing barb; a pleasantly couched message to Jimmy that she *was* capable of handling things on her own. However, her meaning was completely lost on him.

"You'll see, Sara," Jimmy replied, earnestly. "Dad and I will watch over you."

Sara glanced over at Ben. He was biting his lips trying not to laugh, but was failing miserably. "Right," she muttered.

Dewey Middle School's gym was filled with students, parents, and teachers rushing about. The kids making presentations had carefully set up their display tables all around the gym floor. However, it was impossible to miss the center table, which was crowded with pictures and colorful posters. Most were attached to three large pieces of white painted plywood, hinged together so they stood in a huge U on the table.

"See that?" Jimmy told her enthusiastically. "I managed to get the best spot for us. I told everyone you were coming."

Jimmy waved to one of his friends and a moment later several students began to approach them.

Sara watched a small crowd gather around, whispering and jostling for the best view. Whatever Jimmy had told his schoolmates had certainly made an impression. The queen of England herself wouldn't have received more attention than she was getting at the moment.

Sara felt her heart lodge in her throat. "Ben," she whispered quietly, "there's something I want you to do for me, real soon."

"What's that?" He stood close beside her, an enormous grin on his face.

"Teach me how to say no to your kid. If I don't learn that trick fast, he's going to be the death of me."

Before they could even reach the table Jimmy had prepared, a crowd of twelve-year-old boys and girls began to shoot questions at her. Sara tried to answer everyone, though at times it seemed that all the questions were coming at her at once.

"Let her sit down, you guys," Jimmy ordered, then led Sara to her chair. "And give her a break. She can't answer seven questions all at once. Keep them one at a time."

Ben gave Sara a teasing wink. "My kid's determined to look after you," he baited her in a barely audible whisper. "Isn't it wonderful to know you're protected by such a faithful warrior?"

Sara chuckled softly, but then quickly forced herself to look serious as the kids crowded around the table.

One of the smallest boys edged his way to the front of the crowd. "Is it hard to become an inventor? Do you have to go to school forever?"

Sara smiled. "I did go to college, and you do have to take lots of science and math courses."

"Are you very rich?"

Sara choked. "I make a nice living now, but it's not that way all the time. Sometimes business can be so good, there hardly seems to be enough time to get all the work done. Then there's other occasions when it can be very rough, and it's a long time between paychecks."

"Is it easy for you to invent things?" someone in the back of the crowd asked.

"Not at all. Sometimes I get working on a project, know I'm very close to the end, yet I can't quite find all the answers I need. It's hard work, and I very seldom put in a normal eight-hour day."

A tall lanky boy who stood by the edge of the desk leaned forward. "Joey was telling us what it's like for his dad, who's an author. He said that his dad's always putting money in the bank and stuff because he never knows when he's going to get paid next. Is it that way for you, too?"

Sara nodded. "I think it's that way for many people who own their own businesses."

Ben watched Sara pensively. If his son decided to be an inventor, then he'd face the same financial risks Sara was talking about. It would be even more challenging for Jimmy than it had been for Ben himself. Would Classic Parts be able to provide his son with the financial security Jimmy would need until his career was established?

Ben pursed his lips tightly. No matter what it took, he'd fight to save his company. He'd risen from a past filled with financial uncertainty. He'd worked hard to provide for himself and his son. He had to protect Jimmy from losing what was rightfully his. One way or another, he'd beat Paul Tracht.

The next two hours passed quickly, much to Sara's surprise. The kids never tired of asking questions, and when some left, others came to take their places. Patiently, she talked to each one. Seeing the proud smile on Jimmy's face made all her efforts worthwhile.

After the closing thank-you speech by the principal, the students began to gather their things.

"You did great, Sara," Jimmy said with a wide smile.

"That you did. You were the central attraction here tonight," Ben commented, helping Jimmy fold up his display and clear the table.

"Sara, it was really swell of you to come tonight," Jimmy said, then added, "And Dad, thanks for helping me set up my display."

"No problem, son. Anytime." Picking up a batch of rolled-up posters, Ben began to carry them back to the car.

"Dad, how about driving us to the mall? I'd like to treat you and Sara to some flavored ice."

Ben gave Sara a speculative look. "It's up to you. Are you too tired? You did most of the work here tonight."

"I'd love to go," she replied, looking from one to the other. It was hard to resist the circle of love they formed around her.

Ben forced himself not to think about business. Tonight belonged to Jimmy and Sara. "Your science teacher, Mr. McConnell, told me how impressed he was with your page turner robot, Jimmy."

"It works really neat, Dad. They're going to make it a permanent part of the science exhibit out in the main lobby of our school." Jimmy leaned forward, straining against his seat belt. "Sara, you're not sorry you came, are you?"

"Of course not. I'll admit I was nervous at first, but I finally relaxed, after all."

Ben parked near the side entrance of the large shopping mall. "Sara, were the sandwiches Jimmy brought from the buffet table at the Career Fair enough dinner for you?"

She nodded. "A flavored ice would really hit the spot now, though."

As his son bounded ahead of them, Ben draped his arm over Sara's shoulders. "Jimmy was really proud of you tonight, Sara. I could see it in his eyes every time he looked at you."

"I never thought I'd say this, but I enjoyed myself, too," she admitted.

Ben led her toward the small concession stand where Jimmy stood waiting. "You fit so easily into our lives, Sara," he said softly. "You're the best thing that's happened to me in a very long time."

She met his eyes, and was about to answer when Jimmy interrupted.

"Hey, you guys, you want to try their newest flavor? It's apple cinnamon fizz. It sounds really good."

Ben grimaced. "Not for me. I'll have cherry."

"I'll try the cinnamon fizz," Sara ventured.

Jimmy was about to pay when Ben stepped forward. "I'll get it, Jimmy. You deserve it. You did a really good job tonight."

Jimmy smiled, but shook his head. "No, Dad. This is my treat." Jimmy reached into his back pocket and pulled out a blue nylon wallet. Unfolding it carefully, he handed the vendor his money. "Let's go sit on the benches outside, okay? There's something I want to tell you."

"All right," Ben agreed, wondering what was up.

Picking a secluded spot beside one of the entrances, Jimmy sat on one end of the wooden bench, feet folded beneath him. "I just wanted to thank you for coming with me tonight." He looked somberly at his dad, then at Sara. "I don't know what's been going on, but you've both been worrying a lot about something lately. Yet tonight, when I needed you, both of you left work and came to be with me. That really made me feel great, and I just wanted you guys to know it." He took a lick off the top of his flavored ice.

Ben's expression became gentle as he looked at his son. "You're always my top priority, Jimmy."

Sara touched Jimmy's shoulder. "As far as I'm concerned, Jimmy, I got the better end of the deal. I was really flattered, and very honored that you chose to take me to your school."

Jimmy smiled tentatively at them, then focused on his ice, avoiding their eyes. "I know you've been working hard, Dad, so that we can have all the things we need. I guess it's because of the way it was when you were a kid, being poor most of the time and all. I'm really glad I have you to look out for me." He paused, glanced up, then quickly averted his eyes again. "And Sara, I love you for being around for me and Dad all this time. Some of the kids in my class don't have anyone they can depend on or talk to, but I have both of you. We may not be a real family yet, but we sure have something special."

Ben remained quiet for a few moments. Maybe he could learn something from his son. Jimmy, though he'd felt a bit uncomfortable about it, had shown enough trust to speak his mind freely tonight. "I love nights like this," Ben commented. "See over there? That's the Big Dipper. And on the opposite side to the right is Orion, the Hunter. See those four big stars that form sort of a box?" Ben pointed so they could all see. "His bow is made out of those little stars curved in a line to the side."

"Dad, I didn't know you were into astronomy."

Ben took a deep breath. "I watched the stars a lot when I was your age, Jimmy." His gaze drifted over Sara and his son, then settled on an indeterminate spot before him. "I used to sit in front of the window at night, when Dad was late coming home. I was always worried about him when he went to those poker games, and I couldn't really get to sleep until I knew he was back. I used to do a lot of gazing at the stars, and that's when I learned all about the different constellations.''

Jimmy watched his dad. "You never told me about that."

"I guess I didn't, did I?" Ben said quietly.

Sara's eyes misted with tears. She understood what it must have been like for Ben as a boy. His candid revelation had touched her deeply. "Your ice is melting," she told him in a soft voice, handing him her napkin.

Ben glanced at the tiny rivulet trickling off the mound that capped his cup of flavored ice. "I guess you're right," he said, smiling as his eyes met hers.

THE NEXT TEN DAYS passed quickly. The new casting furnace worked perfectly, and the automobile part Sara had cast was already being field-tested in her car. She now expected Ben's project to be completed in less than two weeks. Once she finished testing the part she'd molded using her newly designed process, she would present Ben with the good news and show him the final results.

As her thoughts went to Ben, a worried frown settled on her brow. He'd been so preoccupied lately. She knew that he hadn't made much progress identifying the spy who had been undermining his company.

Well, maybe he'd cheer up when he learned that she was close to completing his project. Sara glanced down the hall. It was a bit before seven, and all the offices were locked and empty. The building was quiet. Only one light besides her own spilled out into the hallway.

Ben was still working. Sara closed and locked her office door, then walked down to join him. She found him poring over some account books.

"Hey, I saw your light was still on, so I thought I'd come down and give you my good news."

"What's that?" He leaned back in his chair. "Have you by any chance discovered that you're completely lost without me?" he teased.

She pretended to sniff the air. "Have you been drinking or smoking something illegal in here?"

"Hey, you can't blame a guy for trying." His eyes danced in the muted light. "What's the good news?"

"I should be completely finished with your project in less than two weeks. In fact, I believe you'll be able to start manufacturing those parts in another month, at the latest."

Ben walked around his desk and pulled her out of the chair into his arms. "That's great news!"

He kissed her very thoroughly. The feel of her soft body, so pliant and so yielding, was enough to lure any man. Damned if he didn't want to make love to her right now.

Trembling slightly, Sara pulled away. This was no time to get sidetracked. He had to finish his work so he could get home to his son, and she had paperwork piled desk high waiting for her.

"How are things going?" she asked, gesturing toward the files scattered across his desk. "Have you made any progress toward stopping that information leak?"

"I've made some, but it's a holding pattern." Ben's expression became stern. "I kept the details of our latest bid completely secret by taking all my papers home with me each night, and I won a major contract earlier this afternoon. That'll boost our profits considerably. Until I find the person Paul's hired to spy on Classic Parts, though, I'll have to continue keeping many of my own people in the dark."

Sara desperately wished she had some news for him about Charlie, but she hadn't managed to collect any evidence about the guard. She'd asked a few discreet questions, but nothing had come of it. She had a feeling that the man was being extra careful, keeping a low profile.

Sara started to ask him for an idea of how to proceed with her own investigation, when the telephone rang.

Ben picked up the phone. "How did you know I was still here?" he asked the caller. "I see." He listened for a few minutes, frown lines furrowing his brow. "How much?" Another pause. "I'll need some time to get that amount together. Where can I get ahold of you?"

He put down the receiver, then stared off into the distance. "That was one of Paul Tracht's executives. He knows that Paul has an inside man at Classic Parts, and he's offered to help me fight back. For a rather large sum of money, he'll make sure I get details concerning Paul's current business deals. Fighting fire with fire, so to speak."

"Ben, you can't resort to buying privileged information," Sara warned. "That would lower you to Paul Tracht's level. You're too good for that."

Ben paced around the office. Pushing his suit jacket open, he jammed his hands deep into his pockets. "I agree, but I don't know what else to do. Maybe this way I can neutralize what Paul's trying to do. If he gets the idea that I'm willing to fight on his own level, he might back off."

"Can the man you spoke to give you the name of Paul's spy?"

Ben shook his head. "That's one of the first things he said. According to him, that's something only Paul himself knows. The caller's going to try and get it, but he made it clear that he can't promise me anything on that score."

"Ben, you can't trust one of Paul's own men! The fact that he's betraying Paul and coming to you in exchange for money establishes his character. You can't do business with someone like that, even in self-defense."

"I'm not out to destroy Paul, Sara. I just want to even the odds. Classic Parts is my legacy to Jimmy. I've got to fight back, and fight hard."

"Yes, but not like this. Let's find another way," she pleaded.

"Sara, I don't know if there is another way. In the long run, I know I'll discover who's betrayed me. However, for the time being, I have to find a way to minimize the damage Paul can do. Maybe I can force him into a stalemate."

"Will you at least discuss this with your top executives? Get their opinion before you make your final decision?"

"All right. Fair enough." Ben glanced at his watch and began to clear his desk. "I've got to get going. I promised Jimmy I'd pick him up at the library and take him home. Are you going to keep working tonight?"

"I have to. I'm not finished yet." She walked with him down the hall. "Ben, consider all the ramifications of what you're doing before you go ahead. Remember that you're going to have to live with that decision."

He nodded. "I realize that." He stopped by her office and escorted her inside. "Sara, make sure you lock the door after I'm gone."

"I will."

He gave her a quick, hard kiss. "Sara, now that I know that Mike and his staff are not part of the break-in, I'm convinced that the person we're looking for is a Classic

Parts employee we all trust. Be very careful, and please, no more investigating on your own. If you see or hear anything suspicious, call the guards.''

"Ben, I won't do anything foolish. Trust me, okay?"

"Sara, please, just stay out of the way. I can handle the problems facing Classic Parts if I know you're safe." He paused. "You wanted me to share my thoughts and feelings with you, and I have tried. You know how much you mean to me. Support me now when I need you, by not forcing me to have to worry about you, too.''

"What would you have me do, Ben? Do you want me to stop working at night, is that it? We've been through this before." She thought that he'd understand her need to be her own person. Had he found her demand impossible to acquiesce to? It was one thing to concede her argument intellectually, but quite another to actually accept it when it was put into practice.

He jammed his hands into his pockets once again. Anger and a sense of helplessness coursed through him. "All I'm asking you to do is exercise caution when you're here late at night. I wish you worked regular hours, but if you don't feel comfortable with that, then at least agree to take every safety precaution you can."

She nodded slowly. "Okay, I'll do that, if you promise to stop worrying about me."

He gave her a wry smile. "I'll try, lady, even though at times you don't make it very easy."

Sara watched him go, then locked the door as he'd asked. She had a very bad feeling about the informer who'd contacted Ben. Resorting to that type of tactic was so against everything Ben stood for. It was bound to take a huge toll on him.

She knew Ben's actions stemmed from the fact he believed he was failing Jimmy by not being able to stop his competitor. His love for his son had clouded his perspective. Sara slumped in her chair. In all honesty, she wasn't at all sure how objective she would have been under the same circumstances.

She was still certain that Charlie, the guard, was their culprit. If only she could convince Ben of that. By process of elimination, Charlie was turning out to be the best lead. The question was how to get him to come out into the open and incriminate himself. Even after she had completed her work for the evening, her mind never really left that puzzle.

CHAPTER FIFTEEN

THE FOLLOWING MORNING, she stopped by Techtronics to have the automobile component she'd cast undergo a final durability check. Sara made arrangements for the engineers to deliver their report directly to her before the end of the day, then left for her lab in a cab. Her car was to be returned to her office sometime in the afternoon. It was eleven o'clock by the time she arrived at her office. The telephone began ringing the moment she came through the door. She dashed to her desk and picked up the receiver.

"Good morning," Ben greeted her. "Can you come to my office? Marc and Joe are here now, and I'd like all three of you to be witnesses in case something goes wrong."

"Witnesses to what?" she asked, then quickly added, "Never mind. I'll be right there."

Two minutes later, she'd said hello to Ben's top executives and taken a seat in the chair closest to Ben's desk. She leaned forward, unable to relax, wondering what was about to happen.

"Paul Tracht's man called this morning and I made arrangements to meet with him tonight. We've worked out a schedule of payments," Ben told the group. Next, he handed them a slip of paper that specified the amounts and when they were to be paid. "If anything goes wrong, I want you three to know exactly where I'll be, and why."

"The problem is that we have no guarantees, Ben," Marc said as he stood and paced before Ben's desk. "Even if he is willing to sell information, there's no telling how reliable that information's going to be."

"Agreed," Ben replied, "but what other options do we have?"

Joe McCallister, leaning against the file cabinet across the room, faced Ben. "We managed to keep the details of the last bid secret. I believe we should continue to take those precautions, and hire someone to investigate everyone connected with Classic Parts."

"I've already done that, and nothing has been uncovered," Ben replied.

"No, what I'm talking about goes beyond background checks. I was suggesting we hire a private investigator and have him go under cover," Marc explained.

"I considered that, but the security chief told me that those methods are usually effective only over a long period of time. They hardly ever work out in the short run," Ben countered.

"Well, for what it's worth, I don't think we have another choice, Ben," Marc said. "We need something to fight Paul with and this is the only avenue we have open to us for now. I say we take advantage of it."

Sara glanced at Ben and studied his expression. Her guess was that he'd already made up his mind.

"I'll be meeting this man tonight," Ben told them. "He wants to be known as Ezra. That's obviously not his real name, but for our purposes it's as good as any. Once I see him in person, we'll try to figure out who he really is by matching his description to Paul's top men."

"Ben, I honestly believe you're making a mistake," Sara said. She could see the strain mirrored in his features.

"Industrial espionage has always been a part of my field, Sara. Up to now, I've never been put in a position where I had to retaliate in this way to stop a competitor's takeover attempt. But if I don't do something, the advantage will be all Paul's. I'll be left trying to hold my own against impossible odds."

Sara started to protest that the answer to Ben's problems lay with his security guard, then stopped. She had a feeling Ben's background check on Charlie had not been thorough enough. However, she really had no evidence, except that the man had apparently been coming out of her office at a time when he'd believed her to be gone, and the fact that he'd had ample opportunity for spying. He was the logical suspect, even if only by process of elimination. Ben's friendship with Charlie was blinding him.

"That's it, then." Ben signaled for Sara to wait as the two men left. "I know you don't approve, Sara, but I have a right to fight for my company."

Sara reached for his hand and laced her fingers between his. He was not shutting her out as he once had, and the change had made her feel even closer to him. "You know what really worries me, Ben? For years you've been living by the same code of ethics that you've tried to instill in your son. You've been honest with everyone, and have based your business dealings with others on your integrity. Now you're going against everything you believe in. I honestly think that you're going to lose more than you'll gain."

"Sara, I don't have a choice."

When she said nothing, Ben walked her to the door, then returned to his desk as her footsteps faded down the hall. She didn't understand. A man had a right to do whatever was necessary to protect those he loved. Circumstances had conspired against him, and had forced him into a corner. Fighting back was a necessity, and he intended to give Paul Tracht the best fight he'd ever had.

He paced, seeking a release from the pent-up energy that was gnawing at him. Sara, with her usual directness, had cut to the heart of the matter. He hated using Paul's methods, even if only to buy himself some time. She'd been right to say that such tactics went against everything he stood for.

Even though industrial espionage was becoming as much a part of the corporate world as film was to Hollywood, he'd always stood above it. He'd never resorted to spying on his competition. Neither had he given those in his employ a reason to use proprietary information against him. For years his employees' salary and benefit packages had been way above the industry average. And he'd always maintained an open-door policy for those who worked for him.

Perhaps that was why this betrayal had left him feeling so bitter. He'd wanted to believe that the spy wasn't someone housed under his own roof, but the facts had been inescapable. Paul Tracht, his most dangerous adversary, had managed to entrench an enemy right within his camp.

Ben checked his wristwatch and stared at the city street below. Until he could find the culprit and prove his guilt, his company would remain vulnerable. So for the time being, he'd resort to methods that left a bitter taste in his mouth.

SARA STOOD IN HER OFFICE, too restless to sit and too tense to work. She had to do something. She couldn't wait passively while Ben was putting himself and everything he stood for on the line. If her suspicions about Charlie were right, then it was time to start the wheels rolling and set up a trap. Waiting for the man to make his next move wasn't working. She'd have to force the issue, somehow.

She spent the rest of the day formulating a good, solid plan. Several times she considered going to Ben and telling him what she was going to do, but on each occasion she dismissed the idea. Ben had enough problems. He liked Charlie, and it might have upset him to know that she was still on the man's trail. Tonight he'd be meeting his contact from Tracht's firm, and didn't need her distracting him now. Besides, at best he'd only humor her about the guard. He was so sure she was wrong that only solid evidence would convince him to take a closer look.

Sara worked at her plan with the same intensity she usually reserved for scientific projects that posed the greatest challenge and had the most possibilities for failure. She couldn't afford to miss anything now.

It was a little after five by the time she'd completed a plan that gave her the widest safety margin possible. First, she'd need to get ahold of a very large packing crate, one that would give her enough room to hide in.

She hurried downstairs, wondering if she'd find the shipping and receiving section still open. Seeing the door ajar, she strolled inside. "Anyone here?"

"Not for long," came the reply from the back. "I'm getting ready to leave right now."

A small, rotund man came to the front and gave her a sheepish smile. "I'm already late. It's my wedding anniversary tonight, and if I don't make it home soon, it's also going to be the anniversary of my divorce. This isn't going to take long, is it?"

She chuckled softly. "Not at all. I just wanted to know if you had a large packing crate I could borrow. I can have it back here by tomorrow morning."

"I'm not supposed to let those go. We reuse them, you know."

Sara tried her best to smile. "Please. I just need it for an experiment I'm running in my office upstairs. I won't damage it at all, I promise, and you can have it back first thing tomorrow."

"Oh, are you the lady inventor?" The man's eyes brightened considerably.

"That's me," she answered.

"Well, in that case, I suppose it's okay. I just didn't want you to use it for moving and then bring the box back in pieces."

"I won't damage it at all. I just need it as a backdrop, really," she said, hedging a bit. Well, it would be in the background, only she'd be inside.

He led her around to the large room in the back. "Take your pick."

Sara spotted a large rectangular cardboard box that looked about the size of a small stove. "This one. Is it okay if I haul it off with me right now?"

"Sure." He glanced at the clock on the wall. "In fact, let's hurry. My wife's probably getting ready to send the marines after me. She made me promise that I'd be home at six, and not one minute later. If I leave right now, I may just make it."

"In that case, I'll get out of your way so you can lock up." She dragged the box out the door and toward the elevator. "Thanks!"

The box was cumbersome, but not heavy. As the elevator doors opened at the top floor, she pulled it out quickly, pushing the box out of the way just before the door slid shut.

"Can I help?" Ben offered, meeting her halfway down the hall.

"Sure." She stood at one end and lifted the box with his help. "This beats trying to drag it," she told him.

"What are you doing with this?"

"I need the box as a containment vessel for one of my experiments." Quickly diverting his attention, she added, "Are you on your way to your meeting?"

He nodded. "Don't worry. I'll be fine."

"Ben, I wish there was something I could say to talk you out of this."

He helped her slide the box into her office. "I don't want to talk about it anymore, Sara. As soon as I get home after the meeting, I'll give you a call to let you know I'm all right."

It was a perfectly natural suggestion for him to make, but she hadn't anticipated it. "Er, I won't be here."

"You won't be working late tonight?"

"No, I've got some errands to run, then I was planning to go home. I'll tell you what. Call me here and leave a message on my machine. I check with it at regular intervals. Then, once I get home, I'll give you a call. Is that okay?"

He gave her a quick kiss. "Sure. Take care." He stepped inside the elevator, then seeing Charlie hurrying toward it, held the doors open.

Sara met Charlie as he strode past her. "Charlie, I'll be leaving some very important papers and equipment in my office tonight. My safe is too small to house anything else, so they're out in the open. Everything will be locked, but it's imperative that you keep a very careful watch and make sure no one, and I mean not anyone, gets in there. I won't be working late like I usually do, so I'm counting on you to take special care and make extra checks to make sure all is well."

"I'd be glad to, ma'am."

Ben smiled. So she'd finally started listening to him! She had given up the idea that Charlie was their culprit and had started to trust him. At least he wouldn't have to worry about Sara tonight.

Charlie rushed to the elevator, then stopped. "Hey, Billy!" he yelled at one of the maintenance men down the hall. "Make sure you let the security men know when you're going to wax the floors. Last night, Pete almost broke his neck stepping out of the elevator on the fourth floor. Apparently you buffed it a little too well."

"It's going to be a beautiful evening, sir," Charlie said, as he entered the elevator and joined Ben.

Sara watched them leave, then returned to her office. Beautiful evening? Not unless she managed to put together all the parts of her plan soon.

She glanced at the clock. It was five-forty. There was plenty of time to track down a video camera and get the equipment set up. She called the rental shop a few streets down, but they had no video equipment she could rent. The next few calls proved just as futile. Her plan hinged on getting a camera, but until now she hadn't anticipated one being so difficult to find.

She remembered seeing video equipment at Ben's home. Picking up the receiver, she dialed quickly.

"Hello?"

Sara heard Jimmy's familiar voice and smiled, a rush of warm feelings spreading over her. "Hi, Jimmy. It's Sara. I'm calling to ask you a favor."

"Sure. Anything!"

"I need to borrow your dad's video camera, and I'll need you to give me a real fast lesson on how to use it."

"Fine. It's really easy to use. Do you have a video cassette?"

"I'll get one on the way over there."

"Does Dad know?" Jimmy asked after a brief pause.

Sara chuckled softly. Jimmy didn't miss much. "Not yet, but I'm sure he wouldn't mind if I borrowed it. I'll tell him about it tomorrow. It's an emergency of sorts."

"Oh, he'd let you borrow whatever you wanted, that wasn't why I asked. I was just wondering if you were playing spy games again."

She choked. "I'm not playing games. I just need it for a few hours." At least that part wasn't a lie.

"Are you going to use it for an experiment?"

"Yes," she replied, wishing she'd never started answering his questions. "Listen, I'll be coming over in about fifteen minutes, okay?"

"Sure. I'll be waiting. Dad won't be home for another hour or so. He called a little earlier and told me not to expect him until after dinner."

"I know," she said, then bit her tongue. Jimmy would know for sure she was up to something now. "I'll be over soon."

SARA PLACED THE test module of the first, unsuccessful casting furnace and a phony formula on her desk, labeling the cover folder Classic Parts Project. That heading was bound to get the guard's attention. Once Charlie took the bait, he'd end up stealing the very evidence that would convict him. Inside the casting furnace was a small radio transmitter, a miniature tracking device that would allow her both to follow the guard using a matching receiver and to identify his contact. The police would then be able to go and arrest them.

The biggest problem still lay ahead. It was imperative that Sara check out at the front with the guard and make everyone believe she was truly gone for the day. Knowing how difficult sneaking back into the building would be,

Sara took steps to resolve the problem. Prior to leaving, she made sure that the latch securing the small basement window was open. No one ever locked the basement door leading out of the boiler room, and with a bit of luck no one would check the window latch to make sure it was really closed until she was through.

Although it was a tight fit, the entire process of slipping back into the building took her less than five minutes.

Once inside her own office again, she crept around noiselessly. Camera in hand, she settled down inside the large cardboard packing crate.

Time ticked by slowly. She heard a guard or someone come by several times and check the lock, but no one tried to enter.

After an hour, her legs began to ache. She tried sitting instead of crouching, but with the camera, there really wasn't enough room for that. Sara shifted uncomfortably.

What if she'd been wrong? How long should she stay? She shook her head, angry with herself for not being more patient. She'd stay cooped up in that box all night if that was what it took.

BEN ARRIVED HOME EARLIER than he'd expected. He saw Jimmy's face light up as he came through the door.

"Hey, Dad! You're early!"

"Hi, son." Jimmy's welcome greeting never failed to please him. It was an affirmation that he'd been missed and his return had been eagerly awaited. How did single people ever get by, coming home to an empty house? Ben knew that he wouldn't be able to stand it. Then again, maybe that was because he had something better.

Jimmy picked up a large manila envelope and brought it over to him. "This came for you a little while ago from one of those Instant Express delivery guys. I signed for it, okay?"

"Sure." Ben loosened his tie and sat on the couch.

"Dad, you look like you're really out of it. Did you have a hard day?"

Ben smiled, and then shrugged. "Wasn't the best I've had, I'll say that." He'd met Paul's man, but then Ben had changed his mind. No matter how tempting the prospect, he hadn't been able to set aside a lifetime of principles for a short-term gain. Had he been a fool? Well, he'd made his decision. Perhaps not the wisest, if one thought strictly in terms of business, but the only one he'd be able to live with. How could he demand that his son live his life based on honesty and a high moral standard, unless he was also willing to do the same?

Ben opened the envelope and began leafing through the report inside. He'd ordered the private investigation firm he'd hired to make a more thorough check on all personnel who had access to keys and information. That had included everyone from his top executives to the maintenance people. He'd hated invading their privacy, no matter how discreetly, but he'd run out of options. The firm had already done what they called a level one check on all his staff, but the level two delved well beneath the surface. The investigators made checks on everything, from bank account activities to personal habits. It had been expensive, but now as he leafed through the contents, he realized just how worthwhile the expenditure had been.

The report opened up possibilities he'd never even considered. Sara had been right to look for opportunity, but she'd gone off the track by believing Charlie responsible. He'd known better than to suspect the man who'd taken care of his son at a time when he hadn't been able to himself. Loyalty like that was hard to find.

He studied the report in pensive silence. One of the maintenance men was turning out to be the ideal suspect. The only thing missing was opportunity. He'd already verified that the maintenance men did indeed work in two-man teams, as they were supposed to.

He read over the report on the maintenance crew carefully once again, mulling over the implications. Though Michael Phillips, who'd been with the company for three years, was married and had a relatively stable life, his assistant was quite another story. Billy Wade was single and apparently enjoyed the track. He spent money freely, in amounts that were equal to or in excess of his take-home pay. From what the investigative team had managed to discover, he'd also lost heavily at gambling. Yet he'd made two very large bank deposits within the last few months.

Ben's hands clenched into tight fists. Gambling. He'd hated that vice since he'd seen the toll it had taken on his father and family while he was growing up. He knew gamblers only too well, and all their wounds were self-inflicted. Memories of his father were no doubt influencing him, but he couldn't get rid of the feeling that he'd found the culprit at last. The question in his mind now was what strategy Billy had used to hide his activities from his work partner.

"Dad?"

His son's voice broke through the dark cloud that seemed to cover him. "Yes, Jimmy? Did you say something?"

Jimmy sat on the arm of the couch and stared at his lap. How could he tell his dad he was worried about Sara without getting Sara into trouble? "Um, Dad, I was wondering about something.... Let's say a friend of mine borrowed some stuff that cost a whole lot, and I think this person is up to something, but I'm not really sure...."

"Wait a second. Start over again. You're losing me." Ben closed the file, forcing himself to concentrate on what his son was saying. Tomorrow he'd have a meeting with all his executives and find out how to deal with what he'd learned.

"Well Dad, you see, it's like this. A real good friend, someone I care about a lot, might be in some trouble."

"Jimmy, you can tell me straight out. You know you can trust me. Are you in trouble?" Ben studied his son's expression, trying to read his thoughts.

Jimmy exhaled loudly. "Da-a-d! I'm not in trouble. It's not me, really, it's a good friend. She, uh, this person, borrowed something, and I have a feeling this person might get herself into trouble. I mean, I don't know for sure, but it's a feeling I've got. Maybe it's 'cause I know her."

"Jimmy, talk straight. Who borrowed what?" The person was obviously a girl. Did his son have a girlfriend? That was the last thing he needed right now.

"The video camera."

"You let one of your friends borrow our video camera?" Ben's voice rose an octave. "Jimmy, that equipment is *very* expensive. What on earth possessed you to do that? You know you're never to loan anything like that unless you check with me first."

"Dad, it's a friend of yours, too," Jimmy admitted miserably. He was really bungling this. Sara would kill him—if Dad didn't kill her first.

Ben leaned forward. He was starting to get a bad feeling. His eyes narrowed, and he stared at his son. "Are we talking about Sara?'' he asked, trying to keep his voice level.

His father seldom yelled. When he was really angry, he shook, but right before that he'd usually get very calm. Sometimes if he was really having trouble keeping the lid on his temper, he'd even smile. Jimmy glanced up. Oh-oh. Dad was smiling. "I think I'll go to my room now, Dad. I've got to study, and I was probably wrong about what I said...."

"Stop right there," Ben said evenly.

Jimmy froze in his tracks.

"Look at me, son, and don't waste any more of my time. I want to know exactly what went on here while I was gone."

Jimmy swallowed. "Sara asked me if she could borrow the video camera. She said it was for an experiment of sorts, but when I asked her if she was playing spy games, she didn't say no. All she said was that she wasn't playing any games. It was the way she said it, Dad. I think she's up to something, but I can't be sure."

Ben would have staked his life on Jimmy's insight. His son was sharp when it came to reading people, particularly those he loved.

Suddenly a lot of things made sense to Ben. Sara had been baiting Charlie, his security guard, by telling him to watch her office, since she'd have important papers in there tonight. He shouldn't have assumed that she'd finally accepted his word that Charlie could be trusted. When had she *ever* listened to him? Sara had been setting Charlie up, of course. Unfortunately, Billy had been mopping the floor only yards away at the time. If he hurt Sara...

A rage as black as the nighttime sky started Ben shaking. He muttered a dark oath under his breath and reached for the telephone. He dialed the police, and quickly explained that he thought there was a theft under way at Classic Parts, and the employees who were still there might be in danger. Asking them to meet him there, he replaced the receiver. Ben grabbed his coat and made his way out the door. Jimmy, lifting his jacket off the chair, rushed after him.

"Son, you can't come with me," Ben said, stopping only for a fraction of a second.

Jimmy had never disobeyed his father before, but there had to be a first time for everything. "Dad, you don't have time to argue, and I'm going to go with you even if I have to catch a cab. I heard what you said on the phone. Sara's in trouble."

"I could lock you up in your room," Ben threatened, opening his car door, and slipping behind the wheel.

Jimmy dived into the passenger's side. "But you'd lose time and you haven't got any to spare. I'll stay out of the way, I promise, Dad, but I've got to go too."

Ben slammed his hand against the steering wheel and started the ignition. Didn't anyone ever listen to him anymore? He glared at Jimmy, then realized that what he was seeing in his son was a lot of himself. "Okay. Buckle your seat belt." He smiled grimly, and with a screech of tires, pulled out into the street.

"Dad," Jimmy asked in a quiet voice, "will you marry her soon? I think it's going to take both of us to keep her out of trouble."

Ben laughed, a short dark sound that echoed in the car. Concentrating on the road ahead, he increased his speed. "I'll keep that in mind. In the meantime, hang on."

CHAPTER SIXTEEN

SARA FELT HER LEG MUSCLES begin to cramp. Great! She'd be walking around looking like Quasimodo for the next week, at least. She shifted, trying to stretch her legs, but it was a useless exercise. Maybe if she lay on her back and stuck her legs straight up... She was busy contemplating the idea when she heard the door being unlocked. Forgetting her discomfort, she stayed motionless, and squeezed the trigger on the camera.

The humming noise echoed loudly in her ears. However, she'd already tested the machine and found it couldn't be heard across the room. Praying that her earlier assessment had been right, she forced herself to remain calm. If her hands continued to shake, she'd never be able to hold the camera steady enough to shoot the videotape.

Sara waited as the intruder came toward her desk. As he leaned over, she saw his face clearly for the first time. It wasn't Charlie. This man was in his late twenties and had dirty-blond hair. The realization took her completely by surprise. Who on earth was this? She continued aiming the camera, and saw the man loading her papers and the dummy casting furnace into a large trash bin. She saw the dark green coveralls and tried to think where she'd seen that uniform.

The maintenance men! Sara squinted through the tiny holes she'd drilled in the box for her eyes. But they worked in pairs. Where was the other man? She continued taping as she tried to sort out her thoughts.

She saw the maintenance man carefully place the lid on the trash bin containing the papers and equipment he'd stolen. Sara was angling her body, trying to get a better shot, when her toe smacked against the side of the box.

The man spun around. In one fluid motion he leaped at the box she'd been using as cover, and yanked the top flaps right off. "You!"

He grabbed her hair and jerked her roughly out of the box, tipping over the entire crate.

Sara tumbled to the floor right in front of him as he released his painful hold. She broke the fall with her elbows in an effort to protect the camera clutched tightly to her chest.

"The game's up," she said in the bravest tone she could muster as she scrambled to her feet. "I know who you are. If you try and hurt me, someone will hear and the police will catch you for sure. The best you can do is give yourself up."

His eyes were cold and filled with malice. "Or I can take you with me, and deal with you later."

"There's no way you'll get me past the guards downstairs. I'll scream so loudly you'll need ear protectors just to be near me. Like I said, the game's up." Sara stood and faced him squarely, holding the camera protectively in her arms, hoping that her knees would hold instead of buckling as they were threatening to.

"You've got guts, lady, but it won't do you any good." With one hand, he grasped her forearm and pulled the camera away from her with the other.

"Let go of me, or I'll start screaming." Sara tried to jerk her arm free, but his grip was like a vise.

"Go right ahead. My partner is one floor down from here, buffing the floor. He'll never hear you over the noise. After everyone's gone we split up and get the work done twice as fast that way. He likes to go home to his family," the man said, sneering. He tossed the camera into the trash on top of her phony papers.

Sara tried to swallow, but her mouth was too dry to aid her parched throat. "What are you going to do?" she asked. Her voice shook, but she quickly brought it under control. She'd fall apart later. Right now, she needed to think of a way out of the mess she'd got herself into. "You can't be completely stupid if you managed to avoid getting caught all this time. Surely you understand that you won't be able to escape unless you leave me here."

"You wanna bet?" He forced her to turn around and slammed her hard against the desk. Her head collided against the wooden top. In the seconds it took to clear her thoughts, he'd tied her hands securely behind her back, using a length of cord from the blinds.

He grabbed a box of tissues on her desk, then taking a handful, stuffed them forcefully inside her mouth. He spun her around, holding her against the desk with his body as he wound masking tape around her head to keep the gag in place.

Deliberately keeping her off balance, he shoved her toward the third giant trash bin that stood on the cart, then picked her up and dumped her inside.

She landed roughly on her derriere, legs sticking straight up in a jackknifed position. Her head throbbed and her hair pulled where it was stuck to the tape. The bin reeked of old cigarettes and pencil shavings. There were other smells too, which she couldn't identify, and which were equally unpleasant.

He reached down and tied her ankles together. "Feel free to make as much noise as you want. I usually go out back with the trash, and deposit everything in those metal dumpsters. No one pays the slightest bit of attention to me when I'm doing that. That's how I managed to steal all the papers and things I've been taking from Classic Parts.''

Sara stared aghast at the man. This was the first time she'd ever truly feared for her life. If he got her out of the building, he could kill her and get rid of her body almost anywhere. No one would be the wiser.

He placed the metal lid over the top, sealing her in. She started to struggle against the cords that held her bound, chafing against her wrists, when she heard him smash something against the side of the container. The blow had been in line with her head. For a minute or two, the ringing prevented her from hearing anything. The sound, amplified inside the metal container, echoed in her ears.

"...and you better behave yourself. Keep in mind that the last thing you want to do is get me angry. A lot of unpleasant things could happen to you in the next few hours. If you cooperate, I'll go easy on you. If not, then I'll have my fun later.''

His voice made her skin crawl. Sara knew she had to escape, and soon. Maybe if she pretended to cooperate with him, he'd slip up, and she'd have a chance to get away.

She felt the cart being wheeled down the hall, then heard the elevator doors slide open. Sara could feel the descent as the elevator traveled downward. No light permeated the trash bin except a sliver around the lid, and no fresh air entered the stifling, oppressive container. Fighting her growing fear, she continued to try and loosen the rope that held her hands behind her back. The exertion made her breathe harder, and the tissues in her mouth almost caused her to choke.

When the elevator came to a stop, she felt the cart moving again.

"Hey, Billy!"

Sara recognized Charlie's voice. She had to get his attention. She began kicking the side of the trash bin as hard as she could.

"What the hell's that? Billy, something is inside that bin!"

Sara held her breath, and continued to kick.

"Hold it right there, Charlie," she heard Billy say.

"What in God's name are you doing with a gun, Billy? Have you lost your mind?"

Gun? Sara felt like crying. First she'd been convinced Charlie was the culprit. Now she'd managed to drag him into the same mess she was in! A feeling of sheer desperation gripped her.

"Take out your pistol with two fingers, Charlie. That's it. Now drop it real carefully into the trash bin in front of you."

There was a pause, then the dull *thunk* of the gun as it came to rest against the bottom of one of the other trash cans. "Okay now, Charlie, push the cart outside. We're all going for a little ride."

She heard the sound of doors being opened, then she felt the bump as the cart was pushed over the threshold. She bounced against the sides of the bin as it traveled over the asphalt parking lot.

"Okay, stop here," Billy ordered. "Open the third trash bin and pull the lady out of there. Then carry her over and put her behind the driver's seat of my car. Untie only her legs when you're done. I'll take care of the rest. She's going to be my chauffeur."

Charlie opened the lid and gently scooped her out. "I'm sorry, Ms Cahill," he muttered.

He lifted Sara and took her to a new model sedan, setting her upright in the driver's seat. Leaning over, he untied the cords that bound her ankles.

"Now I want you to open the trunk." Billy handed Charlie his keys.

Sara watched the men, hoping for some opportunity to escape. Glancing around, she searched in vain for a passerby.

Pushing the car door partially shut as if to shield Sara, Charlie moved slowly toward the back.

"Charlie, quit stalling. Don't play games with me. Just get inside that trunk, then toss me the keys," Billy snapped.

Charlie climbed into the trunk and disappeared from Sara's view. She heard the keys jingle as they landed in Billy's hand.

"Now pull the trunk shut. Move it!" Billy waited until he heard the trunk lid snap.

With a satisfied smile, he started to walk to the passenger side of his car. It was then that two security guards came rushing out of the building, weapons drawn.

"Drop that gun and let her go!" one shouted.

Billy ducked back around the car, using both the vehicle and Sara as a barrier. "Forget it. You two can drop *your* guns, or I'll shoot the woman right here."

Billy crouched and moved the gun up to the level of the window, pointing the barrel directly at Sara's head. Peering over the hood, he watched the guards for a moment.

Before Billy shifted his gaze back to her, Sara bent her legs at the knees, and kicked open the partially closed door with all her strength.

The door slammed against Billy's arm and shoulder, sending him tumbling to the asphalt, the pistol clattering somewhere out of reach. Away from the cover the car provided, Billy had no chance as the security guards rushed forward, their weapons aimed directly at him.

"Don't move. Lie facedown in the parking lot, hands out on both sides of you!" one guard yelled. "Nice going, lady."

As Billy rolled onto his stomach, groaning in pain, a police car screeched to a stop, blocking the parking lot exit. From where she was sitting, Sara could see two officers leaving the car, guns drawn.

Then Sara saw Jimmy and Ben come rushing toward her. An enormous lump formed at the back of her throat. Although she'd never admit it to either of them now, for a while she hadn't been sure she would ever see them again.

They arrived together, silent concern mirrored in their eyes. Ben crouched beside the open car door and carefully removed the tape and gag from her mouth.

"Are you okay?" he asked.

Sara nodded, and leaned against the steering wheel as Ben cut her hands free with a pocketknife. "How did you two know to come? Did the guards call you when Charlie...? Oh my gosh! Charlie's in the trunk."

Ben scooped up the keys that had fallen onto the pavement, and hurriedly unlocked the trunk.

Charlie, looking no worse for wear, came out slowly. "I'm sorry, Mr. Lowell. I didn't do such a good job of protecting Ms Cahill tonight." He gave her a puzzled look. "What I don't understand is what you were doing in the building, Ms Cahill. Our records showed that you'd signed out earlier."

"I was trying to find out who'd been stealing documents from my lab and from Classic Parts," Sara told him quietly. "I rigged it so I could sneak back inside the building without anyone knowing. There's a video camera in one of the trash cans with evidence of Billy's theft." Sara leaned against the side of the car.

"I wish you'd tell me just how you got back inside...." Charlie started to ask, then stopped as Jimmy rushed around him.

Without warning, Jimmy threw his arms around Sara, hugging her tightly. "I was so scared. I was afraid something would happen to you."

Sara pressed Jimmy against her as Charlie walked away to speak to the police. "I didn't mean to scare you, Jimmy. I was wrong to take matters into my own hands like I did. Will you forgive me?"

Looking embarrassed, Jimmy turned his face away. "Only if you promise to take either Dad or me along next time you decide to play your spy games."

Ben placed his hand on his son's shoulder. "Jimmy, remember the advice you gave me about keeping her out of trouble?"

Jimmy's eyes lit up. Was he going to ask her to marry him right now? What an awesome way to end the night! "'Course I remember."

"Well, I think I'll be taking your advice real soon." Ben gave Sara a wary glance. "Only for now, let it stay between us."

Jimmy laughed. Way to go, Dad. Make her sweat for a bit. She deserved it for driving them both nuts worrying about her. "Dad, for once I agree completely with you."

"Hey, what's this all about?" Sara asked as she glanced from father to son.

Jimmy stuck his hands in his pockets and gave her an angelic look of sheer innocence. "Don't ask me. I'm just a kid." He gave his dad a wink. "I'll wait for you two back at the car."

Ben smiled at his son. Jimmy was growing up fast. Had he sensed Ben's need to be alone with Sara for a moment, or had his kid learned to read minds?

Ben's eyes met Sara's in a penetrating glance. "I could have lost you tonight," he said and his voice shook. He cleared his throat and started again. "I couldn't even think straight. I should be furious with you, but I'm so glad you're safe that my anger can wait until later."

He pulled her to him and kissed her hard and possessively. "You're mine and I'm yours, Sara. Accept it. Don't you ever do anything like this again without telling me. For the first time I realized why my keeping things from you hurt so much. We should have faced this together."

Ben was holding her so tightly she could scarcely breathe, yet she'd never felt better. Sara could feel his love flowing out and enveloping her. "I'm sorry I scared you. If it's any consolation, I scared myself, too."

He laughed. "Well, maybe you learned something. Now come on over and sit in my car for a while. After the police get your statement, I'm taking you to the house until I can relax enough to be able to let you out of my sight."

Ben held the door open as Sara entered his car. Jimmy leaned forward between the two front seats, his face in the gap between Sara and Ben.

"Dad, she *is* going home with us, isn't she?"

Ben gave Sara a knowing smile. "Yes, for a while anyway."

"Aw Dad, talk her into staying. We both need to get some sleep, and at least at home we can make sure she's safe."

Sara glanced from one to the other. "Now wait a minute, you two...."

"Dad, don't listen to her. That only starts trouble. That's how she talked me into loaning her the video camera."

"I agree, son. I'll never listen to a word she says. We'll just take care of her whether she likes it or not."

"That's best, I think," Jimmy answered.

"You know, it's a toss-up who's the bigger chauvinist here," Sara commented.

"It's got nothing to do with that," Jimmy protested quietly. "We love you in a special way. We're not trying to push you around, but we want to be there for you when there's trouble. Sticking together is what friends and family do best. Don't you see? You'd be helping us as much as we'd be helping you. Dad and I like to feel needed, too."

Sara swallowed, trying to ease the lump she felt at the back of her throat. For a moment or two she sat silently, unable to speak. She took Jimmy's hand and held it.

Jimmy reached for his father's free hand and placed it over theirs.

Sara basked in the warmth of Ben's and Jimmy's love. She'd never really felt a sense of belonging before, but Ben and Jimmy had changed all that. They were as much a part of her as she was of them. She leaned back in her seat and smiled. "I love you both," she whispered.

Hearing her soft words, Ben and Jimmy exchanged quick glances.

"We know," Ben answered with a smug grin.

THAT EVENING WAS ONE Sara would never forget. Ben and Jimmy catered to her, pampering her and showing her so much love that she felt as if she'd burst with happiness.

"I hate to be a spoilsport, but I think it's time you went to bed, Jimmy," Sara told him, seeing the boy yawn for the third time.

"Tomorrow's Saturday. I can sleep late. Besides, I want to be with you."

"I'm going to ask your dad to take me home. We'll have plenty of time to spend with each other tomorrow."

"Can't you sleep here? I won't mind, and I'm sure Dad wouldn't either," he begged, not wanting her to leave. He rubbed his eyes.

Ben laughed. "I wouldn't mind at all."

Sara smirked. "I'm going home," she replied stubbornly.

Jimmy peered at her through heavy-lidded eyes. "Come on, just this one time, okay? Dad could sleep on the couch, and you could have his room. That's okay, isn't it, Dad?"

Sara stood up, giving Ben a look that clearly indicated she needed help. "Go to bed, Jimmy. You can talk to me tomorrow. We'll have brunch together. My treat. That's the least I can do for my two favorite men."

"Stay, please?" Jimmy pleaded. "After all that's happened, I'd really worry if you weren't here. I'm so tired! Stay overnight, Sara. I'll be able to sleep so much better if you do."

She should have held out, but Jimmy's eyes were almost closing on their own. "Oh, all right. I'm not going to keep you two awake all night discussing this."

Jimmy beamed. "Does that mean you're staying?"

She nodded.

"Dad, you don't mind sleeping on the couch, do you? Your bed's bigger and more comfortable than mine."

"I don't mind, son," Ben replied, after a moment's pause. "Now you go to bed. Sara'll sleep in my room, and we'll all be together again tomorrow."

"That sounds reasonable to me," Sara added, giving Jimmy a questioning look.

"Great, then it's settled." He stood, then gave Sara a quick hug. "I'm glad you're okay."

"I love you, Jimmy. Now go to sleep," she answered softly.

They watched him amble quietly down the hall.

"He looks half-asleep," Sara commented slowly.

"He's had a hard night." Ben sat next to her on the sofa, and shifted until he faced her. "Why didn't you tell me what you were going to do?" Ben's question was level, his voice soft, but his hands were clenched. "You could have been hurt. Didn't you realize that?"

"I never thought it would go as far as it did," she replied candidly. "But as for the reason I didn't tell you..." She paused, and exhaled softly. "I know you didn't believe Charlie was the person we were looking for, but I was convinced that he was," she explained. "I was determined to lay a trap for him and get the evidence I needed to convict him. However, I was afraid if I told you, I'd get you upset. I thought you'd be angry because I wanted to help you by getting involved and because you felt Charlie was innocent. Had you asked me to go home and not go ahead with my plans, I'd have fought you. Then you'd have been worried and angry on my account at a time when you needed to be concentrating on something else. You were about to go meet Paul Tracht's man, a person I was certain couldn't be trusted at all. The last thing I wanted was to distract you."

"Well, I was right, wasn't I? Charlie wasn't the man we were after," he observed wryly.

"I know," she admitted, with a chuckle. "Couldn't resist rubbing it in, could you?"

"Nope." He wove his fingers into the curtain of her hair. "But we're getting off the subject, and Sara, this is much too important to brush aside. You still should have told me. I realize that you were looking out for me, but you denied me the same right. Besides, you gave me your word you'd stop investigating."

She shook her head. "No, I told you I'd take every safety precaution I could, and I did." She took a deep breath. "I love you more than I've ever loved anyone, Ben. If I've hurt you, I'm sorry. You're right, I should have told you anyway. I realize that now." She could feel the warmth of his fingers as he toyed with her hair, allowing it to cascade over his hand. "No more secrets. I'll never keep anything from you again."

"Sara, I give you my word that from now on there will be no more pressure on how or where you work. Monday morning, you move back down to your basement office. It's been ready for a week now. I won't try and stop you doing anything you feel is necessary. You won't have a reason not to come to me, ever again." He stopped, then added, "But I will reserve the right to join you if you're about to do something that's going to make me worry about you."

"It's a deal."

Ben took her mouth in a demanding and unrelenting kiss. He felt her soften in his arms and melt into him. His kiss turned harsh then gentle, then harsh again, his tongue claiming possession of the moist territory. Slowly he released her. Taking Sara's hand in his, he led her down the hall. "Let's check on Jimmy, then make up our beds. If we continue like this, there's no telling what will happen," Ben whispered.

Nodding, her heart still hammering, Sara tiptoed with him down the long hallway to the room at the end.

Ben opened the door slightly and they peered inside. In the muted glow of the moonlight filtering through the curtains, they could see Jimmy's head on his pillow. His deep breathing indicated he was fast asleep.

Closing the door softly, they walked down the hall again, this time to Ben's bedroom, where they gathered a sheet and comforter.

Back in the living room, Ben spoke again. "We don't need to whisper. He's really out like a light tonight. He's exhausted. I bet he was asleep before his head ever hit the pillow."

"He's so very special," Sara commented, helping Ben adjust the bedding on the sofa.

"Just like his father?" Ben took her hand and drew her close.

Sara rested her head against his chest. His heart was racing. The knowledge that she was the cause sent a thrilling shiver coursing through her. "Just like his father," she said softly.

Need and longing made their bodies tremble as they continued to hold one another.

"Sara, I need to feel you naked against me, calling out my name, wanting me as much as I want you. Come to my bed, sweetheart, and let me love you."

"Jimmy," she reminded him with a sigh.

"Is extremely sound asleep," he countered, reaching beneath her pullover and kneading the soft flesh of her breast. "And he's halfway across the house with his door closed. We'll have all the privacy we need."

"I don't know...."

Ben unclasped her bra. Lowering his head, he touched the tip of her breast with his tongue and teased the rosy bud into aching tightness.

Her breath came in one shuddering gasp. "Well, maybe you can move to the sofa later tonight," she managed to say.

Ben lifted her off her feet, carrying her easily in his arms. "Let's make our night special. There's so much I want to show you, so much pleasure I want to give you," he murmured, brushing her forehead with a kiss.

She buried her lips against his neck. "And what about me? Will I get equal time? I can think of many wonderful things I'd like to do."

He felt her shift in his arms, pressing her breasts against his chest. He drew in his breath. "Sara, don't. The night's going to set its own pace if you tease."

"Tease?" She opened his shirt as he carried her into the bedroom. "Not at all. I'm a woman of action. What I promise, I deliver. I thought I'd start by kissing you all over, taking my time over those spots that make you go crazy."

He set her down near his bed, then seated himself on the edge of the mattress and began to undress her at a deliberate pace. As her breasts fell free of their confinement, he clasped her to him, sucking and nibbling at the taut peaks.

Her body turned into liquid fire. She moaned softly, pressing his head against her. "Let me lie down," she requested in a trembling voice. "I can't stand here while you do this. My legs won't hold me."

"One second." Ben yanked at the zipper that held her jeans in place and pulled them out of the way. He tasted the flesh he uncovered, trailing a hot, moist path down the center of her.

Sara gasped and a second later his arms were around her. He placed her tenderly on top of his bed, then walked to the lamp, intending to turn it off.

"No, don't."

He undressed before her, feeling her hungry eyes travel over him. The knowledge that she wanted him filled him with an exhilarating sense of power. He looked down at her, watching her gaze travel the length of him. The driving need to take her pounded through him.

Ben lowered himself beside her on the mattress. He stroked her breasts tenderly, then trailed his hand downward, caressing and exploring all of her. She moaned softly and arched toward him.

His predatory mouth branded each curve, each hollow of her body with deliberately inciting kisses that left her mindless. Tracing a path with his tongue this time, he moved down her body, then stopped. His tongue probed gently, his breath adding to the fires that threatened to consume her.

"No more!" she gasped.

He held her hips in his hands, controlling her movements. "So sweet," he murmured, leading her to the brink again and again.

When at last she lay spent, he comforted her, his hands soothing and his caress gentle.

Though the release had been welcome, her need for him deepened into aching emptiness. A small cry of surprise escaped her lips as he lifted her easily and positioned her over himself. He guided her body down over his and eased himself inside her.

His hands clasped her hips, then moved to the rounded curve of her bottom, directing her movements. "Feel me within you. See how well we fit into each other!"

Despite the restraint his hands posed, she began to yield to her needs and moved at a faster pace.

"Yes. Let me fill you completely," he encouraged her.

She felt his flesh as it penetrated her body over and over again. Soft sounds erupted from the back of her throat as she pressed herself against him.

He wrapped his arms around her waist and shifted, pinning her beneath him. "Take all of me, Sara. More," he growled, burying himself in her once more.

She gasped. "Yes! Oh yes!" Her body felt tight, then suddenly an exquisite weakness spread over her.

With a moan that seemed to come from the depths of his soul, Ben shuddered.

His body, pressed so intimately against hers, felt intoxicatingly sexy. He kissed her tenderly, then turned his head and nuzzled the curve of her neck. With a sigh, she wrapped her arms around his waist and held him. A feeling of utter peace and contentment washed over her.

With infinite care, Ben eased away his weight and lay beside her. He ran his hand over her body, tracing delicate patterns over her skin with his fingertips. "There will never be anyone else for me, Sara," Ben said, and his voice, infinitely masculine, vibrated with conviction.

His lady. Just his. She nestled against him, her cheek brushing against the crisp hairs on his chest. "That's the second-nicest thing you could have said to me."

He laughed softly. "I love you," he murmured in her ear.

"Now you're getting it," she answered, nuzzling the hollow at the base of his neck.

"I want you to be my wife, Sara. Will you marry me?" Ben's voice reverberated with emotion.

Her heart skipped a beat, then slowly she smiled. "Persuade me."

With a throaty growl he bent down, claiming her mouth with his own. "I will. In fact, in a few hours, I may even have you asking me," he added, playfully arrogant.

She chuckled softly. "Sounds promising," she managed to say as she felt the warmth of his breath yet again, weaving downward in searing exploration.

CHAPTER SEVENTEEN

SUNLIGHT FILTERING THROUGH a crack in the curtains nudged Sara awake. She was alone. Ben had returned to the couch hours earlier. Tossing the covers aside, she stood and dressed quickly. There was much she wanted to do today. The time had come to surprise Ben with the final results of the project she'd been working on for Classic Parts.

Creeping about so as not to wake either Jimmy or Ben, who was sound asleep on the sofa, she telephoned for a taxi and left the house. First she'd collect her own car at the office, then freshen up at home. Finally she'd return with what she hoped would be a terrific surprise for Ben.

She felt as if she were walking on air. Sara couldn't wait to see Jimmy's face when he found out that Ben and she were getting married. The knowledge that they would all be a family soon filled her with energy even though she'd scarcely slept a wink the night before. She ran all her errands that morning with such enthusiasm and efficiency that by ten o'clock she was back at Ben's. Readjusting her short-sleeved knit top and pulling it smoothly over her blue jeans, she strode up the walkway leading to Ben's door.

Ben answered before she could even ring the bell. "Where have you been? I tried reaching you at home, and then I called your office. I didn't know what the heck had happened."

Ben looked enticingly masculine in a casual sort of way, as men usually did when they stayed at home on lazy Saturday mornings. He'd left his shirt open, shirttail hanging outside low-slung jeans. He wore socks, but no shoes, yet still towered over her.

"And good morning to you, too," she said. "Are you always this cheerful in the morning?" Seeing Jimmy sitting at the kitchen table, she raised her eyebrows questioningly and whispered to Ben. "Did you tell him about us yet?"

"Yes, he did, and it was about time!" Jimmy's voice carried from the kitchen. "Congratulations! Maybe now that you and Dad are getting married, things are going to be a little more peaceful around here, huh?" Jimmy came over and gave her a big hug and a squeeze.

"I wouldn't bet on it, considering your dad's welcome this morning." Sara stepped back, playfully messing up Jimmy's hair.

"I wouldn't kid around too much with him," Jimmy warned in a low voice, shaking his head. "He hasn't had his coffee yet, because he's been calling everywhere looking for you."

"Are you listening to me? Where have you been? I was worried," Ben said peevishly.

"I've brought fresh coffee I ground myself at home. I also stopped by the grocery store and bought bacon, eggs and the fixings for pancakes," she replied, refusing to allow him to get too serious. "This is a double celebration brunch, so don't be crabby. Otherwise you'll ruin my surprise."

"Saints preserve me from your surprises," he muttered. "What have you done now?"

"It's really big news. I think I should set the scene more, maybe add a drumroll or something."

"Are you trying to bait me, to see how much teasing I can take before I go crazy?"

"Tsk, tsk! You really should work on your patience."

"Sara," Ben said and his voice held an edge.

She laughed and threw her arms around his neck. "I've got the most fantastic news, and you're determined to be crabby. You can be so difficult."

He held his breath as she pressed her body against his. "Sara, will you be serious! I was worried about you, and I don't like having to worry."

"What if I told you that I finished your project?" she asked, and smiled up at him. "The casting furnace works perfectly. I also had an engine part installed in my car a week ago, and I've tested it thoroughly for the past seven days. I had an engineer make one last check on it yesterday, take some measurements and so on. He messengered a report directly to me, and I stuck it beneath a file cabinet for safekeeping. I was certain that no thief would ever think of looking there, even if my office was rifled. According to what I read this morning, the part doesn't even show signs of wear."

Ben grasped her shoulders and held her at arm's length. "Honestly? It's really completed and I can start manufacturing parts?"

She took him by the hand and led him outside to her car. Opening the hood, she pointed to a big toothed ring by the end of the engine. "There. I thought that part would be ideal. It's a flywheel. The starter spins that flywheel, and that makes the engine turn over. Basic, but necessary."

He laughed. "And you've used it all week?"

"It's held up beautifully. I've had it checked several times, and my mechanic and the engineer both say it looks to be more durable than the original part. There's no signs of stress or wear, and it's perfectly balanced."

Ben wrapped his arms around her waist, and twirled her around. "You're terrific."

"I know," she joked. "Does this mean you'll cook?"

Jimmy, who was leaning over the fender of the car, looking down into the engine compartment, made gagging noises. "Don't ask him that. Dad's awful with bacon. He incinerates it every time. And if you'd ever tasted his pancakes, you'd die. He always gets the batter too thin and the griddle too hot. They come out thin and gooey, sort of like soggy potato chips."

"Thanks a lot, kid. Looking for new parents? I'd love to adopt you out," Ben said cynically.

"I'll cook, okay, Dad?"

Sara laughed. It was great. All her life she'd dreamed of being the heart of the family, and that was exactly the way she felt now, snugly nestled between Ben and Jimmy. "Come on, guys. We'll all cook."

Sara helped Jimmy prepare breakfast while Ben opened up the morning paper. He liked having Sara there with them. For the first time since Rosemary had died, the circle of love that held his family together seemed complete. He watched Sara lovingly. She demanded a great deal, but gave everything in return. She was going to be a perfect wife, mother and partner.

"Do you always read the newspaper upside down?" Sara teased, turning it the right way for him, then putting it back in his hands.

Ben laughed. "Only when you're around."

Sara stood behind Ben and gave him a hug. Suddenly her eyes fastened on something. "Ben, will you look at that?" she said, pointing to an article at the center of the page. "Classic Parts is in the news."

Ben scanned the article quickly. "It seems Billy made a full confession. The man who was going to sell me information on Paul's company turns out to be in on it. That's his picture on the left. Paul's claiming innocence. Would you believe it? He's sticking to his story that he didn't know what his people were doing, but the police expect the grand jury to bring down indictments against all three." He set down the paper. "Now it really is over. Where's that celebration brunch?"

Jimmy stared at the sputtering bacon Sara had been frying, and quickly turned off the burner. "Hey, Dad! These look just like yours. Sara just burned the heck out of our food."

AN HOUR AND A HALF passed before the dishes were all put away, and Jimmy left them to play an adventure game on his personal computer.

Sara sat at the table opposite Ben. "What's going to happen to Classic Parts now, Ben? How much harm have these spying incidents done to your business?"

"Classic Parts won the last contract we bid for, though I had to keep most of my people in the dark as to what I was doing. With that, and the process you've invented, I expect the company is going to be doing better than it ever has. In fact, we may even have to expand again. I think this process of yours is really going to make us the number one parts distributor in the States."

"That's great!" Relief flooded through her. "I can't tell you how glad I am that's all behind us." She walked to the counter and poured herself a cup of coffee. "Just in time, too! Tomorrow's Jimmy's birthday."

"I know. I was about to remind you."

"I think we both should devote the entire day to Jimmy, and take him wherever he wants to go. I spoke to Mike at National Labs, and he's going to make an exception and let me take Jimmy to see the labs and work with his computer there. It's one of the most advanced computers in the state. I've programmed it to do some special things he might like. There's an artificial intelligence program someone there has developed, and Jimmy can carry on a conversation with the computer. After that, I thought we'd take him to the city museum. They have a laser and the new holographic displays set up in their special exhibit hall for children. Then, if he wants, we can go out for pizza and maybe see that new science fiction film he's been talking about.''

"It's Jimmy's type of day, all right,'' Ben said cautiously. The problem was, he wasn't sure whether Jimmy would share her enthusiasm. Lately he'd noticed his son becoming even more independent, and increasingly interested in choosing his own activities. A year ago, he would have been certain that Jimmy would love going with Sara and him almost anywhere, but now he just didn't know.

Sara watched Ben's face. "You told me last week that you hadn't planned anything special, so I assumed you wouldn't mind if I made a few arrangements. It is okay, isn't it?''

"Oh, I don't mind at all. It's just that you went through a lot of trouble.''

"Not really,'' she said, minimizing her efforts. "I just wanted to share the day with Jimmy and you. I know he likes visiting with me at the lab, so I thought I'd find things along those lines that he'd be interested in.''

Ben remained quiet. "Sara, I don't want you to be disappointed, but there's something I should tell you. Jimmy's very much his own person. Sometimes he wants me to do things with him, but other times he likes going off and pursuing his own interests. This past month, I've noticed that he's becoming more interested in what some of his friends at school are doing. He's growing up.'' He paused, and with a wince added, "And I think he's also started to discover girls.''

Sara smiled. "Really?" With a shrug, she added, "I was planning to surprise him at the last minute, but maybe you're right. I should check with him." Sara felt her spirits sag, but she was determined not to show it. She'd so wanted to spend Sunday with Jimmy and Ben. She'd wanted to make it a real family day. It was her way of showing Jimmy how much she'd appreciated the love and affection he'd lavished on her.

Had she presumed too much by assuming that he'd want to go to all those places with Ben and herself? Jimmy had spent so much of his free time with her that she'd taken the liberty of making plans without consulting him. She'd hoped that the news would make him as happy as making the plans had made her. "I'll go to the den right now and ask him what he thinks."

Sara joined Jimmy, who was sitting before the small computer playing a game. "Jimmy, tomorrow's your birthday and I was wondering if you'd like to come with me to National Labs. I've managed to get permission for you to use their supercomputer and I've borrowed a few programs I think you might enjoy."

"I'd love to, but does it *have* to be tomorrow? I met this girl in my class who just loves science fiction movies. I asked her to go with me to see *Lunar Android* tomorrow at the Plaza Theater. I want to go with you, but..."

Jimmy sounded so embarrassed that Sara's heart went out to him. "It's okay, we'll do it some other time. I should have known you'd have made plans already." Sara smiled, hoping he wouldn't sense her disappointment. She loved Jimmy as if he were her own son, and the fact that he preferred to spend his birthday without her hurt.

Ben put his arm around Sara, and walked outside with her. "I could see that coming, but I couldn't think of a way to prevent it."

"Jimmy has a right to spend his birthday with whomever he wants," she said. "Still, it hurts that I won't be there to celebrate it with him. These past few months he's given me so much love and made me feel so wanted that this came as a disappointment." She stared into the distance. "I guess I was wrong to assume he'd prefer to be with us."

"You have no idea what an important influence you've been in Jimmy's life, Sara. Before you came along, that kid didn't have the confidence to go out and make friends his own age. He was always by himself, here at home. He adores you, and the fact that you gave him your love in return made him feel special. He began to see his own worth. That was when he started coming out of his shell and socializing with the kids at school."

"So I helped him and pushed him away all at the same time?"

"Not at all. He's crazy about you, but Jimmy's growing up. He needs his independence. That's one of the things that worried me when you kept insisting that you wanted a very close-knit family. To love one another is good, it's the very center of what binds a family together. However, people need a certain amount of room to grow. Jimmy needs to discover his own strengths and weaknesses. You want Jimmy to choose to be with you because he loves you, not because he can't cope without you. You may not realize it, but you have the best type of relationship with my son. Jimmy wants you around, and he also knows you will be. He trusts in your love, and that gives him the freedom to be himself. There is no gift greater than the one you've already given him."

"Ben, what you're saying is true. I do understand. However, I need a bit of time to deal with this. I've spent so many years fantasizing about the type of family I wanted. I saw myself giving birthday parties, and sharing holidays with people who belonged with each other. In my mind, what would make my family special was that we'd all want to be with one another more than we'd want to be with anyone else. Now I'm seeing that the togetherness I envisioned may not be practical, nor always the best way to demonstrate love, for that matter.''

''It can be, but in your desire for togetherness, you forgot that certain things can't be forced. You can't expect everyone's needs to perfectly match your own. A family's strength comes from its willingness to work around the differences that normally separate people and to temper judgments with love.''

Ben started to gather her into his arms when Jimmy came out.

He cleared his throat. ''Am I interrupting?''

''Not at all.'' Sara smiled at him.

''I've been thinking about your invitation, Sara. You must have gone through a lot of hassles getting permission for me to use the computers and stuff, so I'm going to call Penny and tell her that something's come up. I'll go with you guys.'' He looked at her, then stared at his shoes, shifting nervously. He wasn't a total moron. He'd seen the look in her eyes. He sure didn't want to hurt her feelings. Penny would understand how grown-ups were funny and got sensitive sometimes. Besides, Sara was going to be an official part of their family very soon. If she really wanted to spend the time with him on his birthday, then he could do that much for her. She was really a pretty neat lady.

Sara swallowed the lump in her throat. ''Jimmy, it's okay if you want to take Penny to the movies. It's your birthday and your choice. We can go to the lab some other time, really,'' she said. ''It's no problem.''

''You sure?''

''Positive.''

Ben watched as Jimmy gave Sara a quick hug, then returned to the living room.

Sara watched Jimmy through the sliding glass doors for a few moments. "That's some kid you've got there, Ben."

"I do believe you're right. You know, it's funny about kids," Ben observed. "You try so hard to teach them so many things, then one day they end up teaching you." He tilted up her face, then kissed her softly. "I hope you know how much you're loved."

The gentle caress was so tender that it practically became her undoing. With a sigh, she nestled against him. "Hold me for a while."

"Gladly."

Her plans for Jimmy's birthday hadn't worked out, yet she didn't feel a sense of loss. Her thoughts drifted back to the dreams of love she'd held on to as a teenager. She still wanted togetherness, but now she knew the difference between the kind rooted in love, and the kind forced and held by chains. She'd given her love to Jimmy and Ben. Now she had to trust them to return it in their own way, knowing that she'd placed her heart in gentle and caring hands.

"This is what I've waited for all my life. I have everything I've ever wanted, the best kind of love and a family to share it with." Her heart swelled with happiness. They'd be bound by a love that wasn't blind, but based on understanding and affection.

"It won't always be perfect," Ben cautioned, easing his hold slightly, "but I promise that although I may not always agree, I'll always be there to listen and help."

"Excuse me again, guys?" Jimmy asked as he tapped Sara on her shoulder.

"Yes, what is it?" Ben looked down at his son from over the top of Sara's head.

"You remember how you two really trashed brunch this morning?"

"We know, Jimmy." Sara laughed.

"What did you have in mind?" Ben asked with a grin.

"Do you suppose you'd like ham and egg pizzas?"

Laughing in unison, Ben and Sara nodded. "Perfect," said Sara, looking from Ben to Jimmy. "Absolutely perfect."

Harlequin
Superromance

COMING NEXT MONTH

HARLEQUIN SUPERROMANCE BRINGS YOU...

Lynda Ward

Superromance readers already know that Lynda Ward possesses a unique ability to weave words into heartfelt emotions and exciting drama.

Now, Superromance is proud to bring you Lynda's tour de force: an ambitious saga of three sisters whose lives are torn apart by the conflicts and power struggles that come with being born into a dynasty.

In *Race the Sun, Leap the Moon* and *Touch the Stars*, readers will laugh and cry with the Welles sisters as they learn to live and love on their own terms, all the while struggling for the acceptance of Burton Welles, the stern patriarch of the clan.

Race the Sun, Leap the Moon and *Touch the Stars* . . . a dramatic trilogy you won't want to miss. Coming to you in July, August and September.

The Welles Family Trilogy